DREAMS OF FOREVER

NEW YORK TIMES BESTSELLING AUTHOR

BRENDA JACKSON

DREAMS OF FOREVER

A Westmoreland Novel

HARLEQUIN®

entertain, enrich, inspire™

DREAMS OF FOREVER

ISBN-13: 978-0-373-53476-0

Copyright © 2012 by Harlequin Books S.A.

This edition published July 2012

Recycling programs
for this product may
not exist in your area.

The publisher acknowledges the copyright holders
of the individual works as follows:

SEDUCTION, WESTMORELAND STYLE
Copyright © 2007 by Brenda Streater Jackson

SPENCER'S FORBIDDEN PASSION
Copyright © 2007 by Brenda Streater Jackson

www.Harlequin.com

Printed in U.S.A.

CONTENTS

THE WESTMORELAND FAMILY

Scott and Delane Westmoreland

John (Evelyn)

James (Sarah)

Corey (Abbie)
Madison

②	③	④	⑤	⑦	①
Dare (Shelly)	Thorn (Tara)	Stone (Madison)	Storm (Jayla)	Chase (Jessica)	Delaney (Jamal)
AJ, Allison	Trace	Rock	Shanna, Johanna	Carlton Scott	Ari, Arielle
⑥	⑪		⑧	⑨	⑭	⑮

Jared (Dana)	Spencer (Chardonnay)	Durango (Savannah)	Ian (Brooke)	Quade (Cheyenne)	Reggie (Olivia)
Jaren	Russell	Sarah	Pierce, Price	Venus, Athena, Troy	Ruark
⑫	⑬		⑩		

Clint (Alyssa)	Cole (Patrina)	Casey (McKinnon)
Cain	Emilie, Emery	Corey Martin

① Delaney's Desert Sheikh
② A Little Dare
③ Thorn's Challenge
④ Stone Cold Surrender
⑤ Riding the Storm
⑥ Jared's Counterfeit Fiancée

⑦ The Chase Is On
⑧ The Durango Affair
⑨ Ian's Ultimate Gamble
⑩ Seduction, Westmoreland Style
⑪ Spencer's Forbidden Passion
⑫ Taming Clint Westmoreland

⑬ Cole's Red-Hot Pursuit
⑭ Quade's Babies
⑮ Tall, Dark...Westmoreland!

THE DENVER WESTMORELAND FAMILY TREE

Raphel and Gemma Westmoreland

Stern Westmoreland (Paula Bailey)

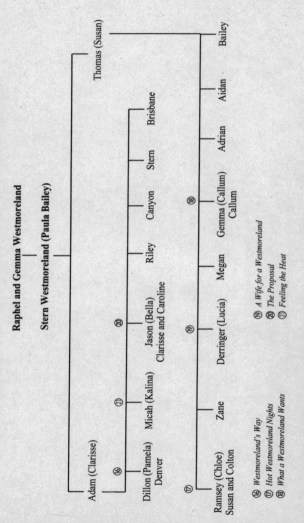

Thomas (Susan)

Adam (Clarisse) ⑯

Dillon (Pamela) — Denver

Micah (Kalina) ㉑

Jason (Bella) — Clarisse and Caroline ⑳

Riley

Canyon

Stern

Brisbane

Ramsey (Chloe) — Susan and Colton ⑰

Zane

Derringer (Lucia) ⑲

Megan

Gemma (Callum) — Callum ⑱

Adrian

Aidan

Bailey

⑯ *Westmoreland's Way*
⑰ *Hot Westmoreland Nights*
⑱ *What a Westmoreland Wants*

⑲ *A Wife for a Westmoreland*
⑳ *The Proposal*
㉑ *Feeling the Heat*

Dear Reader,

When I first introduced the Westmoreland family, little did I know they would become hugely popular with readers. Originally, the Westmoreland family series was intended to be just six books, Delaney and her five brothers—Dare, Thorn, Stone, Storm and Chase. Later, I wanted my readers to meet their cousins—Jared, Spencer, Durango, Ian, Quade and Reggie. Finally, there was Uncle Corey's triplets–Clint, Cole and Casey.

What began as a six-book series will become a thirty-book series when I conclude with all the Denver Westmorelands. I was very happy when Kimani responded to my readers' request that the earlier books be reprinted. And I'm even happier that the reissues are in a great, two-books-in-one format.

Dreams of Forever includes *Seduction, Westmoreland Style* and *Spencer's Forbidden Passion*. These are two Westmoreland classics and are books ten and eleven in the Westmoreland series. Triplet Casey Westmoreland has a thing or two to prove to McKinnon Quinn, and Spencer Westmoreland finds out the hard way that you can't turn your back on love, especially when the woman's name is Chardonnay.

I hope you enjoy reading these special romances as much as I enjoyed writing them.

Happy reading!

Brenda Jackson

Provide things honest in the sight of all men.
—*Romans* 12:17

To the love of my life, Gerald Jackson, Sr.
Happy 40th anniversary. You're still the one!

SEDUCTION, WESTMORELAND STYLE

Chapter 1

Casey Westmoreland entered the barn and paused, mesmerized by the sound of the warm, seductive masculine voice speaking gently to the huge black stallion being given a brush down. She was mesmerized even more by the man himself.

McKinnon Quinn.

In her opinion, he was as gorgeous as any one male had a right to be. Mixed with Blackfoot Indian and African-American Creole, she couldn't help but wish for more time to just stand there and admire what she saw.

Tall and ruggedly built with thick wavy black hair that fell to his shoulder blades, his blue shirt swathed a massive chest, and the well-worn jeans that covered a well-structured butt almost took her breath away when he leaned over to replace the brush with a comb. She didn't need for him to turn around to know what his features looked like. They were ingrained deep in her brain. He had an angular face with eyes as dark as a raven's wing, high cheekbones, medium-brown skin that almost appeared golden, a straight nose, stubborn jaw and full lips. She took a trembling breath and felt the warmth of a blush stain her cheeks just thinking about those lips and her secret fantasy of having her way with them.

Another thing she knew about McKinnon Quinn was that, at thirty-four, he was considered by many—especially now that his best friend and her cousin, Durango Westmoreland, had recently gotten married—to be the most eligible bachelor in Bozeman, Montana, and its surrounding areas. She'd also heard his bachelor status was something he valued with no plans to relinquish.

It was her opinion from their first meeting a little over two years ago that there was a quiet and innately controlled nature about him. Although he shared a rather close relationship with her cousins, there was still something about him that gave the impression that not too many others got close to him. He picked those he wanted to be associated with and any others he kept at a distance. Whenever she was around him she always felt he was watching her, and she could always feel his gaze on her like it was some sort of a physical caress.

"Are you going to state your business or just stand there?"

His words, spoken in a deep, cutting voice, caught her off guard and made her wonder if he had eyes in the back of his head. She was certain she hadn't made a sound, yet he had sensed her presence anyway.

"I know how important grooming time is and didn't

want to intrude," Casey heard herself saying after a moment, deciding to finally speak up.

It was only then that he turned around and she forced herself to continue breathing—especially when a surprised glint shone in the dark eyes that connected with hers. "Casey Westmoreland. Durango mentioned you were here visiting your dad," he said in a voice as intense as the eyes looking at her.

Your dad. That term in itself was something Casey was still getting used to since discovering she had a father who was very much alive after being told he had died before she was born.

"I'm not visiting, exactly. I've decided to move to Bozeman permanently," she said, wishing he wasn't staring at her so intently.

She watched as he hooked his thumbs in the pockets of his jeans—a stance that immediately placed emphasis on his entire muscular physique. Surprise once again lit his eyes. "You're moving to Bozeman? Permanently?"

"Yes."

"Why?"

He all but snapped the question and she wondered why he would care one way or the other. "Corey...I mean, my dad, is hoping that moving to Bozeman will give us a chance to get to know each other better." Even after two and a half years it was still somewhat difficult to call Corey Westmoreland "Dad" as her two brothers had begun doing.

McKinnon nodded and she noted that the eyes studying her were more intense than before. He had a close connection to her father since Corey was the best friend of McKinnon's father. In fact, to her way of thinking, it was a deeper connection than the one she herself shared with Corey if for no other reason than because McKinnon had known her father a lot longer than she had.

"That's what Corey thinks, but is that what you think as well?" he asked, his voice breaking into her thoughts.

What I really think is that it would help matters tremendously if you'd stop looking at me like that, she wanted to say, suddenly feeling like she was under a microscope. Whether he intended it or not, his gaze was provocatively sensual and was sending a heated rush all through her. "I think it wouldn't hurt. I've lived in Beaumont, Texas, all my life and when the lease expired on the building holding my clothing store—and I wasn't given the option of renewing it—I considered the possibility of relocating elsewhere. I've fallen in love with Montana the few times I've been here and agree that moving here will give me the chance to develop a relationship with Corey."

"I see."

Casey doubted that he did. Not even her brothers fully understood the turmoil existing within her after finding out the truth. From the time she was a little girl her mother had painted this fairytale image of the man who'd fathered her and her brothers—the man who'd supposedly died in a rodeo accident while performing, leaving her mother pregnant with triplets.

Carolyn Roberts Westmoreland had made it seem as if she and Corey Westmoreland had shared the perfect love, the perfect marriage and had been so dedicated to each other that she'd found it hard to go on when he'd died. According to her mother, the only thing that had kept her going was the fact that Corey had left her with not *one,* not *two,* but *three* babies growing inside her womb. Triplets who would grow up smothered in their mother's love and their father's loving memory.

It hurt to know her mother had weaved a bunch of lies.

Corey Westmoreland had never married Carolyn Roberts. Nor had he known she was pregnant with triplets. Legally, her mother had never been a Westmoreland. And to make matters worse, Corey had never loved her mother. For years he had been in love with Abby, a woman he had met years before meeting Casey's mom, and Abby was the woman he'd been reunited with and eventually married just a couple of years ago.

"And there's another reason I wanted to move here," she decided to add, getting to the reason for paying McKinnon a visit. "I felt a career change would do me good, and by moving I can do something I've always loved doing."

"Which is?"

"Working with horses—which is why I'm here. I understand you're looking for a horse trainer and I want to apply for the job."

Casey tried ignoring the sensations that flooded her insides when McKinnon's gaze moved up and down her five-foot-three petite physique. His gaze glittered when it returned to her face, as if he was amused by something. "You're kidding, right?"

She lifted a brow. "No, I'm not kidding," she said, crossing the floor to where he stood. "I'm dead serious."

She watched as his jaw tightened and his eyes narrowed and immediately resented herself for thinking he looked infuriatingly sexy.

"There's no way I can hire you as a horse trainer," he said in a rough voice.

"Why not?" she asked with as much calmness as she could muster. "I think if you were to take a look at my résumé, you'd be impressed with my qualifications." She offered the folder she was holding in her hand to him.

He glanced at the folder but made no attempt to take it from her. "Maybe I will and maybe I won't, but it doesn't matter," he said, giving her an intimidating stare. "I'm not hiring you."

His words, spoken so calmly, so matter-of-factly, sent anger coursing through her veins, but she was determined to keep her cool. "Is there a reason?" she asked, still gripping the folder in her hand, although she no longer offered it to him since he'd made it blatantly clear he wasn't interested.

After several tense moments he said, "There're a number of reasons but I don't have time to go into them."

Casey steeled herself against the anger that swept through her body but it was no use. His words had assaulted her sensibilities. "Now wait just a minute," she said, her eyes clashing with his.

He crossed his arms over his chest and to Casey, his height suddenly seem taller than six-three. "Don't have time to wait either," he said smugly, glaring down at her. "This is a working ranch and I have too much to do. If you're interested in a job then I suggest you look someplace else."

Casey, known to be stubborn by nature, refused to back down. McKinnon had effectively pushed her anger to the boiling point. And when she saw he had gone back to grooming the horse, as if totally dismissing her, her anger escalated that much more.

"Why?" she asked, struggling to speak over the rage that had worked its way up to her throat. "I think you owe me an explanation as to why you won't consider hiring me." For a long while McKinnon remained stubbornly silent and Casey waited furiously, patiently, for him to respond, refusing to move an inch until he did.

Finally, after several tense moments, McKinnon sighed deeply and turned back to face her, feeling that he didn't owe her anything. He saw the angry lines curving her lips and thought that from the first time he'd seen her, he had found her mouth as tempting as the shiny red apple Eve had offered to Adam. And he bet her lips were just as delicious and probably even more sinful.

For crying out loud, couldn't she feel the sexual chemistry flowing between them even amidst all that anger radiating from her? And from him? The moment he had turned around and seen Casey standing in the middle of the barn, he'd felt a zap of emotions shoot to every part of his body as well as his testosterone spike up a few notches. The woman was so striking that even the bright sunlight, which rarely showed its face in these parts, didn't have a thing on her.

She exuded an air of sexiness without much effort and although she was frowning quite nicely now, the few occasions he had seen her smile her mouth had a way of curving enticingly that made you want to kiss the smile right off her lips. Even now her angry pout was a total turn on.

Then there were her physical attributes. Dark brown hair that was cut in a short and sassy style complemented her mahogany-colored features, eyes the color of the darkest chocolate that could probably make you melt if you gazed into them long enough, and a petite frame that was clad in a pair of jeans that appeared made just for her body.

He had just seen her last month at her cousin Delaney's surprise birthday party. He was of the opinion that each and every time he saw her she just kept getting prettier and prettier, and his attraction to her that more extreme. She even had the ability to smell good while standing in a barn filled with a bunch of livestock. Whatever perfume she was wearing was doing a number on him and besides that, although he couldn't see her legs right now, he had them plastered to his memory. They were long, shapely and—

"Well, McKinnon?"

He met her gaze as he tossed the brush in a pail and shoved his hands in the back pockets of his jeans. "Okay, I'll give you a reason. This is a horse ranch and I'm looking for someone who can train horses and not ponies. Corey would never forgive me if something were to happen to you."

He inwardly shuddered as if imagining such a thing, then added, "For Pete's sake, you're no bigger than a mite. The horse that needs to be trained is meaner than hell and I need to get him ready for the races in six weeks. As far as I'm concerned, you're not the person for the job. Prince Charming is too much animal for you to handle."

Anger flared in Casey's eyes and she drew herself up to her full five-foot-three. "And you're making that decision without giving me a chance to show you what I can do?"

"Yes, evidently I am," he drawled.

"Then you're nothing but a male chauvinistic—"

"Think whatever you like, but the bottom line is that I'm not hiring you. I'm sure there're other jobs in Bozeman that might interest you. And since you're familiar with running a clothing store, you might want to check in town to see if there're any employment opportunities available in that area."

Casey stared at him as she struggled to control the fury that threatened to suffocate her. He was right. She was wasting her time here. "In that case, there's nothing left for me to say," she said tightly, staring at his impassive features.

"No, there really isn't." And to prove his point he picked up the brush and began grooming the horse again, totally dismissing her once more.

Without saying anything else, an angry Casey strode toward the exit of the barn.

McKinnon watched Casey leave and released a deep sigh of frustration.

He knew she was pretty pissed with him but there was no way he would hire her to work on his ranch. Most Arabians by nature were mild-mannered and people-oriented, but the horse sent here for training lacked a friendly disposition by leaps and bounds. The only explanation McKinnon could come up with was that someone had treated the horse badly in the past, and it would take a skilled trainer to turn things around. He knew Casey had been born and raised in Texas, so chances were strong she was used to horses. But still, if things worked out and he expanded his business to train more horses, she would be dealing with studs that were known to be mean-spirited. He refused to be responsible if something were to happen to her.

Besides that, there was another reason he wouldn't hire Casey. He had decided six years ago after Lynette Franklin had walked out on him that a woman had no place on his ranch.

Just thinking of Lynette sent resentment through all parts of his body. But then to be fair, he couldn't rightly fault her for wanting something he couldn't give her. And when she had left, she had made him realize that a serious relationship with any female was something he would not involve himself in again.

His thoughts grudgingly shifted back to Casey. His attraction to her was more lethal than what he'd had for Lynette. Casey was a woman who, without very much effort, could bring out strong desires in any man. And to make matters worse, she was Corey's daughter and Durango's cousin. That meant she was definitely off-limits.

"Regardless of what she thinks, I did the right thing," he muttered, trying to place his concentration back on grooming Thunder, and not on how Casey's curvy backside swayed when she walked out of the barn. All he wanted from a woman was a short, hot, satisfying affair with no ties. Casey Westmoreland had the words *home, hearth* and *motherhood* all but stamped on her forehead. And that was the type of woman he avoided at all cost.

He refused to let any female become an emotional threat to his well-being ever again.

The moment the sunshine hit Casey's face she inhaled, trying to get her temper under control. She doubted there were any words to describe how she felt toward McKinnon Quinn at that moment. The man was impossible!

She glanced around and grudgingly admitted his sprawling ranch was simply beautiful. The house wasn't as huge as her father's but she thought it had a lot of class and exuded an appeal as strong as the man who owned it. He had adroitly erected the structure on a beautiful piece of land that had a picturesque view of the mountains in the background.

It was a sunny day in early May and the weather reminded her of a day in Texas. McKinnon's men were busy at work and as she walked toward her car to leave, she noted several beautiful horses were being led into a corral. She turned suddenly when one of the men's shouting caught her attention in time to see this huge monstrosity of a horse break free from the man's hold and start charging after him.

When the horse reared up on hind legs with full intent to stomp the man to death, she held her breath and watched as the man made a smart move and fell to the ground, immediately rolling out of harm's way. It seemed the animal was in rare form, and when several of the men ran forward to grab hold of his reins, he tried attacking them and sent them running for cover.

One of them wasn't quick enough and the horse took off, charging after him.

Without any thought of what she was doing or that she was putting her life in danger, Casey raced toward the charging animal trying to get his attention. She frantically waved her hands in the air and whistled. Pretty soon the animal turned huge, dark, flaming eyes in her direction and with a tilt of its head, a flare of its nostrils and a turn of its body, she then became his target. She felt the hairs on the back of her neck rise, putting her on full alert, however, instead of running for cover, she stood still.

McKinnon rushed out of the barn at that very moment. He had heard all the commotion and when he saw Prince Charming turned toward Casey, and she just standing there as if frozen in place, his heart slammed in his chest.

"Casey, run, dammit!"

When he saw she didn't move, he decided to run toward her, knowing that with Prince Charming's speed there was no way he was going to reach her in time, but he would die trying. Suddenly a rifle was shoved into his hands by one of his men and he knew he had to destroy the animal before it took Casey's life. At that moment it didn't matter one iota that the animal he was about to take down had cost Sheikh Jamal Ari Yasir over a million dollars. McKinnon's only concern was doing whatever it took to protect Casey Westmoreland.

He raised the gun to take aim and fire when one of his men shouted, "Wait! Take a look at that."

McKinnon blinked, amazed at what he was seeing.

Fear hadn't frozen Casey in place—she had been talking to the blasted animal and somehow she had gotten through to it. Prince Charming had come to a screeching halt within ten feet of Casey and was now trotting over to her with his tail wagging like they were the best of friends. She was holding her hand out to him and the horse cautiously came up to her and began nuzzling her hand.

McKinnon lowered the rifle. He knew that, like him, everyone was holding their breaths watching, waiting and staring in pure astonishment. Then, once she felt confident that she had gained the animal's trust, Casey grabbed hold of the reins and began walking him slowly back toward a hitching post.

"Well, I'll be. If I wasn't seeing it with my own eyes, I wouldn't believe it," McKinnon heard one of his men whisper behind him.

"Take a look at that," another man said as if awe struck. "That woman has Prince Charming practically eating out of her hands instead of him eating her hands off. Who the hell is she?"

McKinnon handed the rifle back to his foreman, Norris Lane, and shook his head. He'd heard the men's stunned comments. He would not have believed it without seeing it, either. "That's Corey Westmoreland's daughter," he said gruffly.

"Corey's daughter?"

"Yeah," McKinnon said as he watched Casey tie the animal to the hitching post and then lean over to whisper something in his ear before turning to walk away.

Whatever conversation was taking place between his men was lost on McKinnon as he began walking toward

Casey. His heart was still pounding wildly in his chest since he wasn't even close to recovering from the impact of seeing the horse charge toward her. Damn! He felt as if he'd lost a good ten years off his life.

When they reached each other, instead of stopping, Casey glanced at him with unconcealed irritation glaring in her eyes and walked right past.

McKinnon stopped and turned in time to see her walk over to her car, open the door and get in. He cursed silently as he watched a furious Casey Westmoreland drive away.

Chapter 2

Early the next morning, McKinnon was sitting at his kitchen table drinking a cup of coffee before the start of his work day when Norris walked in. He took one look at his foreman's expression and knew that whatever news he came to deliver, McKinnon wasn't going to like it.

"Good morning, Norris."

"Morning, McKinnon. Beckman's quit. He hauled ass sometime during the night and left a note on his bunk stating yesterday was the last straw. I guess that little episode with Prince Charming made him rethink staying on until you found a replacement."

McKinnon cursed under his breath as he set his coffee cup down. This wasn't news he wanted to hear. Gale Beckman had come highly recommended from an outfit in Wyoming. He had taken the man on, convinced he could do the job, and offered him one hell of a salary to train Prince Charming, one of Sheikh Yasir's prized possessions. Evidently Beckman had felt he'd met his match with the horse. Granted, Prince Charming had been in rare form yesterday, but, still, in the world of horse breeding you couldn't expect every horse to be meek and biddable. Far from it. Most were unfriendly and aggressive at best, hot-tempered and volatile at worse.

"Where are we going to find another horse trainer this late in the game?"

Norris's question reeled McKinnon's thoughts back in. He and his best friend Durango Westmoreland had started their horse-breeding business a few years ago because of their love for the animals. McKinnon handled the day-to-day running of the operation while Durango, who was still employed as a park ranger for Yellowstone, managed the books.

When Sheikh Jamal Ari Yasir, a prince from the Middle East who was married to Durango's cousin Delaney, had approached them a couple of months ago about taking on the training of Prince Charming to ready him for the races this fall, they had readily accepted, not foreseeing any problems and thinking it would be a way to expand their business from horse breeding into horse training, as well.

Successfully getting Prince Charming trained was their first major test in that particular area, and their success with that endeavor would assure the sheikh sent more business their way and provided good recommendations to his friends and business associates. But the situation looked bleak since they hadn't made any real progress and valuable time was being wasted.

McKinnon leaned back in his chair. "I guess the first thing I need to do is place a call to my contacts again," he said finally answering, although he was quick to think that his contacts' reliability was on shaky ground since they had been the reason he'd hired Beckman in the first place.

"What about Corey Westmoreland's daughter?"

McKinnon stiffened, pushed away from the table and stood. "What about her?"

"Well, you saw how she handled Prince Charming yesterday. She had that blasted animal eating out of her hands, literally. Do you think she might be interested in the job?"

McKinnon decided now was not the time to mention to Norris that Casey *had* been interested in the job—in fact, that had been her reason for showing up yesterday. Instead he said, "Doesn't matter if she would be. You know my policy about a woman working on this ranch."

Norris stared at him for a long moment before shaking his head and saying, "It's been over four years now, McKinnon. How long will it take you to get what Lynette did out of your mind...and heart?"

McKinnon sucked in a deep breath before saying, "I've done both."

Norris was one of the few who knew the full story about Lynette. He had been with McKinnon the night they'd arrived back at the ranch from rounding up wild horses in the north prairie to find that Lynette had packed up and left, leaving a scribbled note as to the reason why.

McKinnon's brusque words should have warned the sixty-year-old Norris that this was a touchy subject—

one McKinnon had no desire to engage in; but Norris, who'd known McKinnon since the day he was born, paid no mind. "Then act like it, son. Act like you've put it behind you."

McKinnon cursed under his breath. "You actually expect me to ask Corey Westmoreland's daughter to come work for me and live on this ranch? You saw her yesterday. She's no bigger than a mite. Granted, she handled Prince Charming okay, but what about the others to come after that? Some twice as mean. Besides, I need a trainer that I can invest in long term."

"I heard she's moving to town to be close to her father. To me that speaks of long term."

McKinnon's gaze narrowed. Evidently Norris had asked questions of the right people after Casey's impressive performance yesterday. Abruptly, McKinnon walked over to the window and looked out. He had barely slept last night for remembering the sight of Casey standing frozen in place while that blasted animal charged toward her. He hadn't felt so helpless before in his entire life. The thought of what that horse could have done to her sent chills through his body even now.

"The decision is yours, of course, but I think it will be to your advantage, considering everything, to hire her," Norris said behind him. "The sheikh expects that blasted horse trained and ready to race in less than two months. And the way I see it, Corey's daughter is our best bet."

McKinnon turned and shot a hard glare at Norris. "There has to be another way," he said, his features severe and unyielding.

""Then I hope you find it," Norris replied before moving to walk out the door.

He hadn't found another way.

And that was the reason McKinnon found himself arriving by horseback on Corey's Mountain later that same day. Seeing the spacious and sprawling ranch house, set among a stand of pine trees and beneath the beauty of a Montana sky, had bittersweet memories flooding his mind. He could recall the many summers he'd spent here as a young boy with Corey's nephews— all eleven of them. Just how Corey managed all of them was anyone's guess, but those summers had been some of the best of McKinnon's life. He'd been footloose and fancy free, and the only thing he'd worried about was staying away from the blackberries he was allergic to.

These days things were different. He had a lot to worry about. He had both a ranch and a business to run, and now it seemed the woman he'd always intended to keep at a distance would be living on his land, a stone's throw away.... If she accepted his job offer.

And that was the big question. After the way they'd clashed yesterday, would she even consider coming to work for him now? His contacts in the horse industry hadn't been any help and now it came down to eating crow and doing the one thing he hadn't wanted to do— offer Casey Westmoreland a job.

When he reached the ranch house he got off his horse and tied him to a post before glancing around, his gaze searching the wide stretch of land, scanning the fields and pastures. Corey's land. Corey's Mountain. McKinnon shook his head thinking it was rather sad that during those times he and Corey's eleven nephews were spending time on this mountain, somewhere in Texas Corey had three kids he'd known nothing about—a daughter and two sons. Triplets. Being the good man that he was, Corey was trying like hell to make up for lost time.

A sound coming from somewhere in back where the stables and corral were located caught McKinnon's ears, and before moving up the steps to the front door, he decided to check things out. As soon as he rounded the corner a swift surge of intense desire flooded him. He recognized Casey sitting on the back of a horse, surrounded by a group of men—one he recognized as her father.

He stopped walking and stood there, leaned against the house and stared at her, remembering the first time he'd laid eyes on her. It had been here, on this very land, standing pretty close to this same spot, while attending her cousin and his good friend Stone Westmoreland's wedding. It just so happened that Corey, who she had met for the first time that day, was also getting married.

It had been just minutes before the wedding was to begin and he had been talking with Durango and his brothers, Jared and Spencer. He had glanced around the exact moment a group of people had parted, giving him a spacious view of what he thought had to be the most beautiful woman he'd ever seen. He'd heard about Corey's triplets and had already met her two brothers, but that day had been the first time he had set his eyes on Casey Westmoreland.

Every male hormone within his body had gone on full alert and his libido hadn't been the same since. He had stood there, the conversations between him and the men long forgotten as he watched her move around the yard talking with her cousin Delaney. There had been such sensuality in her movement, such refined grace, that he found it hard to believe she was the same woman sitting on a horse now. But all it took was a glance of her face to know that she was one and the same. The same woman determined to stay etched inside his brain.

And then, as if she knew he was standing there staring at her, she glanced over in his direction and their gazes locked and held. He watched her stiffen, felt her anger and knew he had his work cut out for him. Chances were strong that after yesterday he was the last person she wanted to see.

But still he kept staring at her, liking the way the sun was shining on her hair, giving it a lustrous glow against the light blue blouse she was wearing. She had on jeans—that much he could see although his total view was hampered by the men standing around her.

As if wondering what had captured his daughter's attention, Corey glanced in his direction and smiled. He then said something to Casey and a brief moment later the older man was walking toward him. McKinnon shoved off from the wall and moved forward to meet the man he considered a second father. Corey and McKinnon's father had been best friends for years, long before McKinnon was born.

Towering over six-five with a muscular build, Corey Westmoreland was a giant of a man with a big heart, a love for the land and his family and friends.

"McKinnon," Corey Westmoreland said, smiling as

he embraced him in a bear hug. "What brings you up here?"

"Casey," McKinnon said simply. He couldn't help noticing the older man's expression didn't show any surprise. "She came to see me yesterday about a job."

Corey chuckled. "Yes, she told me about that."

McKinnon could imagine. "I'm here to offer her the job if she still wants it."

Corey shrugged. "You're going to have to discuss that with her. I guess I don't have to tell you that you did a pretty good job of pissing her off."

McKinnon nodded. He'd always appreciated Corey's honesty, even now. "No, you don't have to tell me." He glanced over to the area where Casey had been earlier when he heard several loud shouts. He lifted a brow. "What's going on?"

"Casey's about to try her hand at riding Vicious Glance."

McKinnon jerked his head around and practically glared Corey in the face. "You can't let her ride that horse."

Corey shook his head, grinning. "I'd like to see you try talking her out of it. She's been here enough times to know what a mean son of a bitch that animal is, but she's determined to break him in."

"And you're letting her?" McKinnon had both outrage and astonishment on his face. Everyone who had visited Corey's Mountain knew that Vicious Glance— named for the look the mean-spirited animal would give anyone who came close—was a damn good stud horse, but when it came to having anyone sitting on his back, he wasn't having it. More than one of Corey's ranch hands had gotten injured trying to be the one to change that bit of history.

"I'm not *letting* her do anything, McKinnon. Casey's a grown woman who's past the age of being told what she can or cannot do," he said. "I did ask her nicely to back down but she feels Vicious Glance isn't too much horse for her to handle, so we're about to see if that's true. You might as well follow me and watch the show like the rest of us."

McKinnon sucked in a deep breath and for the first time wondered if Corey had lost his mind. This was the man's *daughter*—the same one who could end up breaking her damn neck if that horse threw her. But before he could open his mouth and say anything else, Corey reached out and touched his shoulder. "Calm down. She'll be fine."

McKinnon frowned, wondering who Corey was trying to convince—especially after seeing the expression of worry that quickly crossed the older man's face. "I hope you're right," McKinnon said, pulling off his Stetson and wiping his forehead with the back of his hand. Already he was perspiring from worrying. Dammit, what was the woman trying to prove?

Without saying anything else, he placed the Stetson back on his head and walked with Corey over to where the other men were standing. Casey glanced at him, glared and looked way. Corey shook his head and somberly whispered to McKinnon, "Seems she's still pissed at you."

"Yep, seems that way, doesn't it," McKinnon replied. But at that moment, how Casey felt about him was the least of his worries. Like the other men standing around, he watched, almost holding his breath, as she entered the shoot to get on a blindfolded Vicious Glance's back. She swung her petite body into the saddle and grabbed hold of the reins one of the ranch hands handed to her.

McKinnon's pulse leaped when she gave the man a nod and the action began when the blindfold was removed from the horse's eyes. Vicious Glance seemed to have gone stark raving mad, bucking around the corral, trying to get rid of the unwanted occupant on his back. A few times McKinnon's breath got caught in his throat when it seemed Casey was a goner for sure, but she hung on and pretty soon he found himself hollering out words of encouragement to her like the other men.

She was given time to prove her point before several of the men raced over and quickly whisked her off the horse's back. Loud cheers went up and McKinnon couldn't help but smile. "Who in the hell taught her how to handle a horse like that?" he asked, both incredulously and relieved as he glanced over at Corey.

The older man grinned. "Ever heard of Sid Roberts?"

"What wannabe cowboy hasn't," McKinnon replied, thinking of the man who had grown up to be a legend, first as an African-American rodeo star and then as a horse trainer. "Why?"

"He was Casey's mother's brother; the man Carolyn went to live with in Texas, and who eventually helped her raise my kids. It's my understanding that when it came to horses, he basically passed everything he knew down to Casey. Clint and Cole had already dreamed about one day becoming Texas Rangers, but I'm told that Casey wanted to follow in her uncle's footsteps and become a horse trainer."

McKinnon was listening to everything Corey was saying, though his gaze was glued to Casey. They had calmed Vicious Glance down and she was standing beside the animal whispering something in his ear, and as crazy as it seemed, it appeared the horse understood whatever it was she was saying. "So what happened?" he asked Corey. "Owning a dress store is a long way from being a horse trainer."

"Her mother talked her out of it, saying she needed to go to college and get a degree doing something safe and productive."

McKinnon nodded. "So she gave up her dream."

"Yeah, for a little while, but she's determined to get it back." Corey glanced up at McKinnon. "Just so you know, Cal Hooper dropped by last night and offered her a job over at his place working with his horses."

McKinnon frowned and looked at Corey. "Did she take it?"

"No, she told him she would think about it." Corey chuckled. "I think he kind of gave her the creeps."

And with good reason, McKinnon thought. Everybody around those parts knew that even in his late forties, Cal Hooper, a local rancher, still considered himself a ladies' man and had a reputation for playing fast and loose with women. If the rumors one heard were true, he was also the father of a number of illegitimate children around Bozeman. McKinnon's gaze shifted to Casey once again. She was walking toward them and he could tell from the pout on her lush mouth that she wasn't glad he was there. In fact, she looked downright annoyed.

"McKinnon," she acknowledged when she reached them.

"Casey. That was a good show of horsemanship," he said.

"Thank you." Although she'd said the words he could tell from her expression that she couldn't care less what he thought.

"I agree with McKinnon. You did a fantastic job out there, Casey."

The smile she gave her father was genuine. "Thanks, Corey. Vicious Glance will be fine now. He just needed to know that someone else, namely whoever is riding him, is always in control."

"Well, I need to talk to Jack about how we'll be handling him from now on. Excuse me for a moment," Corey said before walking off, leaving them alone.

A few brief moments after Corey left, McKinnon tilted his hat back and looked down at Casey. His eyes narrowed. Before offering her the job there was something he needed to get straight with her, here and now. "Don't you ever set foot on Quinn land and pull a stunt like you did yesterday. You had no way of knowing what that blasted horse was going to do. You could have been killed."

"But I'm very much alive, aren't I?" she said snippily, deciding the last thing she needed was for this man to dictate what she could or could not do." "You're not my father, McKinnon."

"Thank God for that."

Casey drew in a deep, irritated breath. "I think we've

said enough to each other, don't you think?" She moved to walk away.

"Aren't you curious as to why I'm here?" he asked.

She frowned up at him. "Not really. I assumed you came to see Corey."

He shoved his hands into his pockets. "I came to see you."

She placed her hands on her hips and narrowed her eyes. "And why would you come to see me?"

"To offer you that job you were interested in yesterday."

She glared at him. "That was yesterday. I have no desire to work for a male chauvinist tyrant."

McKinnon frowned. "A male chauvinist tyrant?"

"Yes, that about describes you to a tee. Now if you will excuse me, I—"

"The pay is good and you'll need to stay at the ranch, in the guesthouse."

Casey threw her head back and squared her shoulders. "Don't let me tell you where you can take the pay and guesthouse and shove it, McKinnon. Like I said, I'm no longer interested. Now if you'll excuse me, I have things to do."

He watched as she walked off, swaying her hips with each and every step she took. He couldn't help but admire her spunk, but he refused to let her have the upper hand. "Casey?" he said, calling after her.

She stopped walking and slowly turned around. "What?"

"Think about my offer and let me know within a week."

Her glare was priceless. "There's nothing to think

about, McKinnon. The last thing I want is to work for you." She then turned back around and continued walking.

Her words irritated the hell out of him because deep down he didn't want her to come work for him, either. But dammit, he needed her...rather, he needed her skill with horses. And more than anything he had to remember there was a difference in the two.

Chapter 3

The nerve of the man, Casey thought as she slipped into the soapy water in the huge claw-foot bathtub. Why didn't he understand English? How many times did she have to say she didn't want to work for him to make herself clear?

She settled back against the tub and closed her eyes. The man was simply infuriating and like she'd told him, he would be the last person she worked for. She would consider going to work for Cal Hooper first, even though that man made her skin crawl each and every time he looked at her. At least she could defend herself against the likes of the Cal Hoopers out there, thanks to all those self-defense classes her brothers had made her take over the years.

But when it came to McKinnon Quinn she was as defenseless as a fish out of water. There was just some-thing outright mind-blowingly hot about a tall man in a pair of tight jeans, especially when he had a nice-looking rear end. Add to that an honest-to-goodness handsome face and any woman in her right mind would be a goner. Holy cow, she was only human!

She eased down farther in the water, wishing for the umpteenth time that she could get the man out of her mind. He had made her madder than a pan of hot fish grease yesterday with his how-great-thou-art attitude. But today he'd shown up offering her the job that he'd told her he wouldn't hire her for. Well, that was too friggin' bad. Like she told him, he could take the job and shove it for all she cared.

Deciding to rid her mind of McKinnon Quinn once and for all, she opened her eyes and glanced around. The room Abby had given her to use was simply beautiful. With all the silk draperies, cream-colored walls and extensive decorating, it was obvious the decor of the room had had a woman's touch, as had the rest of the house. Corey's ranch at one time may have been a man's domain, but now it was evident that a woman was in residence, and that woman was Abby.

Abby.

From the first time she found out about her, Casey had figured she wouldn't like the woman who held her father's heart to the point where he hadn't been able to love another woman—not even her own mother who had loved Corey Westmoreland until her dying day. But all it took was a few moments around Corey and Abby to know just how in love they were and probably always had been, even through his fifty-something years as a bachelor, and Abby's fifteen-year marriage to a man she didn't love.

Casey smiled. She had to admit that she had grown fond of the very proper Bostonian her father had married, who happened to be the mother of Madison, her cousin Stone's wife. Since finding out the truth about her father, Casey had come to realize that she'd had a slew of relatives—more Westmorelands, cousins from just about every walk of life—and they had been genuine in opening both their friendship and their hearts to her and her brothers.

She glanced at the clock. Abby would be serving dinner in half an hour and dinner time, Casey discovered, was a big ordeal for Abby since she had a way of making things somewhat formal. So instead of wearing jeans like she usually did, it was during the evening meal that she would put on a skirt and blouse or a dress.

She eased out of the tub to dry off and her thoughts shifted back to McKinnon. She hoped she'd seen the last of him for a while. Although she wouldn't work for him, she was determined to work for somebody. She could only accept her father and Abby's hospitality for so long. Although she knew they wanted her to stay there with them, Casey only planned to live here for so long. She needed and wanted her own place.

She smiled, thinking that in a way her father and Abby were still newlyweds—or at least they acted like they were. More than once she had almost walked up on them sharing a very heated kiss. A part of her was happy for what they shared, but then those times had been a blunt reminder of what she didn't have in her own life.

Although she had dated while living in Texas, most men hadn't wanted what she'd been determined to one day be—a virgin bride. Most wanted to try out the goodies before committing and she refused to do that; especially after being fed from knee-high her mother's storybook rendition of how romantic things had been for her and Corey.

Casey had been determined to find that same kind of special love for herself, and as a result, had decided the only man she slept with would be her husband. But since finding out the truth about her own parents, keeping her virginity intact hadn't meant as much to her anymore. She just hadn't met a man who'd drawn her interest enough to share his bed.

Her thoughts went back to McKinnon and she gritted her teeth, refusing to consider such a thing. The man was as exasperating as he was enticing. And at the moment, she had much more important things to think about—like finding a job.

She sighed and decided that after dinner she would return to her room. She had picked up a newspaper in town yesterday and intended to cover the Want Ads section. It was time she took control of her future. Making the decision to move to Montana to be close to Corey had been the first step. Now finding employment and a place to stay would be her second.

"I'm glad you took me up on my offer to stay the night, McKinnon," Corey said, handing the young man a glass of some of his finest scotch. "Although you're a skilled horseman, it's too dangerous for you to attempt going back down that mountain this late. It would have been dark before you got to the bottom." He then chuckled before tacking on, "And Morning Star and Martin would have my hide if anything were to happen to their oldest son."

McKinnon grinned knowing that was true. He had a very special relationship with his mother and father, as well as his three younger brothers. Matthew was twenty-seven, Jason was twenty-five and Daniel was twenty-three, and all three were unattached with no thoughts of settling down any time soon.

It was hard for McKinnon to believe at times that Martin Quinn was actually his stepfather and not his biological father. He was in his teens when he'd been told that his natural father, a Creole of African-American descent, had died in a car accident before he was born, and that a pregnant Morning Star—a member of the Blackfoot Indian tribe, had gone to work for the esteemed Judge Martin Quinn as a bookkeeper, only to end up falling in love and marrying him before the child was born.

"So, how are things with the horse business?"

Corey's question pulled McKinnon's thoughts back. "They would be a lot better if I can get Casey to come work for me. I know I blew things yesterday but I had a reason for it. You know how I feel about another woman living at my ranch."

Corey nodded. Yes, he did know but then they weren't talking about just any other woman—they were talking about his daughter. He wasn't born yesterday. He knew about the heated sparks that always went off when McKinnon and Casey were within a few feet of each other. In the past they had pretty much kept their distance but things wouldn't be quite that easy here in

Montana, especially since Corey and McKinnon's parents were the best of friends.

"So how are you going to talk her into it?" he asked, knowing that McKinnon would make an attempt. When it came to the art of persuasion, biological or not, he was Martin Quinn's son and Martin hadn't moved up the ranks of powerhouse attorney to circuit judge in these parts without his persuasive nature.

Corey smiled. Poor Morning Star hadn't known what had hit her all those years ago when she'd been talked into a marriage of convenience that had ended up being anything but that.

"Don't know yet, but I won't give up," McKinnon said. "I promised Jamal that I would have that horse ready for him this fall, and I intend to do just that."

"I hate to interrupt such important male conversation, but dinner is ready," said a beautiful Abby Winters Westmoreland as she stuck her head in the door and smiled. "And Casey will be down in a minute."

"We'll be there in a second, sweetheart," Corey said, smiling back at the woman he loved to distraction—had always loved.

McKinnon watched the loving exchange between Corey and Abby, which was similar to what he always saw between his parents. Some people were lucky to find their soul mate and spend the rest of their lives together in wedded bliss. He had long ago accepted that he wouldn't be one of the lucky ones. His future was set without any permanent woman in it.

Casey hurried down the stairs knowing she was already a few minutes late for dinner. One of her brothers had phoned to see how she was doing. Even all the way from Texas, Clint and Cole were trying to keep tabs on her. She smiled thinking she was used to it and although she would never admit it to them, it felt good knowing they still cared about her well-being. Born triplets, the three of them had a rather close relationship, and by her being the youngest, Clint and Cole made it their business to try and be her keepers.

She moved quickly to the dining room and stopped dead in her tracks when she saw McKinnon sitting at the table. She tried to mask her displeasure at seeing him as he and her father stood when she entered the room. "McKinnon, I'm surprised you're still here," she said, trying to keep the cutting edge out of her voice.

She knew the smile that he gave her was only meant to infuriate her, but before he could respond her father offered an explanation. "It would have been too dangerous for him to try going back down the mountain this late, so I invited him to spend the night," Corey said, once both men sat back down after she took a seat.

"Oh." Casey tried not to show the cringe that passed through her body in knowing that McKinnon would be there all night. Just the thought that they would be sleeping under the same roof was nothing she wanted to think about. So she didn't. As soon as grace was said and the food passed around, she tried concentrating on something else. "Everything looks delicious, Abby."

Abby smiled over at her. "Thanks, Casey." The older woman then turned her attention to everyone at the table. "I got a call from Stone and Madison today. They're in Canada on a book-signing tour and said to tell everyone hello. They hope to be able to swing by here in a few weeks."

"That would be wonderful," Casey said, meaning it. She'd discovered that there had been only two females born in the Westmoreland family in her generation—her and Delaney. Delaney lived out of the country with her desert sheikh, but whenever she came to the States she made a point of contacting Casey, and had even traveled once to Beaumont to visit with her last year. But now that Delaney was pregnant her traveling had been curtailed somewhat.

Then there were the wives of her cousins she'd gotten to know. Shelly, Tara, Jayla, Dana, Jessica and Savannah were as friendly as friendly could be. And Madison claimed her as a stepsister instead of a cousin-in-law.

Deciding to completely ignore McKinnon as much as she could, she turned and struck up a conversation with Abby, who was sitting beside her. They got caught up in a discussion about the latest fashions, and who had broken up with whom in Hollywood.

As much as she tried not to overhear her father and McKinnon's conversation, Casey couldn't help but eavesdrop on their discussion regarding the best way to train a horse. She couldn't believe some of the suggestions McKinnon was making. He would be a complete failure in this latest business venture of his if he were to follow through with any of them.

"It might be best if you stuck to horse breeding instead of horse training, McKinnon," she couldn't resist tossing in. "Anyone with any real knowledge of horse training who's keeping abreast of the up-to-date methods would know that using a strap on a horse is no longer acceptable."

McKinnon lifted a brow like he was taking what she said with a grain of salt. "Is that so?"

"Yes, it is so. Although pain and intimidation may have been the way years ago, things have progressed a lot since then. Trainers are using a kinder and gentler approach to communicate with horses," she stated unequivocally. "And it's sad that some horse owners are still under the impression that such techniques as snubbing a horse to the post or running horses in mindless circles until they're exhausted are the way to go and still being used. "

McKinnon leaned back in his chair. "And what if you had a not-so-docile animal like Prince Charming? Or a bunch of wild horses? What would you do then?"

"Same thing since it would make no difference. However, in the case of Prince Charming, I'd say someone, and rather recently I assume, mistreated him. But luckily at one time or another, he had a nice trainer and when I began talking to him to calm him down, he remembered those kinder days. That's the reason he didn't hurt me. I'm against using strong-arm tactics of any kind when working with horses."

"And I appreciate your opinion, Casey, but I have to disagree. Although I'm against anyone being outright mean and brutal to a horse, I still find the traditional way of doing things much better. And you're right—you were lucky yesterday with Prince Charming, however, I doubt that the kinder approach is for every horse. It will be almost impossible to get Prince Charming ready for the races in the fall without using some kind of strict disciplinary method."

"And *I* disagree."

He locked eyes with her. "You have that right to disagree, Casey. But this is Montana and not Texas. We tend to do things differently here."

"But a horse is a horse and why should you do things differently if the results could be the same?" she asked, taking a sip of her lemonade.

She was trying hard to remain nice but McKinnon was making it plum difficult. Why did the man have to be so bull headed? "It bothers me that some horse trainers are only interested in rushing a horse's training in that quest to seek immediate gratification when all it takes is gentle, loving care. If those methods are used over a period of time, a horse will be anxious, willing and eager to give back to its owner."

"You make it sound like a horse is almost human, Casey."

"No, I'm not saying that but what I am saying is that when it comes to horses, there has to be a foundation of trust established upon which all further development and training must be built. Without it, training a horse like Prince Charming to do anything, especially to win a race, will be hopeless as well as impossible."

McKinnon basically agreed with everything she'd said but he wouldn't let her know that. He would continue playing devil's advocate until he had her just where he wanted her.

"I think you're wrong on that account, Casey."

"And I think you're too close-minded to see that I'm right."

He lifted a brow, not taking his eyes off hers. "I dare you to prove me wrong."

"Consider it done," she said without thinking.

He leaned forward in his chair. "Good. And since you're so keen on the idea of the new way of doing things, I'll pay you fifty thousand dollars for your efforts. You have eight weeks and you'll have to stay on my ranch in the guest house."

Casey blinked. What was he talking about? So she asked him.

He smiled. "You just accepted the challenge to prove me wrong with Prince Charming. But if you're not sure of your capabilities I'll most certainly understand and let you back out of it."

She glared at him. "I know what I'm capable of doing, McKinnon."

"So you say but I don't want to put you on the spot. I'll fully understand if you decide you can't handle things."

Casey's glare intensified. "When it comes to a horse, McKinnon, I can handle just about anything."

He shrugged. "You have eight weeks to prove it."

Casey glanced around the table at her father and Abby. They had been quiet during her and McKinnon's entire conversation and were now staring at her. There was no way she could back out now, although a part of her felt that McKinnon had somehow deliberately set her up.

She then turned her attention back to McKinnon, glaring at him. "Fine, I'll show you just what I can do, McKinnon Quinn. I just hope you're ready for me."

McKinnon leaned back in his chair. He decided not to tell Casey that if he lived to be the ripe old age of one hundred, he would never, ever be ready for her.

Chapter 4

The dark blue car caught McKinnon's eyes the moment it pulled into the yard. He'd been walking out of the barn and stopped a moment to look at the woman sitting behind the wheel. Casey had said that she would arrive within two days and she had kept her word.

He still had mixed feelings about her being there, but he had a business to run and hiring her on had made business sense. He would just have to call on his common sense and keep as much distance between them as possible. At least she would be living in the guest cottage out back and not under the same roof, he thought, as he watched her swing those shapely, gorgeous legs of hers out of the car. He sucked in a deep breath.

He glanced around and saw that he wasn't the only one who'd noticed her arrival...or her legs. His men had stopped what they were doing to stare, especially when Casey grabbed a duffel bag out of the backseat.

She was wearing a mint-green blouse that showed off firm, perfect breasts and a waist-cinching skirt whose hem swished around those gorgeous legs.

When she went to the back of her car and lifted the trunk, her luggage made it apparent to anyone looking that she was moving in. Most of McKinnon's men knew of his long-standing rule that a female had no place living on his ranch. He also knew they were staring at her for another reason—other than the obvious male one. The last time she had been there she had earned their respect with the way she had handled Prince Charming. The way they saw it, she had saved Edward Price from getting stomped to death while placing her own life in danger to do so.

When it seemed that every ranch hand who worked for him was now racing toward the car to help Casey with her luggage, almost tripping over each other in their haste, he shook his head. He knew then and there that he would have a very serious talk with his men and make sure they understood that just like them, Casey had been hired to do a job and that was the only reason she was there.

When it became apparent that Jed Wilson and Evan Duvall were about to knock each other over to offer Casey their assistance, McKinnon decided to intervene. "Okay, you guys can get back to work. I'll help Casey with her things."

He saw the disappointed look on the men's faces as they turned and followed his orders, leaving him and Casey alone. He met her gaze. "Casey." He could tell from her expression that she didn't want to be there.

"McKinnon. If you'd be so kind to show me where I'll be staying over the next weeks, I'd appreciate it."

She had managed to temper some of her anger but not all of it. She was still somewhat ticked off. "Just follow me. I'll come back for your luggage later. The guesthouse is out back."

They walked around the ranch house together and not for the first time, Casey thought that McKinnon's ranch was erected on a beautiful piece of land under the warmth of the Montana sky. It was another nice day and again the weather reminded her of a day in Texas. She sighed deeply. She was already missing home.

"Are you okay?"

She glanced up at him. She wished his eyes weren't so dark, so intense, so downright seductive. "Yes, I'm fine. I've been in Montana a little over a week and I'm missing Texas already."

"It's warmer here than usual for this time of the year," he said, his voice dry as he looked ahead and not at her. "That means a colder than usual winter."

She shuddered. "I don't do cold weather very well."

"If you're planning on hanging around in these parts, my best advice to you is to get used to it," he said curtly. "Otherwise, you'll be shivering all over the place. Montana is known for its beauty as well as its freezing cold winters."

Speaking of shivering…one passed through her body at that moment when their arms brushed. Geez. No man had ever given her the shivers before. She couldn't help but take in the beautifully muscled body walking beside her, making it downright difficult for her to breathe.

When they reached what she assumed was the guesthouse, Casey stood aside for him to open the door. He motioned her in and then followed behind her. She relaxed a bit when he moved to the other side of the room and took that time to glance around. The place was beautiful. For a guest-house, it was massive and the living room was neatly decorated in earth-tone colors. The furniture had been handcrafted of a beautiful dark wood and the huge window that showcased the mountains gave the room a comforting effect.

"There's a bedroom and bath down the hall that you can check out while I bring in your luggage."

She turned toward the sound of McKinnon's voice. "Okay."

"There's not a kitchen since most meals are eaten at the big house, but it won't be a problem if you prefer taking your meals here. Just let Henrietta know."

Casey lifted a brow. "Henrietta?"

"Yes, she's my cook and housekeeper."

Casey nodded. "She lives here on the ranch?"

"No," McKinnon said rather quickly, as if such a thing was not possible. "Henrietta and her husband Lewis live a few miles from here, not far from my parents' place. She gets here every morning around six and leaves every evening around that same time." He pushed away from the wall. "I'll be back in a second with your luggage."

He left the room and Casey was relieved to be out of his presence for a little while. Everything about McKinnon exuded sensuality, and as a woman, she was fully aware of him as a man. But more than anything, she was determined to stamp down whatever hot and racy feelings he brought out in her—and fight the sizzling desire that had a tendency to slam into her body whenever he came within a few feet of her.

Deciding to shake those feelings now, she crossed the room to look out the window at the mountains looming in the background. She was here to do a job and nothing more. So how difficult could that be?

As McKinnon had suggested, Casey looked around while he brought in her luggage. When he returned moments later and found her standing beside the massive oak bed, his pulse began racing. There was just something about a beautiful woman standing next to a bed that would do it to a man each and every time.

Casey turned around when she heard him enter the room and could actually feel the sexual tension that surrounded them. That wasn't good. Angry at his inability to control his emotions like he usually did around a woman, he placed her luggage on the bed. "I'll leave you to unpack," he said gruffly. "Since you don't have to officially start work until tomorrow, you can use today to get settled in."

"I will, and thanks for bringing in my things."

"Don't mention it," he said, glancing at the time on his watch. He then glanced back at her. "And knowing Henrietta she'll be dropping by sometime today to introduce herself."

"I'll look forward to her visit."

McKinnon wished he could keep his concentration on what Casey was saying rather than her features which appeared more striking than ever. It was her eyes, her mouth, her hair that was styled perfectly for her face.

"Will there be anything else, McKinnon?"

He gave himself a mental shake and frowned at her question. She had caught him staring. "No, there's nothing else. I'll see you at dinner."

"No, you won't."

"Excuse me?"

"I said you won't see me at dinner. I've been invited out."

Her announcement only added to his irritation. He tried not to wonder who she would be sharing dinner with. Cal Hooper? Someone she'd met since arriving here? Why the hell did he care and more importantly, why did the thought bother him? "Okay, fine. Enjoy your meal." He turned to leave.

"McKinnon?"

He turned back around. For some reason he was feeling annoyed, aggravated, impulsive; like hitting something, breaking somebody's bones, namely whoever she was meeting up with later. "What?" he responded gruffly.

He could tell from her expression that she hadn't liked the tone of his response. "For some reason I get the impression that you really don't want me here but that you're willing to put those feelings aside to utilize my talents," she said, putting her hands on her hips and glaring at him. "That's all well and good because frankly, I don't want to be here, either."

He crossed his arms over his chest and glared back. "Then why are you?"

"To prove a point that all women aren't incompetent when it comes to horses."

His frown deepened. "I never said they were."

"You didn't have to. You made your thoughts known when you didn't hire me that first day."

A part of McKinnon struggled with what she was saying because she was so far from the truth it was pathetic. The reason he hadn't hired her that first day had had nothing to do with what he thought of her abilities as a horse trainer, but what he'd thought of her abilities as a woman. A very desirable woman. He couldn't tell her that though.

"You're wrong, Casey. I have a high degree of respect for women who handle horses. In fact, the greatest horseman I know happens to be a female and she can outride, outrope and probably outshoot any man I know. And I hold her in the highest regard."

Casey lifted a brow, wondering who this paragon of a woman was. "And who is she?" she asked.

"My mother, Morning Star Long-Lance McKinnon Martin," he said before turning and leaving the room.

"Now, aren't you a pretty little thing!"

Casey turned and met the older woman's smiling face. Her smile was so bright and cheery, she couldn't do anything but smile back. "Thanks. You must be Henrietta."

The woman's laughter echoed through the room. "Yes, that's me. And you are definitely Corey Westmoreland's child. You look just like him, just a whole lot prettier."

"Thank you."

"McKinnon gave me strict orders not to bother you until you'd gotten settled in. I thought these might pretty up the place for you even more," she said, handing Casey what looked to be a bouquet of hand-picked fresh flowers.

Casey beamed. "Thanks, they're beautiful."

"You're welcome. I grew them myself. I have a flower garden on the other side of the ranch house." She chuckled. "That's McKinnon's way of making me tow the line by threatening to have my garden mowed down, but he doesn't scare me any."

"He doesn't?"

"Heck no. I've been with that boy since the day he was born. I was his first and only nanny, so I know how to deal with him."

A part of Casey wondered how McKinnon had been as a child but decided not to ask. "And you're still with him now?" she asked while finding the perfect spot on a table in the living room for the flowers.

"Yes, only because he needs me. If I didn't make sure he got a home-cooked meal every so often he would probably starve to death. And speaking of cooked meals, I understand you're passing up the chance for me to fix a special one for you tonight."

Casey grinned, thinking she liked this large, robust woman already. "Sorry about that but I was invited over to my cousin's house for dinner."

Henrietta nodded. "I imagine you're talking about Durango. In that case I understand. I'm still grinning over the fact that boy's married with a baby on the way. That just goes to show that miracles can happen to a devout bachelor when the right woman comes along."

Casey hoped she wasn't throwing out any hints about the possibility of her and McKinnon ever getting to-gether because that wouldn't happen. Ever. The man was too reserved, rigid and resigned for her taste. "Yes, I'm happy for Durango and Savannah. They are very happy together," she said, leaving it at that and hoping Henrietta would, too.

"Well, I guess your decision to eat elsewhere is the reason McKinnon told me I didn't have to cook. Now he has plans for himself. I guess he'll be going into town tonight."

A part of Casey didn't want to think what he would do when he got there and who he would see. "I guess that means you'll have a night off," she said.

"Yes. I'll be leaving in a few hours unless there's something you need me to do. I tried to get this place ready for you as best I could."

"And you did a wonderful job, Henrietta. It's beautiful and I know I'm going to feel right at home for the short time I'll be here."

"And that's what McKinnon wants."

Casey doubted it, but decided not to tell the older woman that. However, there were a couple of things the woman could possibly tell *her,* things she preferred not asking McKinnon about. The less she saw of him the better. But it would help to know how early things got moving at the ranch in the mornings. The last thing she wanted was to be sleeping in while everyone else was up and working. The men employed by her father started their day as early as four in the morning. "How would you like to join me for a cup of coffee? There are some questions I have about the workings of this ranch and I'd rather not bother McKinnon with them."

Henrietta smiled. "I'll be glad to tell you whatever you want to know. You got a coffee pot here?"

"Yes, although there isn't a kitchen to set it in. Since all I needed was an electrical plug, I'm using that table in the hallway. We can sit in the living room on the sofa. I simply love the view from there."

"Isn't it just magnificent?" Henrietta said glancing over at the window. "The only thing wrong with this house is that it doesn't have a kitchen. I told McKinnon that while he was building it, but he said it didn't need one since he intended for it to be a guest-house and not a guest lodge. It's only a few feet from the big house, so anyone getting hungry can come in there to eat."

Casey nodded, not surprised he looked at things that way given his stubborn and uncompromising nature. "Well, you just get settled on the sofa over there and I'll bring the coffee to you."

As she turned to leave she had a feeling that Henrietta would be one of the reasons she would find the time she spent on McKinnon's ranch rather pleasant after all.

McKinnon stopped his truck the moment he pulled into Durango's yard, recognizing the dark blue car immediately. It appeared that Savannah had invited Casey to dinner tonight, as well. So much for the mystery of who she was having dinner with. He then frowned wondering if the newly wedded couple were trying their hand at matchmaking?

A part of McKinnon refused to believe Durango would do something like that. After all, his best friend knew the reason he could never entertain the idea of settling down and marrying. However, chances were Durango hadn't shared anything about McKinnon's medical history with Savannah. Savannah Claiborne

Westmoreland, who he thought of as a sister since she'd married Durango, probably thought he needed an exclusive woman in his life. Once married, some people had a tendency to think everyone around them should be married, too.

He got out of the truck knowing it would be difficult as hell to be around Casey tonight. He should have declined Savannah's offer to dinner when she called, and stuck with his plans to go into town, eat at one of the restaurants and then seek out a little female companionship. He wasn't counting but it had been a while since he'd been with a woman, more than six months. The ranch had kept him too busy to seek out a willing bed partner.

He shook his head, convinced that was the reason he was finding Casey so desirable, but quickly knew that wasn't true. He'd always found her desirable.

The moment his best friend opened the door to his home, McKinnon said, "Your wife hasn't talked you into playing matchmaker, has she, Rango?"

Durango shook his head, grinning. "You know me better than that. In fact, I didn't know you were coming until a couple hours ago. But I shouldn't be surprised. Savannah's decided that you need someone special."

McKinnon frowned. "I have someone special. His name is Thunder," he said of his horse.

Durango chuckled. "I care to differ. A horse wouldn't do well in your bed every night."

"I don't need a woman in my bed every night." A serious expression then covered McKinnon's features. "I take it that you haven't told Savannah that I can't have a special woman in my life even if I wanted one."

Durango met McKinnon's gaze. "No. That's your secret to share, not mine."

"Thanks."

"Hey, you don't have to thank me and you know it," Durango said.

McKinnon nodded. Yes, he did know it. He and Durango had been the best of friends since that botched-up job of becoming blood brothers when they were ten. It was an incident that had nearly sent McKinnon to the emergency room for stitches when the knife they'd used had sliced into his hand too deep.

"But you already know my feelings on the matter, McKinnon. You can always consider—"

"No, Rango. It doesn't matter. I made my decision about things a long time ago."

"Hey, I thought I heard someone at the door," Savannah Westmoreland said, breezing as much as she could into the room as a woman who would be giving birth to one large baby in four months. For a while the doctors had thought she would be having twins but a recent sonogram had shown one big whopping baby—a girl.

She quickly crossed the floor and gave McKinnon a peck on the cheek. "You're looking handsome as ever," she said smiling up at him.

McKinnon lifted a dark brow. In a way he was grateful for Savannah's interruption of his and Durango's conversation. The issue of his medical history was something they couldn't agree on. "Sounds like you're trying to butter me up for something," he said, studying her features for traces of guilt.

Savannah laughed. "Now why would I do that?"

McKinnon crossed his arms over his chest. "That's

what I'd like to know—and don't you dare flash those hazel eyes at me."

Savannah shook her head, grinning, and then with a wave of her hand she pushed her shoulder-length curly brown hair out of her face. "I'm not flashing my eyes, so stop being suspicious of me." Then she quickly said with a smile, "I forgot to mention that I also invited Casey to dinner tonight. She's in Durango's office talking on the phone. Tara just called. She's having her first sonogram in a few weeks and she and Thorn are excited about it."

McKinnon shook his head. "What will your family do with all these babies being born, Rango?"

Durango chuckled. "Nothing but make room for more. I talked to Stone last night and he and Madison are coming through on their way from Canada. I have a feeling there's a reason for their visit."

McKinnon was about to open his mouth to say something when Casey walked into the room. He could tell from her expression that she was surprised to see him, which meant she had known nothing about his invitation to dinner. She had changed clothes and was wearing another skirt and blouse. This outfit was just as alluring as the one she'd had on earlier.

"McKinnon."

"Casey," he said stiffly, returning her greeting.

"Okay, guys," a smiling Savannah said, looking at McKinnon and then back at Casey and ignoring the deep frown coming from her husband. "I hope everyone is hungry because I prepared a feast."

Chapter 5

After dinner was over, McKinnon quickly left. Spending too much time around Casey wasn't good. All through dinner he had found himself looking over at her, feeling his flesh prickle each and every time their gazes connected. And even when she wasn't looking his way, he was looking hers; studying her mouth and thinking of over a thousand-plus things he could do with it. And he kept admiring her well-toned body every time she got up from the table while his mind worked overtime imagining that same beautiful body bare.

He had declined dessert, thanked Savannah for preparing such a wonderful meal and told Durango he would touch base with him sometime during the week. Then he nodded at Casey and left, trying to make it home in record time. There was something about having a sexual ache for a woman you couldn't have that made a man want to burn the rubber off his tires.

Damn, he was lucky that one of Sheriff Richard's deputies hadn't been parked along one of the back roads with a speed trap.

Once McKinnon opened the door to his home, he headed straight to the kitchen for a beer. A half hour later, after enjoying his beer and taking a cold shower, he slipped between the crisp white sheets intent on getting a good night's sleep. But before he could close his eyes his mind went to the past and the reason he was sleeping in this bed alone.

He had purchased this land when he'd turned twenty-five knowing when he had bought the ranch house that he would live in it alone. He'd also known he would be one of those men who died a bachelor—refusing to take the risk of ever having a wife and children—once he'd found out about the rare bone disease his biological father had passed on to him.

When he'd met Lynette, he had fallen for her and thought she had loved him just as much—so much that he had felt comfortable for the first time to ask a woman to move in with him, as well as to reveal the full extent of his medical history to her. He had all intentions of asking her to marry him if she was willing to accept him the way he was. But no sooner had he told her, less than forty-eight hours later, she was gone. She left a letter that merely said she couldn't marry a man who would deny her the chance to be a mother.

He received another letter from her almost a year later, apologizing for her actions and letting him know that she had met someone, had gotten married and was expecting his child.

He cursed as he threw the covers back, got out of

bed and slipped into his jeans. It was nights like this when he needed to escape and become part of the wild. He knew when he walked into the barn and Thunder saw him, his friend would understand. That horse was smarter than any animal had any right to be. Whenever they rode, it was man and beast together, flying in the wind in a way his Ford Explorer couldn't touch. At least not within the confines of the law, anyway.

Tonight he needed speed which was faster than lightning and, in his mind, swifter than any speed boat. Tonight he needed to put out of his mind the one woman he needed to keep at a distance, and stop imagining how she would feel in his arms, how that ultra-fine body of hers would feel molded tight against his. But what was really driving him insane was fantasizing about her taste and how delicious it would be on his tongue.

Damn. Casey Westmoreland was getting under his skin—and that was something he'd sworn not to let another woman do again.

Casey stood at her bedroom window and looked out, clearly seeing the mountains beneath a moon-kissed sky. Shivers ran all through her body at the memory of being in McKinnon's presence tonight, sitting across from him at the dinner table trying to concentrate more on her food than on him.

And then there was the part of the night when she'd helped Savannah clear the table and he'd handed her his plate. The moment their hands had touched she felt a heated sensation shoot from the bottom of her feet all the way to the top of her head. There were also moments she had caught him staring at her like she was the dessert he would get after the meal. Just thinking about that deep look of desire she'd seen in his eyes had heat flaring up inside her and no matter what she did, there was nothing she could do to smother it.

She'd tried sleeping but her thoughts wouldn't let her be. Heat would start in her stomach and move lower down her body while visions of McKinnon Quinn danced in her head. How could she concentrate on getting Prince Charming trained when something else dominated her thoughts?

Knowing going back to sleep was out of the question, she slipped into a robe after deciding to take a walk outside. There was a courtyard connecting the cottage to the main house that was surrounded by the flowers Henrietta had planted. It was a beautiful night and she wanted to stand underneath the Montana sky and smell the flowers.

She had been standing outside in the courtyard for well over fifteen minutes and was about to go back inside when she heard a sound. Her heart jammed in her ribs and her breath caught. She blinked, not sure if she was seeing things or if McKinnon was actually there within ten feet of her, sitting bareback on his huge black horse and staring at her.

She blinked again and watched as he slowly slid off Thunder's back and she realized it wasn't a hallucination.

She shook her head to clear it before her gaze latched on to his. She felt her breathing grow shallow as he slowly moved closer.

The moon overhead cast enough light on him and his devastatingly good looks to make her appreciate that she was born a woman. His hair hung loose and wildly around his shoulders, and he was bare chested and wearing jeans. His body was solid, muscular and for a moment her breath caught because he reminded her of a savage beast. But she knew that the man coming toward her—although private and reserved—was no threat to her. At least not physically. Emotionally was another matter.

"What are you doing out here?" he asked in a deep, husky drawl that sent goose bumps spreading all over her body. He came to stand directly in front of her.

From the moon's glow she could see the intensity in the depths of his dark eyes. "I couldn't sleep and decided to come out here for a spell," she said as her hands automatically went to the belt around her robe to tighten it, fully aware that her meager clothing offered no protection against the heat she saw in his eyes.

"You should go back inside," he said in a gruff voice.

"I was about to," she said, taking a gathered breath. Then she asked, "What are you still doing up?"

At first she thought he wasn't going to respond, but then he said, "I couldn't sleep either and decided to ride Thunder."

"Oh." She inhaled deeply. "Well, I'd better go back in. Good—"

"I know the reason why neither of us can get any sleep," he said, taking a step closer to her.

She stared up into his dark eyes. "Do you?"

"Yes. We need this." And then he wrapped his arms around her and lowered his mouth as his lips captured hers. Then he placed his hands on her hips, molding her body firmly to the fit of him. Without wasting any time, his tongue found hers and he heard her gasp at the contact and immediately knew…at thirty years of age, Casey Westmoreland had never been properly kissed before. And damn it all to hell, he planned on doing the honors, here and now.

His fingers tightened at her waist the moment he deepened the kiss, taking what appeared no man had before, an in-depth taste of her. Being inside her mouth felt soothingly warm and downright delicious. A wave of sexual need entrapped him when she parlayed each stroke of his tongue and his brain cells started to overload. At that moment nothing else mattered except having Casey in his arms, kissing her, devouring her this way.

One part of his mind said he needed to stop, but another part said to continue what he'd started since this would be the last opportunity he would have to do so. Tomorrow she officially began working for him and he would have to be sensible. He would not become romantically involved with one of his employees—especially this one. She was a Westmoreland for heaven's sake! But tonight he wanted as much insensibility as he could get.

A sigh escaped from her mouth into his and he continued on and on, mating their mouths, exchanging their breaths, sharing their taste. His tongue moved all over her mouth, in every direction, sucked, licked, nibbled, dabbed, all while performing some of the most inherently erotic things he'd ever done to a woman's mouth.

With no thoughts of ending it… Instead he wanted to take things further. He wanted to move his mouth from her lips and trace a path past her neck, and open her robe, push her nightshirt out of the way and capture the nipples he'd seen pressed against her tops.

He reached up, slipped his hand inside her robe and touched her breast and let out a satisfied sigh. Even through the lace of her nightshirt he could tell that she was perfectly shaped. Then he loosened the front of her robe, needing to touch her if not kiss her there. The moment his hand came into contact with her breast, every part of him got harder and he felt like he was going to explode right then and there.

He pulled back from the kiss and before she could utter a single word, he leaned down and latched on to a nipple, sucked on it, licked it like a hungry man. He heard moan after moan gurgle up in her throat and she arched her back, giving him greater access to her breasts. He was greedy for her and could tell from the sounds of her moans she was in another world, enjoying his mouth on her. He wondered how she would feel if his mouth moved lower and invaded another area of her body.

He shifted their positions, ready to lift his mouth to find out, when somewhere in the distance a coyote howled and McKinnon pulled back, but only so far. He still lingered over her nipple, took his tongue and traced the outlines of it again before raising his head and going for her lips again, testing her softness, savoring her taste.

"Casey," he said quietly, as if the sound would break the spell they had gotten caught up in.

"Yes," she responded, and he heard several tremors in her voice and inwardly smiled knowing he had placed them there.

"I definitely like the way you taste," he said, pulling back and looking down at her, while putting her lacy tank top back in place and pulling her robe closed. He saw her bemused expression and he wanted to kiss it right off her face. He smiled. "You don't kiss often, do you?"

She leaned forward and pressed her face against his chest as if in embarrassment. When she muttered a few words he couldn't make out, he lifted her chin and tilted her head back so their gazes could meet. "When was the last time a man has thoroughly and completely kissed you?" he asked quietly.

"Never. I've never been kissed like that before. You're the only man who's done something like that to me."

Her words made him tighten his arms around her waist and he lowered his mouth to hers again, needing another taste, one to retain in his memories forever. He deepened the kiss, more than before and actually heard her purr. The sound sent blood racing to all parts of his body.

When they parted moments later they were both pulling in shallow and choppy breaths. Casey took a couple of steps back. "I think I really do need to go inside now."

And before McKinnon could stop her, she took off in the darkness, hurriedly walking back toward the cottage.

High up on a mountain, another individual was finding it hard to sleep. Corey Westmoreland stood at the window gazing out, wondering if all was well with his daughter. She had called earlier to say she had unpacked and liked the cottage she would be living in for the next few weeks. But what she hadn't said and what he couldn't help wondering was how she and McKinnon were getting along.

He turned when he heard the sound of feet touching the floor and smiled as he watched his wife—the woman he loved more than anything—softly walk over to him and right into his outstretched arms. "Sorry, honey, I didn't mean to wake you," he whispered softly against her ear, giving her a peck there.

"You're worried about Casey, aren't you?"

He nodded, knowing he couldn't and wouldn't keep anything from Abby, especially his feelings. "Yes. Clint and Cole are concerned, as well."

"Is it because she's taken the job with McKinnon?"

Corey shook his head. "No, McKinnon and Casey are going to have to work out their own problems in that area. What her brothers and I are concerned about is whether she's come to terms with what Carolyn told her all those years ago. Casey's been going through a lot emotionally since finding out the truth."

Abby nodded as she cuddled closer into her husband's arms. "What I think Casey needs to help pull her life together is the love of a good man—and I believe McKinnon is that man."

Corey shrugged. "He could very well be but he won't let that happen. I told you about his medical history. Ever since he discovered that he's a carrier of that rare blood disease, he made up his mind that he would never marry and father children. It was a hard decision for him. Then, a few years ago he met someone he thought would be the perfect mate, but once he told her the truth about his medical condition and his decision not to ever father any children, she left him high and dry. Mc-Kinnon has had a lot of hurt and pain in his life, Abby."

"And so has Casey. That's why they need each other."

Corey shook his head. "McKinnon won't see it that way."

"I want to think that eventually he will. Everything happens for a reason. I think you and I are living proof of that. If it's meant for them to be together then they will. All they need is time and opportunity, and with her living right there on his ranch, right under his nose, they will have that. McKinnon needs Casey as much as Casey needs him." She lifted her head, looked into Corey's face and smiled. "I have a feeling that before long, you'll become the father of the bride."

Corey returned her smile and pulled Abby closer into his arms. McKinnon was an outstanding young man but right now he was hurt and angry. He just hoped his daughter would be able to handle him. But then if anyone could, it would be a Westmoreland.

McKinnon slipped beneath the sheets after taking his second cold shower that night. He had gotten sweaty riding Thunder and hot after kissing Casey. If he thought he hadn't been able to get to sleep before, he sure as hell wouldn't get any now—not with memories of devouring Casey's mouth and breasts so blatantly vivid in his mind.

She had tasted just like he'd known she would, and with a particular flavor that was all hers. And just the thought that she was a novice sent sensuous chills down his body. He wondered if the overprotectiveness of her two brothers was the reason for her lack of experience. He shook his head, dismissing that assumption. He had gotten to know Casey well enough to know that although Clint and Cole may have looked out for her over the years, it had been her decision regarding the level of her involvement with any man. Most women he knew at her age had been kissed hundreds of times—on every part of their body—and he couldn't help wondering the extent of her knowledge. A part of him would love to find out, but another part—the one that knew maintaining distance between him and Casey was the best thing—fought the idea with a passion.

Passion.

And that was what he was trying not to think about, especially when it came to Casey. He definitely had to toe the line. There was no way he could treat her like he treated other women he wanted in his bed. First of all, he needed to get that idea out of his mind because it wouldn't work. And to be sure of that, he would start keeping his distance beginning tomorrow. The only time he would seek her out was when he needed to know the progress she was making with Prince Charming.

Satisfied that he had at least gotten that much cleared up and settled in his mind, McKinnon sought a comfortable position in bed and hoped like hell he got some semblance of a fairly decent amount of sleep.

Chapter 6

"Casey is doing a downright fine job with Prince Charming," Norris said, glancing over at McKinnon.

"Is she?" McKinnon asked, trying to sound nonchalant but at the same time angry that his pulse rate always seemed to increase with the mere mention of her name. It had been a week since he'd seen her—at least up close. The day following the night they'd kissed, he'd made himself scarce, leaving it up to Norris to give her his expectations regarding Prince Charming.

He knew from Henrietta that she preferred taking her meals alone at the guest cottage, however, it seemed the two women had gotten rather chummy and shared lunch together at the big house every day. Once he'd known Casey's schedule, he had adjusted his to make sure he wasn't around when she was. But that didn't really help matters because there were plenty of things to remind him of her presence. He caught the scent of her each and every time he walked into his home.

She had made things a little easy for him this past weekend by leaving on Friday evening to spend time on her father's mountain, not returning until late Sunday. He had kept himself pretty busy going over breeding records but had found that every so often he would get up and look out the window as if anxiously awaiting her return.

And then at night whenever he went to bed, all he had to do was close his eyes to remember the feel of his mouth on hers, his tongue in that mouth and the flavor of her that seemed to be embedded in his taste buds. The bottom line was that he wanted to be with her the way a man needed to be with a woman.

Hell, he'd even gone into town a couple of nights ago to his and Durango's old hangout, Haley's Bar and Grill, but hadn't seen a single woman he wanted to sleep with. The only woman he wanted was the one living in his guest cottage—the one who was definitely off-limits to him. But still, that didn't mean he couldn't dream about her at night, wishing she was in bed with him while he stripped her naked and…

"Damn." McKinnon cursed when he saw the cut on his hand, thanks to the barbwire fence he was trying to repair on a section of his property. He should have been concentrating on what he was doing instead of fantasizing about Casey.

Luckily for him the cut wasn't deep, which meant it shouldn't require stitches. But it would require him putting something on it. He had taken off his gloves to get a better grip on the pliers when the thing had slipped.

"You okay, McKinnon?"

He glanced over at Norris. "I got a cut from this barb-wire and need to go up to the house to put something on it. I'll be back in a minute."

Norris looked at the cut, saw the amount of blood and lifted his brow in concern. "Maybe you need me to take you into town so Dr. Mason can take a look at it."

"No, I'm up on my tetanus shots and it doesn't need stitches. I'll be fine."

"You sure?"

"Yes, I'm sure."

"Okay. I don't want Morning Star and the Judge to have my ass if something happens to you. Why don't you stay at the house and let me and the boys finish things up here."

McKinnon lifted his brow, wondering if Norris was about to accuse him of being more of a hindrance than a help again. He would be the first to admit that his mind hadn't been focused lately for thinking about Casey but still… "And you sure you and the guys will have the fence repaired by morning?"

Norris chuckled. "Look McKinnon, I was repairing barbwire fences before the day you were born." And for good measure the older man then added, "And I'm yet to get a cut on any of my fingers. Now go."

"All right, I'm going," McKinnon said, moving toward Thunder.

"I don't know where your mind has been lately, but it's been wandering quite a bit," he heard Norris say, but refused to acknowledge the man's comment by turning around.

A half hour after cleaning his wound, applying antiseptic and putting on a bandage, McKinnon walked out of the bathroom, glad Henrietta had gone into town to do her weekly grocery shopping. If she'd seen the cut on his hand, no matter how minor the injury, she would have harassed him until he went into town for Doc Mason to stitch him up.

He turned when he heard a knock at the door. Remembering that Henrietta wasn't in, he moved through the living room to open it. Immediately his breath caught at the same time his pulse escalated and he felt a tightness in his jeans. Casey was standing there and the sight of her, the scent of her, suddenly made his skin feel overheated.

He cleared his throat, forced the lump down. "Casey, is there anything I can do for you?" he said as normal as he could while trying to force from his mind all the things he would love doing for and to her.

She seemed just as surprised to see him as he was to see her. "No. I was about to leave to go into town and wanted to know if Henrietta wanted me to pick up anything."

It was then that he took in what she was wearing—a dress that that he bet would ruffle around her legs when she walked. It was light pink and the color made her look totally feminine, alluring and desirable. And she had light makeup on, and even added a dash of color to her lips. Lips he remembered kissing once and would love kissing again.

He cleared his throat for a second time before saying, "Henrietta isn't here. She went into town to pick up the weekly supplies and groceries." Then he checked his watch. "You're through for the day all ready?"

He regretted asking the question before it left his mouth—especially when he could tell from her expression it got her dander up. "Yes," she replied, rather stiffly. "I put in a couple of extra hours this week and asked Norris yesterday if I could finish up early today. I have an appointment in town."

He frowned. "An appointment?"

"Yes. A real estate agent has a couple of places to show me."

His frown deepened. "You're moving? Our deal called for you to stay here in the guesthouse."

"I know what our deal called for, McKinnon," she said, locking gazes and tempers with him, "and I plan to honor it," she snapped. "I'm looking for a place to stay once my job here is finished."

"What about Corey's place?"

"What about it?"

"I assumed that's where you'd be staying since the reason you decided to move here was to get to know him better."

"But that doesn't mean I have to be underfoot. Besides, he and Abby need their privacy," she said, like that should explain everything.

In a way it did. McKinnon knew exactly what she wasn't saying. The couple was openly affectionate, but he was used to such behavior because his own parents were the same way.

"I can't live there permanently," Casey added. "I need my own place. If I were to get a job I can't be coming back and forth off Corey's Mountain everyday."

McKinnon nodded. To get on or off the mountain you could only drive so far and then had to travel the rest of the way by horseback. At least that's how things had been before Serena Preston had moved to town and started a helicopter business. In addition to doing private tours, she provided air transportation to and from those ranches higher up in the mountains twice a week. But using air transportation on a frequent basis could get rather expensive.

"What happened to your hand!" Casey's words cut into his thoughts and he glanced down to notice it had started bleeding again through the bandage.

"I cut it on barbwire earlier."

"Aren't you going to the doctor?" she asked, her voice sounding somewhat panicky.

"Hadn't planned on it," he said, leaning in the doorway. "I've put something on it."

"But it's bleeding."

"I noticed."

She looked at him with total exasperation on her face. "Your need to see a doctor for your hand, McKinnon. If you want I can take you there since I'm going to town."

He lifted a brow. "What about your appointment?"

"It's not for a couple of hours. The reason I was leaving so early was to do some shopping, but I can do that anytime. Getting your hand taken care of is more important."

McKinnon gazed at her for a moment, saw the concern etched on her face. This was the woman he had avoided for a week. The woman he went to bed dreaming about each night. The woman whose kiss still lingered in his mouth. The woman he wanted with a passion.

The woman he could not have.

But he wanted to spend time with her this afternoon. Find out how things had been going with her. He didn't want to hear it secondhand from Henrietta or Norris. He wanted to hear her voice, smell her scent, invade her space…

"McKinnon, do you want me to drive you to the doctor's office in town or not?"

Her words interrupted his thoughts and as he gazed into her eyes he made a decision. He would spend a couple of hours with her today but then tomorrow it was back to business at usual. He would put distance between them again. "You sure it won't mess up your appointment time?"

"Yes, I'm sure."

He nodded. "Then hold on, let me grab my hat."

Casey drove while McKinnon sat in the seat next to her not saying anything, just absently staring out the window at the endless miles of scenic meadows, pastures and mountains they passed.

He was frowning—as usual. She wondered how often he smiled. She'd seen him do so once when he had been standing in a group talking to her cousins. Spencer had shared some joke and all the men, including McKinnon, had laughed. But other than that one time, she was yet to see the corners of his lips crinkle up. She couldn't help but wonder about both the sadness and anger she often saw in his gaze. She had asked Durango about it once but he'd shrugged saying he didn't know what she was talking about.

And it was obvious McKinnon had avoided her this

week. Even now she could tell that he was tense and angry about something, but she didn't know how to go about breaking through his defenses. She was used to dealing with moody males, thanks to Clint and Cole. The moodiness she could deal with, but not the anger because she didn't understand the reason for it.

A part of her knew it had something to do with the kiss they'd shared that night a week ago. Why had he gotten upset about it? They were both adults and he was the one who'd suggested doing it in the first place, saying a kiss was what they needed to sleep, and of course she'd gone along with it since kissing him was something she'd wanted to do for a long time. And he'd been right about the kiss. She had slept like a baby and had awakened the next day with a longing to see him, but he'd evidently regretted what they'd shared and had other ideas and began putting distance between them... until now.

"So, how are things going with Prince Charming?"

The sound of his voice jerked her back to the present. She glanced over at him. He wasn't looking at her but his muscular body was reclined back against the seat staring straight ahead and the Stetson he wore low on his head shielded his eyes. Tight jeans were stretched across his thighs and the blue shirt accentuated a strong, sturdy chest. His hair was pulled back in a ponytail and his profile was just as sexy as the rest of him.

Unwanted images were forming in her mind—especially of how wild and untamed he'd look that night in the courtyard. She wished the kiss they'd shared could have gone on and on since she had enjoyed it so much. No man had ever kissed her that way before and...

"Casey?"

Abruptly she was snapped back to reality. He was looking at her with those dark eyes of his and suddenly she was filled with this urgent, compelling hunger to kiss him again.

"Yes?"

"I asked how things were going with Prince Charming."

And naturally when you asked I was thinking about something that I shouldn't be. "We're in the getting-to-know-you-better stage," she said, forcing the words from her mouth through thick abated breath. "I'm walking him a lot to get a feel of his balance and taking note of those things that might distract him, make him not alert as he should be. I'm trying to develop a good impression with him—one that will last. He's still somewhat tense and I'm trying to rid him of that. Once that happens then the bonding can begin."

"What about working on his speed?"

Casey could see from out the corner of her eye that McKinnon was still looking at her but she refused to look back when she responded. "He has speed, McKinnon, otherwise Jamal would not have purchased him to use in the races. Once I get rid of the tension and the bonding starts, then he'll do some amazing things, including increasing his speed. You'll see."

McKinnon got quiet again for a while. He thought about the reason she was going into town, frowned and then said, "Have you considered moving in with Durango and Savannah instead of getting your own place somewhere?" For some reason he was bothered by the thought of her living in the city alone. "I bet they'd be glad to have you as a guest for a while."

Casey's hands tightened on the steering wheel. "For goodness sakes. They're still newlyweds. I would feel like I'm imposing on them."

He nodded. "Yeah, I can see your point. Even with Savannah being pregnant, it seems every time I drop by they're either getting out of the bed or getting into it."

Lucky them, she wanted to say but changed her mind.

"You could stay with my folks," he suggested.

Casey glanced over at him and met his gaze. Once again she felt the sizzle and tried to ignore the heat swirling around in her stomach and between her legs. She quickly placed her eyes back on the road, tightening her hands on the steering wheel and squeezing her thighs together. She didn't fully understand these sensations that always swamped her when he looked at her a certain way.

She tried to get a grip and think about what he'd just said about her moving in with his parents. How she could tell him in a nice way that his folks were just as bad as her father and Abby? She hadn't known that older couples could be so openly affectionate.

She cleared her throat and glanced back over at him. "I would feel like I'd be imposing on them, as well."

McKinnon smiled. "Yeah. Like Corey and Abby, they do take being touchy and feely to a whole other level, don't they."

"And it doesn't bother you?" she asked.

"No, my brothers and I are used to it. My parents

love each other very much and have no problem openly displaying that love. I think it's kind of special."

She'd been led over the years to believe what her parents had shared had been special, too. Boy, was that wrong. Wanting to change the subject, she decided to ask him about what was still bothering her. "Why wouldn't you entertain the thought of me working on your ranch that first day, McKinnon?"

He glanced over at her, grateful her eyes were still on the road and not on him. He didn't want to look into her face when he lied. He couldn't be completely honest when he told her the reason behind his decision not to hire her. That he'd figured his constantly being around her, having her live on his ranch was a temptation he couldn't deal with.

So instead he said, "Like I told you, if anything happened to you I would have Corey to deal with, not to mention all those other damn Westmorelands."

She shook her head smiling. "There *are* a bunch of them, aren't there?"

He lifted a brow. "Bunch of *them?* Need I remind you that you are one of them."

The smile on her face suddenly vanished. "Yes, and it took me all of twenty-eight years to find that out."

McKinnon heard the bitterness in her voice. It was his understanding that she still had issues regarding the lies her mother told her about her father. For some reason, she couldn't let go and move on.

"There might have been a reason your mother did what she did," he said quietly, recalling the reason his mother had never told him that Martin wasn't his biological father until she'd been left with no choice.

"There are some things we aren't meant to understand, and what happened between your mother and Corey is probably one of them."

Casey sighed deeply. She wasn't surprised that he knew the whole story—their fathers were best friends and had been for years. But then, given Corey Westmoreland's popularity, she was certain that everyone in these parts had heard about his long-lost triplets.

"Don't try and make excuses for what she did to me and my brothers, McKinnon. All those years we thought our father was dead but he wasn't. Just think of all that wasted time when we could have known him."

"But you're getting to know him now. I hate to say that old cliché but better late than never, fits in this case."

Casey frowned. "No, it doesn't fit, and I prefer that we change the subject." A few minutes later she said, "We'll go see the doctor first to get you all fixed up."

McKinnon shook his head. In addition to being feisty, she was stubborn. "Whatever."

A couple of hours later, as they walked out of the doctor's office, Casey glanced over at McKinnon. "Are you sure you don't want me to take you back to the ranch now?"

He frowned. "I only got two stitches, Casey, not twenty, and I still don't think I needed them. And that damn tetanus shot wasn't necessary, but then Dr. Mason has always been heavy-handed when it comes to needles."

After he opened the car door, slid onto the seat and

buckled the seat belt, he glanced over at her. "Will you still have time to make your appointment?"

"Yes, the area isn't far from here. The first place is an apartment that's over an empty building."

He turned and looked at her like she'd lost her mind. "Why would you want to live in a place like that?"

After snapping her own seat belt in place, she glared over at him, not liking his tone. "It's not that I *want* to live in such a place, McKinnon, but when it comes to available housing, Bozeman isn't overflowing with it."

He sat back and stared out the window saying nothing. Why did he care where she decided to live? It was her business and not his.

She was right—it didn't take long for her to get to where they were going. The real estate agent, an older, stout lady with a huge smile on her face, was waiting for them and once they were out of the car and introductions were made, she ushered them up the stairs to the apartment.

McKinnon glanced around, immediately not liking the place already. He knew the area. It wasn't bad but then it wasn't good, either. It was close to a business district with a bar on the corner. The place could get pretty rowdy, especially on certain nights of the week, not to mention on the weekends. She would never be able to get any rest.

When they reached the top of the stairs, the Realtor, who had introduced herself as Joanne Mills, moved aside to let them enter. "Nice place," Casey said, placing her hands on her hips while she glanced around the huge room. "I can see potential."

McKinnon couldn't, and while Casey continued talking he tried concentrating on what she was saying and not on what she was doing. Having her hands on her hips had drawn his gaze to her small waistline, curvy hips and thighs. A waist he had touched the night they'd kissed, and thighs and hips that he'd molded against his own.

"McKinnon?"

He quirked an eyebrow at her. "What?"

"What do you think?"

"I don't like it," he said in a gruff voice. "There's too much work to be done before it can be occupied."

Casey frowned. "It wouldn't hurt for you to be a little positive."

"Just speaking the truth." He turned to Ms. Mills. "You don't have anything in a more settled residential area? I don't like the fact that there's a bar on the corner."

Before the woman could answer, Casey said in an irritated voice, "You don't have to live here, McKinnon. That bar won't bother me." She then turned to Joanne. "But the size of the kitchen does. It's too small. I like cooking on occasion and there's not enough cabinet space. What's next on the list?"

McKinnon didn't like the next couple of places, either, and Casey had to admit that neither did she. It was late afternoon when they'd seen the last apartment and Ms. Mills promised to call when other listings came up.

"You might do better just to buy a piece of land and build on it," McKinnon said as they headed to the car.

"I might have to do that," she said, but knew that building a place would take even longer. She glanced up at the man walking beside her, thinking that although he had gotten on her last nerve a few times today by being overly critical of the places they'd seen, she had enjoyed spending time with him. "How's your hand holding up?"

He glanced over at her. "I told you my hand is fine. To prove that point, I'll drive back to the ranch."

Casey didn't have a problem with that since she'd found concentrating on the road and not him rather difficult. She'd been too distracted by his mere presence, and now that he had removed the rubber band from his hair, the curly mane flowed freely down his back, making him look more savage than tame. And then there were his smoky, dark eyes that would lock with hers. More than once while sitting in the doctor's reception room she'd glanced up from the magazine she'd been flipping through to find him watching her with an unreadable expression on his face. Each time their gazes connected her desire for him intensified that much more, and although she tried looking in another direction, it seemed her eyes kept inexplicably returning to his, only to find him still staring.

She handed him the keys. "If you want to drive, that's fine with me."

"Thanks." McKinnon opened the car door for Casey and stood back to let her get inside, trying to ignore the way her dress raised a little when she sat, showing a nice amount of thigh. He was attracted to her something awful and spending time with her had only intensified that attraction. Sitting and watching her at the doctor's office had been challenging. He was sure he had made her nervous but he hadn't been able to help it. She was take-your-breath-away beautiful and while staring at her he wondered about a number of things. How she would look naked. What sounds she would make when she came. Visions of them wrapped up together in tangled sheets had immediately materialized in his mind.

He composed himself as he moved around the car to get in on the driver's side. He was used to seeing what he wanted and going after it, but had to constantly remind himself that with Casey came limitations. Hell, forget limitations—with Casey Westmoreland there was a no-fly, total hands-off zone, which he'd already breeched with that kiss. But he was determined to try and adhere to it from now on, no matter what.

"Hey, McKinnon, wait up!"

McKinnon gritted his teeth as he turned around. Rick Summers, who'd always been a pain in McKinnon's and Durango's sides, was approaching at a rapid pace. Rick wasn't someone they considered a friend. In fact, from the time he'd moved into the area a few years ago, he'd practically made it his business to try and compete against them where the ladies were concerned. He really thought a lot of himself, and when it came to the treatment of women he could be a total jerk.

"Rick, what can I do for you?" McKinnon asked, annoyed when the man reached the car.

Rick gave him a smooth smile. "I was on my way to visit a friend and thought I recognized you coming out of the house that's for sale. Thinking about moving into town, McKinnon?"

"No."

The man then peered through the open window to where Casey was sitting and all but licked his lips. "I also saw your lady friend. Aren't you going to introduce us?"

McKinnon stopped short of saying "no" but knew he really had no choice. "Casey, I'd like you to meet Rick Summers, and Rick, this is Casey Westmoreland."

A surprised look appeared on Rick's face. "Westmoreland?"

"Yes. She's Durango's cousin and Corey Westmoreland's daughter."

A smile touched Rick's lips and McKinnon knew the man was giving Casey what he thought was his most flirtatious smile. "Nice meeting you, Casey," he said, opening the car door to shake her hand.

Casey returned the man's smile. "Nice meeting you, too, Rick."

"Are you just visiting a spell?" Rick asked curiously.

"No, I'm moving to Bozeman."

McKinnon knew by the darkening of Rick's eyes he had definitely latched on to that response. "To live with your father up on his mountain?"

Casey chuckled. "No, somewhere here in town."

McKinnon watched as Rick's smiled widened into a look McKinnon compared to a wolf on a hunt. "In that case, I hope we run into each other again…real soon." He tipped his hat and walked off smiling.

McKinnon shook his head, and when he slid into the driver's seat, he slammed the door shut as his protective instincts kicked in. If Rick Summers thought for one minute he would be adding Casey's name to his little black book, he could think again. Although who she dated was none of his business, the thought of her getting mixed up with the likes of Summers didn't sit well with him.

"He seems like a nice guy."

McKinnon glanced over at Casey. "In this case looks are deceiving because Rick's not a nice guy. He's an ass and I suggest you stay away from him." He could tell by her expression that she didn't appreciate his suggestion.

And as he drove toward the highway that would take them back to the ranch, he decided that whether she liked it or not, he intended to keep Summers away from her.

Chapter 7

"What are you doing for dinner?"

Casey stiffened as she got out of the car. Now that they were back at the ranch, surely he wasn't going to invite her to eat with him. "The usual," she heard herself say. "Henrietta usually fixes me something, and I eat it at the guesthouse while doing journal entries of Prince Charming's daily progress on the computer. Why?"

"Just asking. Thanks again for the ride into town."

"Don't mention it."

Common sense told McKinnon that this is where they would part ways. She would go to the guesthouse and he would go to the ranch house, and if he was real smart he would avoid her again this week. He'd spent some time with her today. He'd heard her voice and inhaled her scent and now he had gotten her out of his system for a while. Hell, not by a long shot. But as he forced himself to keep walking toward his front door, something made him turn around.

"Casey, how about if—"

Whatever words he was about to say died on his lips. She was gone, having made a swift exit to the guest-house. His disappointment quickly turned into annoyance. Evidently she'd taken as much as she could of him for one day. He wished he could say the same but couldn't. He could have taken more of her…a lot more. He had been constantly aware of her as a woman—a woman who probably didn't know the extent of her own sensuality or sexuality. And he was a man who would love tapping into what she didn't know; expose her to a few things. Hell, more than a few.

Thirty minutes later, after taking a shower and being careful to keep his stitches dry, he made his way to the kitchen to warm up his food. He'd been following this same routine for years, ever since Lynette had left. He was used to it and preferred things this way. He was about to stick his plate into the microwave when the phone rang.

He reached over and picked it up. "Yes?"

"How are you, McKinnon?"

He smiled upon hearing his mother's voice. "I'm fine. How are you and Dad?"

"We're both doing well. We just got back today. We've been up on Corey's Mountain visiting, which is why I'm calling. Abby and I decided it would be nice to give a party for Casey."

He tensed. "A party? Why?"

"To welcome her to the area. A lot of our neighbors know about Corey's triplets and some have even met

Clint and Cole. But very few have had a chance to meet Casey, and we think a party will be a wonderful way to arrange that, to welcome her to the community."

Sounded like his mother and Abby had their minds made up. "So what do you need me to do?" Nothing, he hoped.

"In addition to not working her too hard where she's too tired to attend her own party and enjoy herself, how about making sure she gets here."

McKinnon stiffened. He had endured one car ride with Casey and wasn't sure he would be able to do another anytime soon. It seemed the scent of her was still all over him. "When is this party?"

"Next Friday night, here at our ranch at eight. Can I depend on you to help?"

He sighed. There wasn't too much Morning Star Quinn couldn't get out of him and she knew it very well. "Yes, I won't over work her that day and I'll make sure she gets there."

"Thanks, McKinnon. I appreciate it. By the way, it's not a surprise or anything like that. I just finished telling Casey about it and she's fine with it."

"That's good," he said with grim resolve before hanging up the phone.

Another night and Casey couldn't sleep. Nor could she get McKinnon off her mind. He had invaded her dreams and she didn't like it.

Actually, that wasn't true.

She *had* liked it. So much to the point where she had awoken filled with desire so intense she felt it deep in her belly. She'd heard of belly aches before but nothing like this one.

She slipped into her robe and, as was the norm whenever she found she couldn't sleep, decided she'd take a stroll around the courtyard and enjoy the beauty of the night.

A few moments later she went out the front door and onto the brick paved walkway. A flood light off the front of the ranch house glowed, but just enough to illuminate some of the new flowers Henrietta had boasted of planting this week.

"Couldn't sleep again tonight?"

Casey placed her hand over her chest. Just like the last time, she hadn't heard McKinnon's approach. She slowly turned, thinking what she really needed was to find a reason to go back inside the guesthouse. It didn't take much to remember what had happened the last time they'd been out in the courtyard together.

However, instead of taking off, she answered, "No. I have a lot on my mind."

The eyes staring at her were dark, intense...sexy. "You're thinking about the party?"

She raised a brow. "The party?"

"Yes. Mom called and told me about it."

"Oh." It was on the tip of her tongue to tell him that the party his mother and Abby had planned for her was the last thing on her mind. She'd been thinking about a party all right, a party of two. There were no party hats—just a big bed, silken sheets and plenty of heat between two naked bodies. "No, I wasn't thinking about the party," she said. And that was all she intended to tell him.

He came closer into the moonlight, into her line of vision. His hair was flowing around his shoulders and she wanted to hook her finger around a few strands and pull his mouth down to hers, to take possession of his tongue the same way he had taken hers that night. She wanted to—

"The stars are really out tonight."

McKinnon's comment brought her back to the present which was just as well, since her thoughts were going places they had no business venturing. Following his gaze, she tilted her head back and glanced up into the sky. "Yes, they are, but in my book if you've seen them once, you've seen them all."

"Hey, you better not let Ian hear you say that. He's the astronomer in the Westmoreland family."

Casey smiled. "Oops, I forgot. And speaking of Ian, I guess everyone is getting prepared for his wedding next month. I hear it's supposed to be one grand affair at the Rolling Cascade Casino."

McKinnon nodded. "Yeah, and I bet Lake Tahoe won't be the same when Brooke becomes a permanent part of his security team." A few moments later he added, "And speaking of Lake Tahoe, you looked good that night at Delaney's birthday party."

A tiny tremor passed through her. She doubted he gave many compliments. "Thank you. You looked rather dashing yourself." And he had. They hadn't said more than a few words to each other that night, but she had noticed him and it seemed from his compliment that he had noticed her, as well.

"I talked to Norris when we got back from town. He

said that our fathers dropped by to check on Spitfire while we were gone."

"Spitfire?"

"Yes, she's the mare that Thunder impregnated. Corey's the one who gave her to me a couple of years ago. We agreed then that he would get her first foal."

Casey glanced up at him. "You like Corey a lot, don't you?"

He glanced over at her wondering why she'd asked the question. "Yes. He and my dad were friends before I was born. I can't remember a time when he wasn't a part of my life."

He smiled and Casey blinked thinking that was the first smile she'd ever seen on McKinnon Quinn's lips. "Do you know what one of the things I admired most about him while growing up is?"

"What?"

"His love for his family. He was a young single man, yet every summer he would invite all of his nephews and his one lone niece to spend the summer months with him, and he would always include me."

"Sounds like all of you had a rowdy good time every year."

McKinnon chuckled and Casey found the sound rich and sincere. "Trust me, we did. Especially those times Delaney got left back in Atlanta and we could get into all kinds of trouble without anyone telling on us."

Casey smiled. "Sounds like Corey would let all of you get away with murder."

"Oh, we knew how far to take things with him. But he would make everything we did fun for us. How he kept all of us over those summers months without going insane is beyond me."

Casey paused a moment to digest his statement. Had her father known about her and her brothers, they would have been included in those summers, as well. But he hadn't known.

When a few moments passed and she didn't say anything, McKinnon said softly, "Sorry. Maybe I shouldn't have mentioned those summers."

Casey glanced up at him. It was as if he'd read her thoughts. "No, it's okay. Besides, you can't rewrite history, McKinnon. I don't begrudge any of you for the times you spent with my father when Clint, Cole and I didn't. It's not anyone's fault." *But my mother's,* she wanted to scream.

McKinnon brushed a lock of hair back from her forehead, thinking the short, sassy style looked cute on her. The glow from the moon highlighted her features in a way he found incredibly sexy.

"McKinnon?"

"Yes?" He heard that little tremor in her voice; the same one that had been there right before he'd kissed her.

"I think I should go back inside now."

"Why? I kind of like it out here, don't you?"

"Yes, but…"

He heard the apprehension in her voice at the exact moment his gaze was drawn to her mouth. "But what?"

She sighed, and he watched the sound escape through her lips. In fact, he actually felt the warm breath against his own lips, which meant he had subconsciously lowered his head closer to hers.

"The last time we were out here together," she finally said, "something happened to make you avoid me for a week." She decided not to spell it out to him since she was sure he knew what she was talking about. "If you're going to have any regrets about anything we do, then I'd rather we didn't do it."

"Anything like what?" he asked, inching his lips even closer to hers.

"Whatever," she said, nervously chewing her bottom lip.

As quick as she'd ever encountered, he darted his tongue out and slowly began licking around her lips, trailing a path from corner to corner. "By anything, do you mean something like this?" he asked as his tongue continued to toy with her lips.

"Yes," she whispered, barely able to get the word out. "Something like that."

"And what about this?" he asked, reaching up, drawing her face closer with his hands, so close she could see the dark intensity in his eyes. He began nibbling on her lips, gently, thoroughly, seemingly partial to the plumpness of her bottom lip. After hovering there for a few seconds, he then moved to her top lip, giving it equal play.

She felt her stomach clench, felt the heat forming between her legs and wished he would stop torturing her and just go in for the kill—she was dying a slow, sensuous death with every teasing stroke of his tongue.

"I like kissing you," he whispered against her moist lips.

She could tell and wondered if he realized he wasn't exactly kissing her, just tormenting her. Then, without warning, she had a fantasy flashback of him doing this very thing in her dream, almost making her beg before finally giving her what she wanted. She had never experience lust before now. Didn't have an inkling of how profound and potent it was. Had never known how it felt to want a person to an extent that was mind-blowing.

But what was making her feel heady was the fact that she knew he wanted her, too. The tightness in his jeans, the large bulge she felt pressed against her was evidence of that fact. And the more he tortured her mouth, the more he was working the both of them into a state of extreme arousal.

Deciding she'd had enough, she gripped a section of his hair. He stopped, looked at her, their eyes just as close as their lips. She saw the desire, the need, the outright hunger in his gaze, and then none too gently tugged on his hair and pulled his mouth down to hers.

She opened hers over his, not knowing exactly what she was doing but having a good idea of what it was she wanted. And when he parted his lips, she inserted her tongue, determined to find that pleasure she'd found before.

She didn't have long to wait.

He launched into the kiss full speed, demonstrating his ability and flexibility; an impact she felt all the way to her toes. The fact that all the blood in her body had rushed south would explain her recklessness, her desire, this ingrained need to have her way with him, she decided. Sensations ratcheted through her and she was driven to satisfy this hunger she had never felt before, this need to—

"Sorry to interrupt."

Casey and McKinnon quickly ended their kiss but he held onto her tight, refusing to allow her to put distance between them. "What is it, Norris?" he asked in an irritated tone, ignoring the curious look on his foreman's face. It wasn't the first time he'd been caught kissing a woman and it probably wouldn't be the last.

"Spitfire's in trouble."

"Damn." McKinnon muttered under his breath, easing Casey out of his arms. "What's wrong with her?" he asked in a rough but worried voice.

"She's in labor and having problems. I called Paul but Beth said he's over at the Monroe's spread taking care of their sick cattle. She's not sure when he'll be able to get here."

Casey had regained her senses enough to absorb most of the conversation between McKinnon and Norris. She knew that Beth Manning was a park ranger who worked with Durango and that her husband, Paul, was the vet in the area. Before she could think of anything else beyond that, McKinnon, ignoring Norris's presence, brushed his lips with hers and then whispered against her moist lips, "I have to go." And then he was gone, rushing beside Norris to the stables.

"Is she all right, McKinnon?"

McKinnon glanced up as Casey walked into the barn. She had changed from her nightgown and robe into a pair of jeans and a top. The outfit was more practical and, in his book, just as sexy.

He swallowed deeply and glanced back at the mare in the birthing stall. "I hope so, but it seems her first foal is giving her one hell of a time."

"Oh, poor baby."

"Yeah, and the daddy over there isn't handling things too much better," McKinnon said as he glanced over at Thunder who was anxiously prancing back and forth in his stall. "If you'll take care of Spitfire and try keeping her calm, I'm going to move Thunder to one of those empty stalls in the back. The less he knows about what's going on, the better."

"Sure," Casey said, moving closer to the mare. McKinnon had talked like Thunder was a person rather than a horse, and she knew her brothers felt the same way about their horses.

Alone with Spitfire, she spoke gently to the mare, trying to keep her calm. She had been around pregnant horses enough to know when the time came for them to deliver, they had a tendency to increase their anxiety levels, just like humans. Having a baby, no matter who was doing the having, was no picnic.

"She's okay?" McKinnon asked, stepping back into the stall sometime later.

Casey glanced up at him. "Yes, she's doing fine. Have you heard anything from Paul?"

"He called my cell phone while I was moving Thunder. He's left the Monroe's and is on his way, so hopefully he'll have something to calm Spitfire down."

McKinnon came to stand closer to Casey. "You're probably tired after all you've done today. I have a feeling it's going to be a long night. Why don't you go back up to the guesthouse and go on to bed."

Casey stared up at him. He was trying to get rid of her, to put back into prospective what he thought their relationship should be yet again. "I'm fine, McKinnon and since tomorrow is Saturday, I can sleep late if I want."

He met her gaze for a long moment and said nothing, but she felt him putting his guard back up. She couldn't help wondering why he refused to let her get close. A part of her said let it go, that if that's the way he wanted to be then so be it. Another part, the part that felt there was more to it than what she was seeing, decided not to let it go. There was a reason for McKinnon's behavior and she intended to find out what it was.

"Isn't he a beautiful colt?" Casey said excitedly about the foal Spitfire had given birth to a couple of hours earlier. Both mother and baby were doing fine, and proud Poppa Thunder had whined proudly.

"Yes, he most certainly is," McKinnon said as the two of them walked back toward the house. "And I know your dad is going to be pleased."

"I'm sure he will be." After Paul arrived, everyone got busy and there was no time to concentrate on anything but the business at hand. But now they were back to square one.

"You mentioned something about sleeping late in the morning. Does that mean you plan to stay on the ranch all weekend?" McKinnon asked, his voice neutral as if he didn't care one way or the other.

"My parents are off the mountain visiting with yours for the weekend. In fact, I'm going with both parents to a play in town tomorrow night. You're welcome to join us if—"

"No, thanks. I'll have work to do."

She nodded, knowing this was his way of putting

distance between them again. "All right. Then I'll see you later."

Before he could comment, and whether he intended to do so was doubtful, she turned and walked quickly toward the guest house.

Savannah called and invited Casey over for Sunday dinner. Durango would be working that day and she hated eating alone. Casey appreciated the invitation to get off McKinnon's ranch for a while since once again he had made himself scarce where she was concerned. Besides, Casey appreciated the company of a female close to her age, and since meeting Savannah at Chase's wedding the two had developed a close friendship.

They talked about a lot of stuff but Casey would be the first one to admit their current topic was one she wouldn't mind changing. She glanced over at Savannah as she finished her meal. "Why do you think something is going on between me and McKinnon?"

Savannah tilted her head and smiled. "Because there is," she said simply. "You can deny it all you want but it's there. But honestly, I think you really don't recognize it for what it is."

Casey knew that was definitely a possibility since she had little experience with men. "And how do you know it's there?"

Savannah's smile widened. "Because I've seen the two of you at several functions. I've watched how you look at each other when the other's not noticing. I know firsthand how that is because that's how things started with me and Durango. Things got so intense between us that we were in bed together the day after we met."

She then rubbed her stomach and grinned. "And as you know, the rest is history."

Casey chuckled. "But the two of you are so much in love, which means the marriage didn't happen because you got pregnant."

"That was supposed to be the reason but that's the clincher," Savannah said, smiling broadly. "We didn't know we were in love. Or maybe deep down somewhere we knew it but were afraid to acknowledge it. I'm just glad we came to our senses. I can't imagine my life without Durango and I want the same thing for you and McKinnon."

Casey shook her head. "Whoa, back up, hold on. I think your eyes are so full of love for Durango that you think everyone else's eyes should have that same glow. But to set the record straight, there's nothing going on between me and McKinnon."

"If you think so, but I believe otherwise. Whenever the two of you are together, it's like spontaneous combustion just waiting to happen. And I don't think you fully understand just how explosive that can be."

Umm, after two kisses, which she had no desire to discuss at the moment, she did know how explosive passion could be. "Okay, I'll be the first to admit I'm extremely attracted to McKinnon. What woman wouldn't be? But an attraction is as far as things go. He has chosen the life of a bachelor and right now I'm trying to figure out what I want to do with my own life. So much of it has been filled with nothing but lies."

She chuckled harshly. "Do you know I was so wrapped up in all that fairy-tale stuff my mother used to feed me about her and my father that I wanted that same type of love for myself to the point that I'm still a virgin?"

Casey sighed deeply. There was no turning back now—she'd revealed her secret. In a way she was glad to get it out. She'd never had a sister and her brothers were the last people she could talk about something like that.

"I think it's wonderful that you're still a virgin," Savannah said, shifting to more comfortable position in her chair. "I wished I had saved myself for Durango. My one and only guy before him was a selfish bastard and I regret the day I ever met him, let alone slept with him."

She glanced over at Casey before she continued. "But then I had no reason to believe in tales of romance and love. My father was the biggest bastard of them all. Trust me when I say he didn't set a good example."

"Yes, but at least you hadn't been fed lies your whole life," Casey said softly.

"No, but I still think you have a lot to be thankful for. Your mother took very good care of you and your brothers. That couldn't have been easy for a single woman, and it seems you were all raised with good values. Not all kids can claim that, Casey. And before she died, your mom wanted all of you to know the truth when she could have carried the information to the grave. Although you missed not having a father around while growing up, you did finally get to meet him, and look what a wonderful man he is. I'll trade Jeff Claiborne for Corey Westmoreland any day."

Silence engulfed the room for several seconds before Savannah spoke. "There might be something else you're overlooking."

"What?"

"Why your mother fabricated the story that she did. That could have been her way of coping with life, of dealing with the realization that the one man she loved more than life itself had a heart that belonged to another. That had to have been hard on her."

Casey gazed at Savannah, thinking she'd never thought of it that way. For the past two years she had been so angry at what her mother had done that she'd never given thought to the pain her mother must have endured knowing that no matter how much she loved Corey, he hadn't loved her back.

"I want you to promise me something, Casey."

Casey lifted a brow. "What?"

"If you ever do come to realize you care for Mc-Kinnon, don't give up on him and walk away, no matter what. I'm not a psychic by any means, but I feel something. Even when he appears happy I can detect his sadness and I don't know why. It's like there's something private eating at him but I have no idea what it could be. I've caught him looking at me and Durango during some of our play times with a pensive look in his eyes. And although he claims he doesn't ever want to marry and have children, I think that deep down he really does. I've tried talking to Durango about it but he refuses to discuss certain things about McKinnon with me. But then I have to respect that the two of them share this special bond."

Casey nodded. She knew of the bond the two men shared.

"Well, I've said enough," Savannah said, getting up

from the table. "Just promise me that if the time comes, you'll remember what I said."

Casey sighed and met Savannah's gaze. "I promise."

Chapter 8

In the comfort of his office McKinnon tossed a report on his desk. The white stallion he had imported all the way from the Blue Mountains of Australia had arrived earlier that day. Crown Royal was a magnificent animal with stunning looks, exceptional athletic ability and temperament. After his capture, he had spent time with renowned horse trainer Marcello Keaston and was more than ready for the task intended for him to do, and the brood mare selected was of the highest quality and value. McKinnon had no doubt that Crown Royal's first crop of foals would bring in a pretty penny at any auction.

He stood and stretched, and automatically his gaze drifted across the room to the calendar on the wall. It had been four days since he'd interacted with Casey. He had made it a point to keep his distance and it seemed she was doing likewise. The woman had a way of pulling his emotions in a way he couldn't afford to indulge.

He glanced toward his office door when he heard a knock. "Come in."

He smiled when Durango walked in. "How are things going, Rango?"

"Fine. I dropped Savannah off at a hair salon in town and thought I'd come here to kill some time. I just saw Crown Royal. Man, he's a beauty."

McKinnon chuckled proudly as he sat back down. "Yes, he is and I intend for him to make us plenty of money over the next few years. I've gotten a call from Mike Farmer already."

Durango's smile widened. "News travel fast."

McKinnon nodded. "Which is fine with me as long as it's in our favor, and you know Mike. He wants to be the first in everything and has the money to make it happen. He's hinted at acquiring the entire crop of Crown's first foals, now that we've selected Courtship as the mare." Courtship, a product of Thunder and a valuable Australian mare name Destiny, had already proven her worth as a magnificent piece of horseflesh and was known for her speed.

"And I got a call from Jamal today, as well," McKinnon said, smiling.

"Did he want to know how Prince Charming was coming along?" Durango asked, leaning against the closed door.

"Yes, and he wants me to meet with a couple of his associates who'll be in D.C. this week. They're interested in our breeding program."

Durango nodded. "Will Jamal be attending this meeting?"

"No. Delaney's condition is keeping him in Tehran for a while. They'll attend Ian's wedding next month but other than that, Delaney's doctors don't want her jet-setting all over the world."

Durango chuckled. "I can understand that since we have a lot of pregnant Westmorelands. So, will you be traveling to D.C.?"

"Yes, I leave first thing in the morning and probably won't be back until Saturday."

Durango nodded again. "Sounds like you'll miss Casey's party."

"There's a pretty good chance that I will." McKinnon didn't want to add that perhaps that was a good thing. "Would you like something to drink?"

Durango shook his head. "No, thanks. Savannah's cooking tonight and I don't want to spoil my appetite. You're invited, by the way."

McKinnon thought on Durango's invitation. If he was invited then chances were Casey had been invited, as well. He quickly decided to pass on the invitation. The last thing he wanted was to torture himself by looking across the table at her, knowing he couldn't touch her. "Thanks for the invite but I have a lot of paperwork to do before taking off in the morning."

Before Durango could comment that his reason was a lame excuse, McKinnon quickly added, "While you're here, Rango, can you look over the books? I'm sure you'll find everything in order."

"Don't I always?" Crossing the room, Durango took a seat at the extra desk.

When they'd decided to enter the partnership they had known that horse breeding was a risky business, but the risks were now paying off. In just a few years, not only had M&D earned the respect of their colleagues in the horse breeding world, but it was showing more of a profit than either Durango or McKinnon had imagined.

"So how is Casey working out?" Durango asked a few minutes later.

"Good. She's using a different approach that takes longer, but I have no doubt it will work. She knows what she's doing, that's for sure." McKinnon decided not to mention how, on numerous occasions, he would often stand at the window in this office and watch her interact with the horses. But mainly he watched *her.* And each time he saw her he thought about the heated kisses they had shared.

Damn it to hell, the need to feel her mouth beneath his again was almost overwhelming, although he'd been fighting the craving for days. Even now he could distinctively remember the warmth of her lips and how they would automatically part under his, the swift breath she'd take just seconds before his tongue mingled with hers and—

"And how are you handling her being here on the ranch?"

McKinnon gave Durango a look that grimly said he wasn't handling it very well. "Your cousin is a beautiful woman who can be a distraction if I let her be one, Rango."

Durango nodded. "And for you that's a bad thing, isn't it?"

McKinnon let out a deep sigh. "You of all people

know that it could be if I were to let anything get out of hand. As long as we maintain an employer-employee relationship, we're fine," he said, knowing he hadn't even been able to really do that. "I made a decision a few years ago that I knew would affect any future relationship I had with a woman. At the time I felt it was the right one to make. I still do."

"Yes," Durango said, closing the accounting books. "I understand and like I told you then, I support your decision. But having that procedure done wasn't the end of the world. Why don't you want to consider your other options?"

McKinnon didn't answer. At least not immediately. When he did his voice was filled with the anguish he sometimes felt. "I *have* considered those options but I can't expect every woman I meet to want to consider them, as well, Rango. Lynette didn't. Trust me, it's easier this way."

Durango leaned forward in his chair, his gaze fixed on his best friend's features. "Choosing a life where you'll spend the rest of your days alone isn't the way, McKinnon. At one time we both thought living like that would work for us, but since having Savannah in my life, I'm glad things happened the way they did. I probably would have died a very lonely and miserable man. Besides, it can't be as easy as you claim if I read correctly what I saw in your eyes whenever you looked at Casey that night at dinner. You want her in a bad way—that much was obvious, at least to me. But I think it might be a little deeper than that. I think you might be falling for her, McKinnon."

"No," McKinnon growled, denying Durango's allegations as he narrowed his gaze at him. "You're dead wrong on that one."

Durango was silent for a moment and then he leaned back in his chair. "We'll see."

"Damn it, there's nothing to see." Exasperated and angry that he'd allowed Durango's false assumption to needle him, he pushed out of his chair. "I'm going out," he said tersely.

Durango lifted a brow. "Where?"

"To ride Thunder."

He spun around on booted heels and before Durango could blink, an angry McKinnon had walked out of the room.

Casey squinted against the brightness of the May sun when she saw the horse and rider slowly approach. She held her breath when she recognized it was McKinnon. Beneath the Montana sky, his hair was loose and hung around his shoulders, touching his chambray shirt. His jeans were worn and as far as she was concerned he looked perfect, all the way down to his boots, as he sat atop the huge horse with the rugged mountains as a backdrop. She swallowed and tried to downplay the fluttering that was going on in her chest. Seeing him reminded her of the heated kisses they'd shared, each one seemed to get bolder and more daring.

"Hello, McKinnon," she said when he stopped close to where she was standing with her horse beside the stream. She had finished with Prince Charming early and decided to do a little riding. At least today she wouldn't be eating alone since Savannah had invited her to dinner.

"Casey. You decided to go out riding, I see," he said, eyeing her. His tone was cautiously polite.

"Yes, and before you insinuate otherwise, I did give Prince Charming a good workout today."

"I wasn't going to insinuate otherwise. From what I hear his speed yesterday was even better than what Jamal assumed, which means your way of doing things is working."

"I told you it would," she said pointedly, crossing her arms over her chest.

He nodded. "Yes, you did." A few minutes later, after dragging in a deep breath, he said, "I'm leaving in the morning for D.C. and I probably won't be back until sometime Saturday. If you need anything while I'm away see Henrietta or Norris."

The thought of him leaving, knowing he wouldn't be around—although she knew he had been avoiding her again—made a part of her stomach dip, but she inhaled in swift denial. Why should it bother her if he was leaving town? He meant nothing to her and she meant nothing to him. "Thanks for letting me know," she said, trying to keep her voice steady. "Have a safe trip."

Tightening his hand on the reins, he turned Thunder to leave and as he did Durango's words slammed into his ears. Even before his best friend had spoken them, McKinnon had come to suspect the allegations were true. His feelings for Casey had been growing since the day she set foot on the ranch, and that wasn't good because nothing could ever come of it...of them. But still, there was no way he could get on a plane tomorrow without taking the memory of another kiss with him.

He trotted a couple of feet before bringing Thunder

to a stop and turning the horse around. The reason he had left to go riding was to escape the memory of her. But here she was. She stood there, meeting his gaze as an electrified silence stretched between them. With a will he couldn't resist, he climbed off Thunder and slowly began walking toward her, eliminating the distance separating them.

Casey watched McKinnon. His handsome features were hard as granite in one sense, but filled with a sensuous longing in another. She had sworn after the last time they'd kissed and he'd made himself invisible afterward that he wouldn't get near her again. But the closer he got, the more she suspected what she had begun feeling for McKinnon was too bone-deep to deny him anything.

Casey's gaze flicked to his features when he came to a stop directly in front of her. She could tell by the way his hands were balled into fists at his sides that he was fighting the urge to take her in his arms. So she decided to make it easy on him and take him into hers.

She reached up, cupped his face with her hands and on tip-toe, leaned forward, intent on giving him something to think about while he was away. First she readied his lips with a couple of quick swipes of her tongue, ignoring his sharp intake of breath with each stroke.

She decided this was her kiss and she would go slow, be gentle and savor every moment. Working more on instinct than experience, she brushed her fingertips against his jaw and on a deep sigh, his mouth opened and she inserted her tongue and began lapping him up like he was the tastiest morsel she'd ever devoured.

And when his tongue joined hers, something that mirrored a quake caused her insides to rumble with a need she felt only while in his arms. She felt herself drowning and quickly grabbed hold of his shoulders to keep from falling.

She released his mouth when she heard one of the horses, either his or hers, make a sound. She rested her forehead against McKinnon's as they both tried to regain their breath.

Moments later, McKinnon stepped back and she watched as he rubbed a hand across his eyes and down his face. Then he muttered something that sounded a lot like "damn" before waking away. She watched as he remounted Thunder and then rode off like the sheriff's posse was after him.

"You okay, Casey?" Savannah asked later that afternoon while the two of them were sitting outside on the porch, enjoying the view of the mountains. Durango was inside watching a basketball game on television.

Casey glanced over at Savannah who had cooked chicken and dumplings, a Westmoreland recipe she had weaseled from Chase Westmoreland, the cook in the family. Chase and his wife owned a soul-food restaurant in Atlanta. And it just so happened that Chase's wife, Jessica, was Savannah's sister. To say the least, the meal had been delicious.

And speaking of delicious…her thoughts shifted to McKinnon. He was probably back at the ranch packing to leave in the morning. She wondered if he was still thinking about the kiss they'd shared earlier that day as she was.

"Casey?"

Casey sighed. "Yes, I'm okay. I was thinking about something."

Savannah glanced over at her and smiled. "Some*thing* or some*one?*"

Casey smiled. It was definitely someone. McKinnon Quinn had a knack for kissing her crazy one minute, then putting distance between them the next. "I just don't get it," she said softly.

"Get what?"

Casey's gaze flicked to Savannah. "Why would a man who acts like he enjoys kissing me one minute put distance between us the next? As if he regretted what he's done?"

Savannah chuckled. "Sounds like he's afraid of getting in too deep. Do you have a problem with him kissing you?"

"Yes. No. I—I don't know," Casey muttered, clearly frustrated. "But our kisses don't mean anything."

"And what makes you think that?"

Casey rolled her eyes. "Trust me, they're just kisses. If they meant something, he wouldn't regret doing it the next day."

Savannah nodded. "McKinnon evidently wants you but is working hard to apply the brakes. I'm wondering how long he can hold out on not having you."

Casey shrugged. "I can't be worried about something like that."

Savannah gave a ladylike snort. "Casey Westmoreland, aren't you the least bit interested to know why he's afraid to get into a serious relationship?"

"I'm not as naive as you might think, Savannah. I

have two brothers, remember, so I know why some men prefer not getting into serious relationships. It's called commitment phobia. McKinnon is full of testosterone with a capital *T*. And like Clint and Cole, I'm sure he accepts the concepts of sex and intimacy as a way of life. I used to watch how my brothers would operate, changing women as often as they changed their shirts. I was the one whose head was filled with romantic illusions of forever love and till death do you part."

"But still, if a man showed interest in me one day then tried acting like I didn't exist the next, I'd like to know why," Savannah said. "That way I'd know how to handle him."

While driving home from Durango and Savannah's home Casey inwardly admitted that Savannah had raised a pretty good question. Why was McKinnon putting brakes on anything developing between them?

There was only so much kissing a couple could do before kissing turned into cuddling, stroking, getting naked…and then what? Did he think they could continue to kiss without ever wanting to take things further? Already whenever he took her into his arms she felt emotions she hadn't experienced before. Her body would get hot and bothered like it had recognized it's mate—as if that in itself wasn't the craziest thing.

Or was it?

Her chest heaved at the possibility and heat was spreading to all parts of her body. Could McKinnon be her true mate? Her mother always claimed that a woman would know the man that was meant for her. And although her mother had filled her mind with lies about her and Corey, all Casey had to do was look around to know true love did exist for some people—like Durango and Savannah, her father and Abby, and McKinnon's parents, to name a few. Then there were all those West-morelands who were happily married.

She was determined when she saw McKinnon again that she would get some answers. If he was playing a game with her then he would find that she was a worthy opponent. She wasn't all that experienced when it came to man-woman stuff, but she was not a woman to take lightly.

McKinnon glanced out his bedroom window the moment he heard Casey returning. He took advantage of his position near the window to study her unobserved. It was dark, but the flood lights around his home provided enough lightning to clearly see her.

She was wearing a pair of jeans with a V-neck green blouse. She had on what appeared to be a pair of sturdy boots and her short hair seemed tousled or windblown, giving one the impression she had just gotten out some man's bed or had driven home with the car window down. He wanted to lay blame on the latter and not the former. The thought of her in any man's bed beside his was a very disturbing one.

When she went inside the cottage and closed the door, he moved away from the window, wondering how he could feel so possessive toward a woman that wasn't even his and could never be. Any man who knew his situation would have the common sense and the decency to leave her alone. In fact, any man with a lick of sense would not have kissed her in the first place, let alone kiss her a few more times after that. He knew the score.

He also knew he wanted her.

There was no rhyme or reason as to why he felt the way he did considering everything. But he would give anything to take her into his arms one last time and brand her his, even if it was only for a minute, an hour… a night. He had found out the hard way that when it came to Casey, kissing her would not be enough. She was able to arouse a desire in him so strong and potent that it didn't take much to make his body hard with one hell of a relentless throb.

Like it was doing now.

He inwardly swore as he slammed his luggage shut. He wanted to feel the hardness of her nipples pressed against his chest. He wanted to fit her body to his, position her as close as she could get to relieve his ache, stop the throbbing. He wanted to kiss her again, slide his tongue into her mouth, devour her, savor every stroke as he feasted on her taste…or let her control things the way she'd done earlier that day by the stream. As inexperienced as she was, her technique had been flawless and had his loins blazing to the point the fire was still burning now. He had this connection to Casey that he just couldn't shake. A man with a whole lot of sense wouldn't act on it but around her he seemed to be senseless.

Even now he could picture her getting ready for bed, taking a shower, letting the water stream over her naked body. More than anything he wanted to be in that shower with her, take her against the tile wall, hear her call his name the moment he made her come.

Warning bells went off in his head, reminding him of the reason there could never be anything serious between them, but he dismissed the reason with a low, husky growl as he made his way out of his bedroom toward the back door. At the moment he was too far gone to even think straight.

Casey heard the loud knock on her door the moment she stepped out of the bedroom. She tightened the sash of her robe as she crossed the room, wondering if anything had happened to Prince Charming.

She glanced out the peephole and saw it was McKinnon and quickly unlocked the door and opened it. "What happened?"

"Nothing happened."

Casey met his gaze, saw the unmistakable intensity of an aroused man in his eyes—a man who fully intended to get stimulated even further. She couldn't decide if she should snatch him inside and have her way with him, or run for cover. She quickly recalled her talk with Savannah, and even more recent, the talk she'd had with herself while driving home. She swallowed hard, fighting the desire and the urge to give this man any and everything he wanted. She had to stand her ground and not make things easy for him. Well, not too easy.

She tilted her head back and tried not to focus on that look in his eyes. "Then, why are you here, McKinnon?" She couldn't be more direct than that, she thought.

McKinnon stared at her. She was as he'd thought, still damp in some places from her shower and ready for bed. He reached out and caught her hand in his before she realized what he was about to do. He felt the shiver that passed through her, heard her sharp intake of breath. "I'm here because I'm leaving in the morning and I wanted to kiss you goodbye before I left."

"Why? So you can have a reason to ignore me when you get back on Saturday?"

Her words were sharp and sliced right through him. She had taken his behavior after every kiss as a rejection of her, but he'd only been trying to preserve his sanity by not starting something with her that he'd known he couldn't finish. He had seen putting distance between them as the only answer. Where he saw it as a positive, she'd taken it as a negative. But now he was past the point of trying to be noble. There was an air of intimacy surrounding them and they were both breathing it, being consumed by it, nearly drowning in it.

"No, that's not the reason why. I want to kiss you so I can carry the taste of you with me."

She inhaled sharply, thinking he knew exactly what to say to make her come unglued. When the warmth of his fingers closed around hers, she knew she was loosing the battle. But she refused to give in until she had the answers she sought. "Why? Why did you stay away after each time we kissed, McKinnon?" she asked softly.

He stared at her for a second and knew he had to be honest with her, as much as he could. "I didn't see it as staying away from you, Casey. I saw it as distancing myself from temptation. It was either that or make an attempt to take you to bed every time I was around you. I wanted you just that much."

"And you saw that as a bad thing?" she asked, needing to understand.

"I damn sure don't see it as a good thing. You're

Corey's daughter, Durango's cousin. To me the Westmorelands are like family. I can't see starting something with you that would lead nowhere. I doubt any of them would appreciate it if I did."

"And you're sure it would have led nowhere?" she asked quietly.

"Yes. I don't intend to ever get serious about a woman. Marriage is not in my future."

"May I ask why?"

"No. That's one topic that's not up for discussion. Just take my word that it's not and let's leave it at that."

His words were a sure sign that some woman had hurt him. Was that the reason he was still bitter and hell-bent on not giving his love to someone else? "So, why are you here, McKinnon? I'm still Corey's daughter and Durango's cousin, and you're still not looking for anything permanent in your life."

He released her hand to lean in the doorway and took a moment to let his gaze rake over her from the top of her head to the toes of her bare feet. She looked sexy in her short silk black robe. "Because," he said softly, meeting her gaze again, "in addition to being Corey's daughter and Durango's cousin, I can no longer deny that you're also a very desirable woman."

He reached out and placed a knuckle beneath her chin, forcing their eyes to meet when he added, "And a woman I want in my bed."

The huskily spoken words sent more shivers through her body, made the nipples of her breasts press tight against her robe and made heat stream down her stomach to settle between her legs. "And you made that decision, just like that?"

"No," he said easily. "It took me almost three weeks and only after you took the initiative and kissed me earlier today, making me realize and accept that you're a woman with needs, as well."

Casey wondered what he would think if he knew that he was the one defining those needs, because the "needs" he was referring to had never been awaken until now. Not only had they been awaken, they were stirring to life and seemed to have a mind of their own. She nervously nibbled her lips.

"Wouldn't you rather nibble my lips?"

Casey swallowed against a massive lump in her throat. His question had her imagining such a thing taking place. She was suddenly aware that she was losing ground with him. He had a way of stirring up her emotions and her passion. She drew in a shaky breath and took a step back He followed, closing the door behind him.

He stood tall, broad-shouldered. His muscular chest was covered in a tan shirt that seemed to highlight his golden-brown skin. His mane of hair flowed around his shoulders and the dark eyes staring at her had an intensity that nearly took her breath away. McKinnon Quinn was definitely any woman's fantasy.

Before she could take another step he reached out and snagged her arm, bringing her closer to him. "When I said I wanted to take your taste with me, I meant it."

Then McKinnon leaned down and captured her mouth with his, swallowing her sigh of pleasure in the process. With the sound, a fission of heated desire flowed through his veins and he intensified the mating of their mouths, erasing the physical distance they had endured the past weeks, as well as the one they would encounter over the next three days. He devoured her mouth like a hungry man who needed the taste of her as much as he needed to breathe, and when he wrapped his arms around her, bringing her luscious curves closer to the fit of him, he pressed against her, wanting her to feel just how much he needed her, wanted her.

She reciprocated, as if wanting him to know the same by slipping her arms around his waist as he continued to feast on her mouth. The taste of him always amazed her. He had the scent of man but the taste of sweet chocolate.

She felt herself being lifted into his arms but instead of taking her into the bedroom as she assumed he would, he carried her over to the sofa and gently placed her there. He stood back and looked down at her. She looked back at him, seeing the thick bulge behind the zipper of his jeans as well as the dark look in his eyes.

He slowly eased down on his knees in front of her and leaned over and opened her robe to discover she wasn't wearing anything except her panties. His gaze met hers just seconds before he lowered his head to capture a nipple into his mouth, feasting on it with as much intensity as he had with her mouth earlier. Each pull on her nipple sent a sensuous tug through her abdomen and heat escalating in her center. He braced his hands on both sides of her as he continued a hungry path down her body with his mouth. When he reached her stomach, he kissed her navel, drew circles around it with the tip of his tongue, before moving lower.

She assumed her panties would stop him but she soon discovered he didn't intend for them to be a deterrent. She stiffened when he used his hands to ease the flimsy material down her legs, exposing the area of her that he sought. Then he touched her there and the moment he did, she shuddered as intense heat consumed her.

His fingers moved through the dark curls, teasing the sensitive nub, testing the wetness between her legs before he slid a finger inside and began stroking her.

"McKinnon."

She said his name on a sensuous purr as he continued to stroke, sending shock waves of pleasure straight through her, making her incredibly aroused and filled with a need that was mind consuming.

He lowered his head and she made a move to get up until she felt the sharp tip of his tongue invade the area where his fingers had been. The sensations that single swipe of his tongue made were so potent she thought she would pass out. And when he gently lifted her hips to position her closer to his mouth, she moaned out his name from deep within her throat.

He relentlessly stroked her with his tongue, stimulating every sensory nerve within her, making her tremble all over. He had started a fire within her that she doubted could ever be extinguished. And just when she thought she was about to burn to a crisp, sensations overtook her, making her cry out before she could stop from doing so.

She closed her eyes, thinking that would soften the impact, but it made it that much more forceful, turning her entire body inside out. A heartbeat of a second later, something inside of her exploded and her body shattered into a million sensuous pieces.

When he finally removed his mouth from her, she opened her eyes and met his gaze. Before she could say anything, he kissed her, letting her taste herself on his lips.

Moments later when McKinnon pulled his mouth free, he stood as he gazed down at her. His body was throbbing and ached to be inside of her but he knew tonight was not the time. She had to accept him on his terms before that could happen.

"McKinnon?"

He leaned down and gently pulled her up to hold her in his arms. When he released her, he met her gaze. "Before we can go beyond this, Casey, I need to be sure that you understand that this is all we can ever share. I have to know that you can be satisfied with that. Think about it while I'm gone." His mouth then came down on hers as if he was branding her; kissing her with a desperation that had her moaning all over again.

He pulled back and not saying a single word he turned and headed for the door. And without looking back he left.

Chapter 9

"McKinnon, you're back," Morning Star Quinn said, surprised and smiling up at her oldest son. "We weren't expecting you until tomorrow and thought you'd miss the party altogether."

"I was able to wrap everything up a day earlier," he said, glancing around. This wasn't a small party. His mother and Abby had definitely done things up on a larger scale than he'd expected. But then he really shouldn't have been surprised.

As he scanned the room he was looking for one person in particular—the honoree, the woman who'd been on his mind every day since he'd been gone. He smiled when his gaze was snagged by Stone Westmoreland. Evidently Stone had arrived in Montana while McKinnon had been away.

He nodded at Stone, then moved his gaze on. A group of invitees standing in a crowd parted briefly, allow-ing a better view, and McKinnon's body stiffened when he saw Casey hemmed in a corner by Rick Summers. She looked simply beautiful in a latte-colored skirt and matching blouse.

"McKinnon, would you like something to drink?"

His mother's question momentarily pulled away his attention and he glanced down at her and forced a smile. "No, I'm fine. I think I'll mingle." Mingle hell, he thought, moving straight to the area where Casey and Summers were standing. Neither of them had noticed his arrival.

"McKinnon. I thought you weren't returning until tomorrow," Durango said, appearing out of nowhere and blocking his path.

"Not now, Rango," McKinnon all but snarled. "The only thing I want to do is put my fist in Summers' face."

Durango lifted a brow. "Why would you want to do something like that?" he asked in a low tone.

"Because Rick Summers is a—"

"Bastard," Durango said, finishing the sentence for him. "That's nothing new. Come on, let's grab a couple of beers and go somewhere and chill."

McKinnon narrowed his gaze at Durango. "I don't want to chill. I want to—"

"Smash Summers' face in, I know, but you need to cool down and tell me why seeing Casey with him has gotten you all worked up. She's my cousin so I have a valid reason to be interested in the proceedings—especially knowing the ass Summers is—but whether you've noticed or not, I'm not the only Westmoreland here tonight. Stone's here. So are Corey, Clint and Cole."

McKinnon glanced around. "Clint and Cole are here?"

"Yeah, but maybe they're keeping an eye on the wrong man. Maybe they should be keeping an eye on you. The last time we talked you claimed you weren't falling for Casey. If this isn't falling, I'd like to know what it is when a man wants to smash another's face just for talking to a woman who means nothing to him? Maybe instead of smashing up Summers' face, you need to give what I just said some serious thought."

Then Durango walked off.

Casey quickly concluded that she wouldn't be able to hide her annoyance much longer if Rick Summers continued to deliberately hog her time. In less than twenty minutes she'd discovered the man was so full of himself it was a shame. He had an ego a mile long and at some point during his lifetime, some woman had convinced him he was every female's ideal man.

She glanced around. Where were Clint and Cole when she needed them? She'd been hoping one of them would come and find some excuse to take her away, but so far that hadn't happened.

She continued to glance around the room when her breath suddenly caught as her gaze locked with McKinnon's. Adrenaline was mixing with surprise and making all kind of weird things happen to her body. She hadn't expected him back until sometime tomorrow but seeing him now, standing across the room talking to one of her brothers while slowly raking his gaze over her, was only increasing her adrenaline level. It didn't take much to recall the intimacy that had transpired between them the night before he'd left. Just thinking about it sent a quaking shiver through her body and caused heat to settle in one particular place between her thighs.

"Would you like to go outside with me for a spell?"

Rick's words invaded her thoughts, which was a good thing since she was about to melt from all the heat McKinnon's look was generating. She broke eye contact with McKinnon to glance up at Rick. "No, I don't want to go outside, Rick. I like being inside much better. Besides, I'm the guest of honor and it wouldn't look good if I went missing."

He shrugged. "Who cares about these people."

Her frown deepened. "I do. Most of them are friends of my father's."

Seeing he had ticked her off, Summers tried to backpedal into her good graces. "I didn't mean it that way..." he protested. "I can certainly understand if now isn't a good time, but before the night is over maybe we can slip—"

"May I have this dance?"

The deep, husky voice had both Casey and Rick turning around. Rick's surprise quickly transformed into annoyance. "Where did you come from, McKinnon? I thought you'd be out of town until sometime tomorrow."

McKinnon gave a smile that didn't quite reach his eyes. "See what happens when you think, Summers," he said. He turned to face Casey and held out his hand to her. "Will you dance with me, Casey?"

"No, she won't dance with you. As you can see, she's with me," Summers all but snarled.

"Is that a fact?" McKinnon asked, holding Casey's gaze.

Knowing there wasn't a decision to make, Casey placed

her hand in McKinnon's. "Welcome back, McKinnon, and I'd love to dance with you." She then turned to Rick. "Excuse us, please."

Casey could feel the heat of Rick's anger burn her back when she walked off but at the moment she could care less. And when McKinnon pulled her into his arms, threaded his fingers possessively with hers, Rick was nothing more than a very blurred memory.

It seemed McKinnon had timed it right; a slow number was playing and she couldn't imagine being anywhere but here, in his arms as they swayed slowly to the rhythm of the music. That wasn't true, she decided quickly. She could imagine being somewhere else with him—in his bed. After he'd left that night, after doing all those wondrous things to her body, she had laid there, too overwhelmed to move.

She had done a lot of thinking over the three days since he'd been gone. She wanted McKinnon Quinn. Pure and simple. There didn't have to be promises of forever-after or any pretense of something that wasn't there. At least not on his part since she knew how she felt. She loved him. All it took was waking up that next morning, remembering that special intimacy that had taken place the night before and knowing he was somewhere miles away that made her accept what she'd been trying to deny. Regardless of how he felt about her, she could admit that she loved him and unlike her mother, she wouldn't pretend about what wasn't there. Instead, she would accept what she could and be happy.

When the music came to an end, he leaned down and softly whispered, "Would you step outside with me for just a minute?"

His dark eyes were filled with so much heat that it almost singed her spine. Unlike when Rick had asked her that same question, she'd felt no hesitation when giving McKinnon her response. "Yes."

Taking her hand, he led her out the door. Once they were on the porch, he tugged her closer, slipped his hand around her waist, and he led her somewhere only he knew. This used to be his home, she thought. The place he'd been raised as a child. He knew of secret places and she had a feeling that tonight he intended to share one with her.

"This is a good spot," he said, coming to a stop on the dark side of the barn, away from prying eyes. He turned her in the circle of his arms.

"A good spot for what?" she asked as shivers of awareness and desire caressed her skin.

"For this." And then he leaned down and captured her mouth while gathering her closer into his arms. Their kisses seemed to always get hotter and hotter, more intense, bolder and more profound. Her heartbeat kicked up and her love for him increased ten fold. There was a reason she'd been so attracted to him from the first and now she understood it all.

Moments later he slowly released her mouth and she glanced up at him, her nostrils filled with his sexy scent. "That's the welcome I needed, Casey," he whispered against her moist lips. "The kind I thought about getting once I returned."

"I hope I didn't disappoint you," she said, smiling up at him.

He gave her one of those rare McKinnon smiles and said, "You could never do that." Then, moments later, he asked, "Have you given any thought to what I asked you to think about while I was gone?"

"Yes."

"And?"

She knew what he wanted to hear. "I accept your terms, McKinnon. There will be no expectations, only enjoyment."

He stared at her for a long moment before nodding. "And you can live with that?"

"Yes, I can live with it."

He nodded. "How did you get here tonight?"

"Cole came and picked me up."

McKinnon was glad it hadn't been Rick. "I'll let your brother know that I'll be taking you back to the ranch when the party's over."

"All right."

He leaned down and kissed her again before reluctantly pulling away. "I guess we need to go back inside now," he said in a tone that said he would rather stay out there with her. "And I guess it wouldn't be a good thing for me to dominate all your time tonight," he said, taking her hand.

"I wouldn't complain if you did."

A long, tense silence stretched between them and Casey wondered what he was thinking. She had no idea but she knew what was on her own mind. She would make sure that after tonight the thought of putting distance between them again would be the last thing McKinnon would want to do.

She intended to turn the tables on him and hit him with a little taste of seduction—Westmoreland style.

* * *

Never before had McKinnon thought the distance between his parents' home and his was so long. It seemed
like he'd been driving for hours instead of minutes. He
should feel relaxed, relieved by Casey's decision for
them to get involved in a no-strings-attached affair, but
all he felt was tension and a deep desire for the woman
sitting beside him in his car.

After arriving from the airport he had parked his
truck and decided to take his toy, an '85 Corvette he'd
restored a couple of years ago. It provided him a type
of horsepower that Thunder couldn't. He took a quick
glance sideways at Casey. She hadn't said much since
they'd left the party.

When they had gone back inside after their kiss,
it hadn't surprised him that Rick Summers had tried
seeking her out again, determined to stay glued to her
side. But she had handled Summers by saying that as
the guest of honor she had to spend time with everyone and not just him. McKinnon smiled, remembering
that that hadn't gone over too well with him and he'd
eventually left.

He also remembered the second dance he and Casey
had shared nearly at the end, which had prompted them
to leave the party as soon as they could without raising any eyebrows. The moment he held her close to
him, knowing that later that night she would be his in
every way that a woman possibly could, had set his
loins on fire. And from the way she had shivered in
his arms, he'd known she'd been acutely aware of his
aroused state.

He inhaled deeply and instead of the fragrance of bitterroot, the purplish-pink flower that was abundant in the area, his nostrils were filled with the scent of Casey and he became drenched in a wave of intense yearning. He wanted her. He wanted her in a way he had never wanted any woman before, including Lynette.

His hands tightened on the steering wheel as he felt a deep ache in his gut. On the flight back to Montana from D.C., he had thought about the moment when he would hold her in his arms, kiss her…make love to her. He hadn't been able to stop his mind from going there. Whenever he closed his eyes he thought of her in his bed, burying himself inside of her so deep that—

"I was really happy to see Spencer come in," she said of Durango's brother who made his home in California. "And I found it interesting that he's in the process of buying a winery somewhere in the Napa Valley."

Her words, spoken in a soft tone, floated all around him. He wanted to glance over at her again, but if his eyes were to connect with hers he would be tempted to pull to the side of the road and put an end to his pain and agony.

"So did I, but then Spencer has always been the financial wizard and investment genius in the Westmoreland family," he said.

"And that was wonderful news that Stone and Madison shared with everyone, wasn't it?" she asked moments later. "I'm so happy they're pregnant."

"So am I. Abby is ecstatic at the thought of becoming a grandmother."

Casey smiled. "And my father will become a grandfather. Another Westmoreland baby. I think it's wonderful."

McKinnon didn't say anything for a long moment but then asked, "I take it you want children someday?"

"Of course." She chuckled. "I don't particularly want a houseful like Madison says she wants, but I'd like at least two."

Disappointment swept through McKinnon and he tried to fight it back. He couldn't blame Casey for her desire to one day want a child—a child he would never be able to give her.

"Was your trip to D.C. a productive one, McKinnon?"

Her question brought him back. "Yes, I believe it was. Jamal's friends are impressed with the American way we do things, especially in breeding horses. They've formed a partnership and want to breed champion thoroughbred race horses. They're also interested in breeding Black Sterling Friesians."

"Those are beautiful horses. My uncle bred and trained one once."

"How did it go?"

"It went okay. Uncle Sid was a very patient man. The horse's name was Roving Rogue and it suited him. He had an eye for one particular mare, and no amount of coaxing could get him to cooperate with his training until he had his way with her."

McKinnon knew what she meant but wanted her to expound anyway. "Had his way, how?"

He could feel her gaze slide over to him and the force of it was a heated caress. He wondered if she would explain, go into details, paint one hell of a vivid picture.

"I wasn't supposed to be watching that night when it happened but I sneaked out of my room and got a chance to watch anyway. I was only fourteen and I guess Uncle Sid thought the sight of horses mating would be too intense for my delicate eyes," she said, and he could hear the smile in her voice. "It was to be a private affair with only my uncle and Vick, his head trainer, watching. Uncle Sid and Vick were stationed in a hiding place, out of Roving Rogue's line of vision so they wouldn't interrupt the proceedings, but I doubt Roving Rogue would have cared if he had an audience that night. He wanted the mare that much and to finally be put in a stable, with her at his mercy, was just what he wanted. I think at first, when the mare saw the intent in Roving Rogue's eyes it might have frightened her somewhat. She kept backing up, shaking her head and mane as if to say no way. And then…"

"Y-yes," he breathed in. "What happened then?"

"He seemed to be coaxing her to relax by prancing around her, whining a few times. Then I guess she felt comfortable, or she just wanted him enough that she allowed him to get close enough to sniff her out. Evidently he got a whiff of just how hot she was and before she could blink an eye, he reared up on his hind legs and took her. I had seen horses mate plenty of times before, but never like that."

McKinnon swallowed. He had seen horses mate plenty of times before, too, especially since he'd been around them all his life. He couldn't help wondering how this mating had been different. To keep his mind from getting clouded with all kinds of ideas, he decided to ask.

"What was so different about it?"

"The mare evidently was in heat in a pretty bad way

and was just as hot as he was. I overheard Vick call her a flirt, saying she was like a typical woman, almost driving Roving Rogue to the point of madness before she decided to give in. Good thing Roving Rogue was prime breeding material."

"What was the mare's name?" McKinnon asked, barely able to get the question out.

"Hot Pursuit."

Figures. "Continue," he said, still wanting his earlier question answered. "How was it different?"

"Hot Pursuit got just what she wanted. By the time Roving Rogue mounted her, holding her captive with his front legs while…uh…getting it on, she neighed and trembled the entire time while he thrust vigorously back and forth, pumping his seed into her. I actually thought she was in dire pain, but listening to my uncle and Vick talk, they claimed she was in sheer bliss."

And after listening to her, McKinnon was hard as a rock. His entire body felt hot and solid, and he could visualize in his mind the picture of the two horses mating.

They got quiet for a while, which was all right with McKinnon since he needed to cool down. Moments later they pulled into his yard. "We're here," he said, hoping he hadn't sounded as incredibly aroused as he felt.

He couldn't wait to get her inside the house and with tomorrow being Saturday, there would be no need to get up early in the morning. That meant he could make love to her all night as well as all day. First he would take her hard and fast. Then slow and easy. Then hard and fast again. By the time Monday rolled around he intended for any encounters she'd shared with anyone else to be totally erased from her mind.

Hell, he'd never felt this obsessed before, this filled with sexual need. Even now, before bringing the car to a complete stop, he could imagine touching her breasts, widening her thighs to slip between them and then inside her, pumping in and—

"McKinnon?"

The sound of her voice jerked him erect, in more ways than one. He brought the car to a stop before turning to her. His body hardened even more from the sound of her throaty tone when she said, "Would you like to come to the guesthouse for a nightcap?"

His mind raced ahead, thinking of going to her place for more than a nightcap. McKinnon released a heated sigh and said, "I'd love to."

The way he figured it, he should be feeling some guilt since the only thing he would be offering her was an affair that would lead nowhere. But the decision had been hers. He'd told her what she was in for and he hadn't made her any promises. She had accepted his terms and knowing she was a Westmoreland, the only thing that had made him decide to move ahead was in knowing she wanted him as much as he wanted her.

He knew it. It was there in her gaze each time they'd made eye contact at the party. No matter who he had been conversing with, he had known every moment her gaze had sought him out. He had felt it and the heated warmth of it had sizzled his skin whenever it had slid over him.

Getting out of the car, he walked to the other side to open the door for her. After leaning down and undoing her seat belt, he tried not to notice how the hem of her skirt had ridden up, or that he could see a nice portion of her creamy dark thighs. He felt tension tighten in his belly and tried to get a grip on his control. He offered her his hand and the moment they touched, his pulse immediately kicked up a notch.

"Thanks."

That did it. Instead of releasing her hand when she stood directly in front of him, he tugged on it, tumbling her into his arms. Every part of him was ready, especially his mouth that immediately snatched the breath from hers.

The tension eased from his body the moment their tongues touched, mingled, mated. It was like a homecoming and he spread his hands wide across her bottom to illustrate his point. He needed to kiss her, feel her, touch her, and at the moment it didn't matter that they were standing in the middle of his yard in the dark while he had his way with her mouth.

The only thing that mattered to him was that she was letting him. Not only letting him, but participating in a way that had hot blood running through his veins. The kiss then got so intense he thought it was time to take it indoors before he was tempted to take her right there against his car. He slowly pulled his mouth away. His arousal had increased as a result of her wild and reckless response to him.

"Let's finish this inside." He closed the car door, took her hand and they walked toward the guesthouse.

Chapter 10

It took every ounce of willpower Casey possessed to walk beside McKinnon on sturdy legs. She had deliberately baited him by making the tale of Roving Rogue and Hot Pursuit sound as erotic as she could. And while he'd tried keeping his gaze glued to the road, her gaze had been glued to him—at least to that area where his crotch was located.

She had watched him get aroused, larger than anything she'd ever imagined. And as she had observed the transformation, a tingling of desire had slid sensuously down her spine. What would take place once they were behind closed doors would not come as a surprise to either of them, but what would be a shocker to McKinnon was the next step in her plan of seduction.

When she had dressed for the party she hadn't a clue that he would return tonight, but her undergarments were sexy nonetheless. And from the way he had looked her up and down a few times at the party, she was well aware he liked her outer garments, as well. The above-the-knee skirt had handkerchief-hem tiers of tawny chiffon with a matching fluttery tunic-style blouse. The moment she had looked in the mirror after slipping it on earlier, she'd felt feminine and sexy. And from the looks that several men had given her, they'd thought the same. But none of their interest had meant anything to her. McKinnon's awareness was the one that mattered.

Casey did her best to slow down her racing pulse when they reached the door. While she inserted the key into the lock, instead of standing back, McKinnon stood so close behind her that she could feel the hardness of his middle pressed against her bottom, letting her know how much he wanted her.

She tensed in anticipation while opening the door, and the moment she stepped over the threshold and he followed her inside and closed the door behind him, he reached out before she had a chance to go too far. "Don't you go anywhere," he whispered huskily, his arms gently tightening around her waist as he pulled her to him and turned her around. "I want you."

And then he was kissing her with more hunger than ever before, pleasuring her mouth while his tongue provided frantic strokes all around the inside. The movement of it intensified and the taste of him was delicious and so teeth-chattering good.

When he pulled back moments later, she automatically moaned out her protest and he placed small kisses along her lips and jaw in consolation. "Let's get you out of these clothes," he whispered as he proceeded to undress her, first taking her blouse and pulling it over her head, and then getting down on one knee to catch hold of her waist to tug the skirt down. She stepped out of it, leaving her exposed in just her matching thong, bra and high-heeled sandals.

Instead of standing, he glanced up at her on bended knee and, reaching out, ran a slow finger up her leg and thigh to her center, the area barely covered by her thong. "Do you know that I carried your taste with me to D.C., and it was the only thing that held my sanity together those nights I slept in that hotel bed wanting you with a desperation that kept me hard all night?" he said while sliding the thong down her legs. "I didn't know what your final answer would be when I returned, but after tasting you here that night..." he said as he caught her off-guard when he leaned forward and quickly swiped his tongue across her exposed womanly core, "...you became mine, Casey. All mine."

He tilted his head back and looked up at her. "And that's why I was filled with so much anger when I arrived at the party and saw you with Summers," he admitted in a low voice.

Almost blinded with need, Casey met his gaze. "He means nothing to me and after you finish taking off my clothes, I'm going to prove it to you."

He smiled as he stood. "I'm holding you to that," he said as he reached out and undid the front clasp of her bra. When it released, her breasts sprang forth as twin delectable globes. "I like the taste of these, as well," he said, bending over and swiping both nipples with the heat of his tongue, leaving them wet as he slid her bra off.

Casey moaned. The sensations McKinnon's tongue evoked were causing every place on her body to tug at her center and she felt a deep longing all over, especially in the area between her legs.

"Now prove it," he said in a quiet yet challenging tone as he took two backward steps.

He glanced at her naked body up and down, and Casey fought for control as cool air touched her skin followed by the heat of his gaze. She had no qualms in proving anything to him. She had made up her mind earlier tonight to treat him to a little Westmoreland seduction, and although she'd never used her tempting wiles on a man before, with McKinnon Quinn she intended to give it her best shot and then some. She might be a novice but when she finished with him he would see that she did have a lot of potential. So much that he would definitely want to keep her around.

She knew from overhearing her brothers' conversations that men preferred women who were bold and daring, and she was about to whip up as wanton as one could get.

"Did I ever tell you what a great rider I am?" she asked, taking a step forward and reaching out and pulling his shirt from his jeans.

The moment she began unbuttoning it, one button at a time, he inhaled deeply when her fingers slipped a couple of times touching his bare chest. "You didn't have to," he said huskily. "I've seen you ride several times."

She looked at him and lifted a brow. Other than that one time at her father's place, if McKinnon had seen her ride she hadn't been aware of it. As far as she'd known he had never been around when she'd mounted a horse. Did that mean he'd been somewhere watching her without her knowing it?

"Yes, that might be true," she said, undoing the last button and pushing the shirt off his shoulders. "You might have *seen* me ride before, but you've never *felt* me ride…have you?" she finished off sweetly.

She watched the darkening of his eyes and thought that now was not the time to add that no man had ever felt her ride before, but if she was an ace in riding a horse, it couldn't be much different in riding a man. And she'd had a couple of sexually active female friends back in Beaumont swear that men loved women who rode them and weren't hung up on the traditional way to make love.

"No, I haven't felt you," he said, his irises getting even darker and his breathing getting deeper.

"Would you like to *feel* me, McKinnon?"

He nodded, not taking his eyes from her as he kicked off his shoes. "Hell, yeah."

"Good. But first I need to finish removing your clothes," she said, removing his belt and tossing it aside to join his shirt. She then proceeded to unzip his jeans slowly while noticing the huge bulge pressed against them. "Ooh," she moaned seductively. "It looks like someone is ready for that ride."

She got down on a bended knee, like he'd done earlier, to tug the jeans down his hips but didn't stand back up when he kicked them aside. Instead she reached out and cupped him, testing the solidity through his briefs. "Now to get rid of the final piece," she said, easing the briefs down his legs as she got down on the other knee, as well.

And when he stood in front of her stark naked, she leaned back on her hunches and admired his physique, especially one particular area. "W—wow," she said admiringly, easing the word out slowly. She then glanced up beyond his center to take in all the man. He was tall and unerringly handsome with thick, dark hair flowing wildly around his creamy dark-skinned shoulders, and had a muscular chest that was sprinkled with strands that formed a path down to the center of him. The part of him she intended to ride.

One good thing about having brothers and positioning yourself to overhear their supposedly private conversations was the ability to learn a lot about men and file that information away to use at an opportune time. She'd always thought the time would be right when she married the man destined to share her life forever. But now, she knew that man was McKinnon, even if what they shared only lasted through the night.

Her brothers had once whispered about men having certain pleasure points on their body and according to them, a man's staff was one of them. Mmm, she would see if that bit of information was true. Remembering all the wonderful and delectable things McKinnon had done to her earlier in the week, she decided when it came to love, anything was fair play.

She reached out and shamelessly took hold of him, intent on getting a taste of him like he'd done with her. Using her tongue, she started by doing swirls and swipes all over his throbbing member like it was a lollipop. But before she could close her mouth over him, he quickly pulled her up into his arms. "No more. I need to be inside of you."

Cuddling her in his arms, he headed toward the bedroom. Once there he tumbled her on the covers before joining her, pinning her down beneath him. The eyes bearing down on her flared with heat, desperation and intense need. She frowned up at him, wanting to be the one in total control, wanting to be the one who did the seducing. "I want to ride you, McKinnon," she said, pushing against him.

"Whatever you want," he said, shifting their bodies so she could be on top.

And when she proceeded to straddle his body the same way she did a horse, she smiled down at him. "I see you're ready and able," she said, placing her center right over his straight-as-a-rod erection. She made a delicious moan as she eased down, lowering her body on his. Their gazes held, locked, and she could feel the thick head of him slowly entering her wetness.

"Oh…it feels better than I ever dreamed of," she whispered, balancing on her elbows and lowering herself upon him even more.

While her eyes were still locked with his, she knew the exact moment he detected a barrier but before he could open his mouth to utter a single word, she shook her head. "No. Don't say anything, McKinnon. Get the deed done. It's what I want so just push up a little and go through it."

She saw the corner of his mouth edge into a stubborn frown as he fought to hold his body rigid. Funny thing about men, she quickly decided—they didn't like surprises, but she was determined to make this one he enjoyed. She wiggled her body and knew from his sharp intake of breath she had managed to touch another pleasure point. Then she leaned down and licked the frown from the corner of his lips and she kept licking and licking and...

"You should have told me," he growled through gritted teeth.

"I'm telling you now," she said matter-of-factly. Why did the horniest of men want to become so noble at a time like this? "Besides, it's not you who has anything to lose," she said, deliberately writhing her body while thinking of her almost-lost virginity.

"Stop that."

"Mmm, make me." Like it or not she intended to give herself to him. A second passed, then two. Evidently he saw she meant business or maybe his willpower ran out, she wasn't sure which. All she knew was that she felt the moment he lifted his body upward a little, then a little more, breaking through the barrier. And she lowered her body down to meet his, glad he had decided not to be difficult after all.

"You're going to pay for this," he said when he was finally buried inside her to the hilt.

She inhaled deeply. Connected to him this way felt good. The pain had been minimal and now she intended to take the pleasure to the max. "And I'm about to make you glad of your decision."

Casey may not have had experience in pleasuring a man the traditional way, but if what she'd overheard her brothers whispering one night was true, then she was about to make up for it. Closing her eyes, she imagined the Montana sky over her head, flowers all around her and mounting what she considered the best piece of male-flesh to ever walk the face of the earth. He was everything she wanted in a man and more. And she loved him. She lifted her hips, lowered them, moved them around, writhing, twisting and bucking on top of him, while he tried keeping up by moving in and out of her.

Somehow he bent forward, captured a breast in his mouth and sucked while she continued to ride like the devil was on her heels, loving the way he felt beneath her as she rode him.

Moments later she felt her first electrical jolt at the same moment she remembered something neither of them had thought of. "McKinnon," she said in a strained, panicky voice, barely getting the words out. "We didn't…"

Before she could finish he gripped hold of her hips and plunged deeper inside of her, roaring out her name. The intensity of the climax she felt coming from him caused her to cry out as he continued to push inside of her, deep, hard and fast, making her own body explode.

Never had she felt anything so exhilarating and mind-blowing. And she refused to stop bucking into him the same way he was bucking into her. This was one ride she wouldn't fall off. She felt crazy, she felt wild, she felt like a woman who had gotten what she'd waited almost thirty years for, and with the man she loved. And from the pleasure contorting his face, she knew he was enjoying this mating as much as she was.

She felt more spasms hitting her, hitting him, and she cried out his name once again, the same moment he cried out hers. She quickly decided that though this was her first time, it most certainly wouldn't be her last. But only with McKinnon. She may have orchestrated this seduction, Westmoreland style, but he had concocted a technique guaranteed to zap the life out of her with so many overwhelming sensations. And when the spasms finally ended and she dropped seemingly weightlessly to his chest, she didn't think she would ever be able to move again.

"You okay?"

Despite all her efforts, Casey didn't even have the strength to raise her head to look at McKinnon. She was exhausted. She could barely breathe. And from the sound of the air rattling in his chest, neither could he. But she would answer his question. "Yes, I'm okay."

She felt her head being lifted, but not under her own strength. McKinnon was raising it for her and pulling it closer to his as he kissed her deeply. He released her mouth moments later, only to be pulled back to her lips like a magnet to kiss her again, then again, like he couldn't get enough of her.

But then she couldn't get enough of him, either. She sighed in his mouth when she felt his hand move to her hips, to tighten the hold on their still-connected bodies. It was then that she again remembered that important element. She pulled her mouth away from his and met his gaze. "We didn't use protection, McKinnon."

He stared at her for a long moment and she thought she saw something flash in his eyes. Finally, he leaned up and lightly kissed her lips and said, "It's okay, don't worry about it."

Don't worry about it? She lifted a brow, not understanding. "I don't understand," she said, voicing her miscomprehension out loud. "Why shouldn't I worry about it?"

"Because I'm safe and I have no reason to think you aren't, either."

"No, but what about an unplanned pregnancy?"

He took a deep breath and blew it out. "Is it the time of the month that such a thing could happen for you?"

She thought about it, frowned as she calculated in her head. Then she smiled with relief. "No, I should be okay."

"Good enough." And then he pulled her face to his down for another kiss.

McKinnon came awake at the first sign of dawn, grateful it was Saturday and he didn't have to stir until he was ready, which didn't say a lot for a certain area of him which was stirring already.

All it took was for him to close his eyes to remember how, on the second go round, he had been the one doing the riding as he showed her his skill by pumping back and forth inside of her. Withdrawing, plunging forward over and over again, feeling her inner muscles contract around him as she drew him even deeper into her body. Being inside of her felt so right, a place he could have stayed forever. Each time he glanced down at her face, had seen the pleasure that took over each of her features, he'd been encouraged to double the pleasure, triple the passion and quadruple the need driving the both of them. In all his thirty-four years he had never experienced anything so amazing, so deep-in-your-gut right.

And she had been a virgin.

The thought of what they'd shared—that she hadn't shared it with another male—made it that much more special to him. She was one of the few women around who had waited until they'd been ready, and whose decisions to explore their sexuality with a partner had not been driven by society's standards, but by their own desire to abstain until they felt it was right for them. And evidently Casey hadn't thought the time was right until last night.

He glanced down at her. She was in a deep sleep and uncovered, displaying her nakedness for him to see and enjoy. He was tempted to bend forward and lick the nipples of her breasts but he knew doing so would lead to other things and he would continue licking her elsewhere which would eventually awaken her and after a night of nonstop lovemaking, she needed her rest.

And he needed to think.

For a brief moment last night when she had panicked at the thought of them not using birth control, he had considered telling her the real reason why he hadn't been concerned about her getting pregnant. But all it took was for him to remember the confession he'd made to Lynette. And in knowing the risk of doing that, how he had painstakingly made the decision at twenty-three to never father a child and had ensured that fact by having a vasectomy.

He loved children, had always wanted some of his own, but it would not have been fair to bring a child into the world knowing what medical problems he or she could be up against. He had assumed that Lynette would understand, but the letter he received weeks after she'd left had explained that she was a woman who wanted to one day be a mother and only a child born from her own body would do. Simply stated, she could not marry a man who could not give her that.

Lynette's rejection had hurt deeply and knowing that most women probably felt as she did—and wanted to bear their own children and not entertain any thoughts of adoption—he decided to live out the rest of his days indulging in meaningless affairs, and to put an end to his dream of ever meeting a woman he would marry.

Even now, as he studied Casey's nakedness, he knew he would give anything to one day see her pregnant with his child. The idea had crossed his mind the moment she brought up the fact they hadn't used birth control. But beyond that, he could see her as some child's mother, and as long as that vision stood out in his mind, there could be no place for her in his life. Other than here in his bed.

He wanted to scream out in anger, hit something in despair, but he had discovered years ago to accept any blows life dealt you and move on, not look back, not indulge in pity parties because somewhere in this universe was someone in a worse situation than you.

Casey was his present but she could never be a part of his future. He knew it and he would find a way to accept it. What they were sharing was short-term. It was that simple and he intended to keep it uncomplicated. This arrangement would work out quite nicely for him and he intended to make sure it worked out in a positive way for her, as well.

He heard her sigh and looked at her face to see she had awakened. A tempting smile touched the corners of her lips. "Good morning, McKinnon," she said in a sleepy voice that was filled with enough passion to cause heat to flow up his spine and his erection got harder. "What's up?"

"Umm, funny you should ask," he said, responding with a wicked chuckle before leaning over and capturing her lips.

Chapter 11

McKinnon was no longer avoiding her.

That thought made Casey smile as she dismounted Prince Charming after a good day's workout. Two weeks had passed since the night of her party when he had made love to her all night long. Even now, the thought of that night sent heated shivers through her.

Of course it was a given that during the day he had his work to do and she had hers, but at night it had become a foregone conclusion that they would share a bed, whether at the big house or the guesthouse. In fact, she was becoming a regular fixture in his household. After that first almost embarrassing morning when he had talked her into another lovemaking session before leaving his bed and returning to her own—and she'd run smack into Henrietta on her way out—Casey no longer tried the sneak-and-retreat routine. She and McKinnon were adults, and if they decided to indulge in a lead-to-nowhere affair, then it was their business and no one else's.

But still she was grateful that no one, especially her family or his, was questioning the obvious—that the two of them were lovers. They ate breakfast together each morning and dinner together in the evenings. They even visited their families together often, and both his parents and Corey seemed to accept that they were adults to do as they pleased.

It was now the beginning of June and the sun was hotter today than usual, she thought as she walked Prince Charming back to his stall. Because of the heat, she'd decided to end her workday a little early. In a few weeks she and McKinnon, as well as a number of Westmorelands, would travel to Lake Tahoe to attend her cousin Ian's wedding, and she knew anyone who hadn't heard by now that she and McKinnon were lovers would find out since they planned to share a suite.

"Hey, beautiful. Do you want to take an evening ride with me?" McKinnon's deep, husky voice called out to her, catching her unaware. She glanced around and saw him a few feet from the corral, sitting on Thunder's back. The sun poured over him, catching the long, dark, silky-looking strands that flowed over his shoulders. Today, more of his Blackfoot features stood out and he looked nothing like the man who had made love to her that morning. Now he appeared to be a fierce warrior ready to take her captive if she refused his request.

"I'd love to go riding with you. Just give me a few minutes to saddle Runaway Child." A few moments later they were headed at a brisk pace across the quiet, open range.

"It's a nice day for riding, isn't it?" Casey said when they slowed their mounts after reaching the edge of a lake that was located on McKinnon's property.

"Sure is, and I thought it would be kind of nice to get away for a while. For me it's kind of like a deserving treat. I sold six of my stallions today, which brought me and Durango a pretty nice profit."

"Oh, McKinnon, that's wonderful. Congratulations."

"Thanks."

As they continued to ride together, side by side, she decided to ask him something she'd been meaning to but had never got around to doing. "What made you get into the horse breeding business?" They had brought their horses to a stop and she watched as McKinnon whipped off his hat to wipe sweat from his brow before placing it back on his head.

"When I got this place I thought ranching would keep me busy enough, but it didn't," he said, tilting his head and looking at her. "Durango suggested starting the business because he thinks I have a gift when it comes to handling horses."

"Do you?"

He shrugged. "Probably, but then so do you. I consider what I have as a natural instinct more than a gift. I've discovered that if you breed quality horses there are bound to be serious buyers in all corners of the globe who're ready to do business with you. Which is one of the reasons the M&D is doing so well."

McKinnon glanced over and watched how the evening breeze ruffled the ends of Casey's hair. The urge to run his hand through and tousle it some more took hold of him and he tightened his grip on the reins. If he were to touch her, it wouldn't stop there. He would want to kiss her, pull her off her horse onto his, carry her somewhere private and have his way with her. He ran a hand over his jaw thinking that wasn't such a bad idea and he knew just the place. "Do you want to go play, Casey?"

His deep voice floated over to her and she tilted her head sideways to look at him. "Play?"

He smiled. "Yes. There's a private place not far from here where we can play."

She returned his smile. "And just what will we be playing?"

He chuckled. "How about cowgirl and Indian?"

The shade of his Stetson brim shielded his eyes but she didn't have to see them to know they had darkened at the thought of all the possibilities such a game would entail. "Cowgirl and Indian, huh?"

"Yes."

"You do recall that I'm from Texas, right?"

"Meaning?"

"I'm a true cowgirl in every sense of the word."

McKinnon didn't doubt that since he'd been the recipient of her *rides* a number of times. "And?"

"And I'm no easy prey if that's what you think."

His smile deepened. "We'll see. So do you want to play or not?"

She grinned over at him. "Yes, McKinnon. I want to play."

* * *

"Just where are you taking me, McKinnon?" Casey asked, glancing around. She knew they were still on McKinnon's land but where they were she hadn't a clue. He had taken her beyond the rolling hills and they were now going through a maze of bluffs and ravines.

"Getting nervous, cowgirl?" he asked, chuckling.

She frowned over at him. "Of course not, but hasn't anyone ever warned you that it's not good to back a woman up against a wall?"

McKinnon grinned at a vision of that very thing happening—except the woman in his mind was a naked Casey. "I beg to differ. In fact, I can think of a lot of good reasons to back a woman—namely you—up against the wall, Casey."

His voice had gone low and his eyes had darkened, so she had a pretty good idea just where his thoughts were. She forced her gaze away from his eyes to look the area over. During the past two weeks she had taken the art of seduction to a whole new level. She had come up with signals—both verbal and non-verbal—and had gotten an extreme sense of satisfaction knowing McKinnon had enjoyed being the recipient of her racy seduction each and every time. Her actions had been more on instinct than experience, which added to the aroused feelings and excitement. Sensuous shudders would pass through her every time she thought of how McKinnon had taken her from virgin to vixen.

She glanced back over at him. He was watching her intensely and for some reason she had a feeling he was about the turn the tables—he was about to become the seducer. She hated admitting it, but there was an electrical thrill floating through her veins at the thought of his sexual attentions focused mainly on her.

"We can stop riding now."

Casey halted her horse just as McKinnon took the Stetson off his head and dismounted. He then walked over, reached up with his hand and helped her off Runaway Child.

"You still aren't going to tell me where we are?" she asked when her feet touched the ground. Her pulse kicked up knowing his body had pinned her between him and the horse.

"No, not yet. Come with me. We have to walk the rest of the way." He took her hand in his and led her to an area that seemed to have been grazing land at one time but over the years the melting of ice and snow, along with the fall of rocks and boulders from the mountain, now hid it from view and made it impossible terrain for normal travel.

Casey stopped dead in her tracks when she saw what else the elements had done. A cavern had been carved deep in the surface of a huge mountain. She almost became breathless as she took in the splendor of nature's handiwork. She turned to McKinnon. "I didn't know you had a cave on your property."

He smiled. "Rango's and my secret. We came across it one day years ago while we were in our early twenties. I decided then that if this land ever went up for sale, I wanted it. As soon as it did years later, I bought it with my parents' help. In addition to a loan from them, I had to take out two mortgages to pay for it. Now I've paid my parents back and owe the bank on just one loan, but I feel I own some of the most beautiful land in Montana."

Casey nodded. She had to agree. "Do you come here often?"

"Not as much as I'd like but it's nice to get away every now and then. Come on and take a look inside."

When Casey hesitated he raised a brow. "What are you afraid of?"

"Bats. Bears. Should I go on?"

He chuckled. "Trust me. There aren't any bats or bears in there. Rango and I got rid of them long ago when we made this place into a secret hideaway."

Deciding to take him at his word, Casey let him lead the way while she followed, at least until she came to the cave's opening that was protected by a pull-down metal security gate. But what caught her attention was the thick layer of tobacco dust surrounding the entrance. She stopped walking again and McKinnon turned and saw what had her attention. "That's to keep snakes and other unwanted animals out," he explained.

Casey nodded. That's what she was afraid of.

After unlocking the security gate, he called back to her, "Come on, cowgirl. You can handle it."

Casey sighed. She wasn't so confident anymore but decided not to let McKinnon know it. Once she followed him inside, her breath caught. It was definitely a cave, but McKinnon had transformed it into just what he'd said—a private hideaway with a sturdy-looking made-up bed, a chair and a dresser. There were even a couple of tables with kerosene lanterns and several Native American rugs hanging on the stone walls.

She turned to him, amazed. "McKinnon, it's beautiful."

Coming to this place was hard on horseback, so she couldn't help but wonder how he had managed to get furniture in here. He smiled, evidently knowing her question. "It wasn't easy and more than once Rango and I questioned our sanity. We had one hell of a time but we managed it."

His lips turned into a mischievous grin when he added, "At the time we thought it would be the ideal place to bring female acquaintances."

She raised a brow. "Did you?"

He laughed. "Trust me, we tried to, but those we got as far as the entrance wouldn't go any further once they picked up the scent of the tobacco dust. Everyone around these parts know what it's mainly used for."

Casey snorted. "They were nothing but scaredy-cats. Evidently they weren't true cowgirls."

McKinnon chuckled. "Evidently."

Casey crossed her arms over her chest as she shot him a pointed look. "So, McKinnon, why did you really bring me here?"

His eyes glinted with a kick of satisfaction. "I brought you here to give you a taste of your own medicine."

She lifted a brow. "Meaning?" she asked, releasing a quivering sigh.

"Meaning that you've become the queen of seduction. Well, today I'm going to be the king of takers and I'm going to take you, Casey," he said huskily with a half smile that made heat form between her legs. "I plan on taking you on that bed, against that wall, on that table. Hell, I plan on taking you all over the damn place."

Casey swallowed the lump in her throat as her gaze flew around the cavernous room. The heat between her legs had intensified with his words. If he was trying to get her wet in a certain spot, it was definitely working. The thought of spending time out here alone with him was sending sparks of fire all through her.

She glanced back at him, met his dark, penetrating gaze. He was standing in the middle of the room with his booted feet braced apart. His hands were tucked in the waistband of his jeans and whether he'd wanted it to or not, his stance placed emphasis on his swollen groin area, which showed just how aroused he was.

"So you think you want to take me all over the place, do you?" she asked, holding his gaze.

"Be forewarned, Casey Westmoreland. It's not wishful thinking on my part, either. That's what I intend to do."

A flirty smile touched her lips as her hands went to her shirt. She slowly began undoing the buttons. "Okay then, King Taker. I guess we need to get started and get what you came here for, don't we?"

McKinnon crossed the room with a boy-you-are-gonna-get-laid smile on his face, and Casey decided then and there that he wouldn't just be taking her, she would be taking him, as well, because she wanted him just as much as he wanted her.

He came to a stop directly in front of her. "Need help getting out of your clothes?" he asked meaningfully.

"No. You can stand there and watch or save time by getting out of your own clothes."

He grinned and began following her lead, quickly dispersing with his clothing and kicking them on the pile to join hers. When he raked his gaze over her naked body, he thought as he always did that she was an extremely beautiful woman.

He slipped his hand around her waist knowing just where he wanted to start. "So you're a woman who doesn't like getting backed against a wall, huh?" he said while walking her backward. "That's a pity because with the right person such a thing could be a very pleasurable experience."

He came to a stop when her back was pressed against the stony wall. Luckily for her this particular wall was covered with a huge finger-weaved Native American rug. He moved his hands from her waist to her hips and, grabbing hold of her rump, he hoisted her up and she wrapped her legs around him.

"Guide me in, sweetheart," he whispered against her lips.

And she did. Taking him in her hands she positioned him at her womanly entrance and met his gaze. "I need you *here,* McKinnon."

He pushed against her, easing himself inside. The moment he felt her wet heat, as well as her feminine muscles clenching him, he gritted his teeth and said, "No, baby, I'm the one who needs you *there.*"

And then he plunged deeper into her, ripping a scream of pleasure from her throat, which proved she was every bit as needy as he was. And it seemed every time he pounded into her body, her senses went on overload, her desire for him sharpened and every cell she possessed begged for more. She was struck by one sensation after another. They kept coming, he kept pounding and her muscles tightened around him with each

thrust as she tried to lock him in. And when an orgasm
struck, she screamed loud enough to scare off any animal nearby. But that was only the beginning, and another orgasm followed on the tail of the first.

She knew every time he detonated, she could feel the
liquid heat of him shoot to all parts of her body, and like
her, he kept coming and coming. And when he leaned
down and captured a nipple into his mouth and began
a sucking motion that she felt all the way to her womb,
she let out more screams.

He grabbed her hips each time he rocked against her
so as not to bruise her back and although she may not
be able to walk tomorrow, today she didn't care. And
when he threw his head back and roared, she came again
just from the mere sound of it.

Afterward she sagged against his chest as he kissed
her, placing what she knew was a hickey on her neck,
branding her. Although she knew it took effort since
he had to be weak himself, he managed to pick her up
in his arms and carry her over to the bed. He placed
her on it then fell down beside her, cradling her in his
arms. "We'll take a short nap and then I'm taking you
in this bed."

Casey closed her eyes. She had no reason not to believe him.

"How are things going with you and your dad?"

Casey cuddled closer to McKinnon in the bed. She
glanced toward the cave's opening to see it was getting
dark but neither of them had made a move to get up and
start getting dressed. Good to his word, he had taken

her all over the place and she wondered if any part of her body would ever be the same again.

"Fine," she said, finally answering his question. "I'm discovering just what a thoughtful, kind and considerate person he is. And he's understanding to my feelings and I appreciate that. But…"

"But what?"

"It hasn't been as easy for me as it is for Cole and Clint to establish close relationship with Corey, but I'm trying. There're just some things I still need to put behind me."

"I understand. I know how I felt when I found out Martin wasn't my natural father."

She turned to him. "When did you find out?"

"At sixteen. At first I felt like I'd been betrayed."

Casey knew the feeling. "So what did you do?"

"After hearing my mom's reason for not telling me, I slowly began to accept things since what she'd done was her way of trying to protect me. My paternal grandparents had never approved of her marriage to their son, and when Martin adopted me at birth, she felt it was best to move on so I wouldn't be hurt by their rejection."

He didn't say anything for a few moments but then added, "She did feel I should have something from my natural father, which is why she named me McKinnon, which was his last name. So in a way I have the best of both worlds as a McKinnon and as a Quinn. Each time that I see my name I'm reminded of the two men I'm honoring."

"Did you ever get the chance to meet your grandparents?"

"Yes, I met my grandmother when I was eighteen.

My grandfather had passed on years earlier so I never got the chance to meet him, though. My father had been their only child and my grandmother wanted me to know what would be mine upon her death, like that was the only thing that mattered. It saddens me when I think of all those years I could have gotten to know them, developed a relationship with them, but they didn't want that because of my mixed heritage. They'd been a part of New Orleans' elite wealthy society, and my mother had not been the woman they wanted for their son. What they never accepted was that they really didn't have a say in the matter. That he was old enough to make his own decisions."

Casey nodded. "You and Mr. Quinn are so close that I can't imagine him not being your natural father. I was surprised when I heard that he wasn't."

"He's the only father I know. My mother says that John McKinnon was a good man and they had a good marriage. Short but good. They had met at one of those cultural day events at the Nation's Capital. She was there as a representative of the Blackfoot Nations and he was there representing the Creoles of Color from Louisiana."

McKinnon pulled her tighter to him. "I gather you never had a stepfather."

She shook her head. "No. Mom never dated, although I know there were men interested in her. Her heart belonged to my father until the day she died."

McKinnon shook his head, thinking what a waste. But then wasn't he doing the same thing? Hadn't he decided to sacrifice sharing a real relationship with a woman for a reason he felt was important to him?

Although he no longer loved Lynette, because of her he had turned his back on ever loving anyone again. "Ready to head back?" he asked moments later.

"Yes." She smiled up at him as she flipped on her back. "Thanks for bringing me here, McKinnon. It was special."

He leaned down and kissed her cheek. "No, you're special." Then he went for her lips. Casey sighed in pleasure the moment their mouths touched. They needed to head back and the last thing she needed from him was a long, drugging kiss, but she had a feeling that was what he was about to give her. And of course there was no way she was going to deny him.

A couple of days later, Casey got a surprise visit from her father. She had heard a knock at the door and opened it to find him standing there. "Corey? This is a pleasant surprise."

He nodded, smiling. "I dropped by to see how Spitfire and her colt were doing and wanted to check to see how things are going with you, as well."

"I'm fine. Would you like to come in?"

"Thanks."

Casey stood back and watched as he entered, not bothered that he had found her at McKinnon's home and not the guesthouse. "I was just about to sit down and eat lunch. Would you like to join me?"

He glanced around. "Where's Henrietta?"

Casey smiled. "She and her husband went to Helena for the day. She'll be back tomorrow. McKinnon and I usually eat lunch together but he met his brothers in town to help them with supplies, so I'd love the company."

"Thanks. I'd love to join you."

"Wonderful. Just make yourself at home while I get everything ready."

Back in the kitchen, Casey thought her dad's visit was perfect timing. It was time they had a talk to bury the past, something she hadn't been able to fully let go of until now. Her talks with McKinnon had helped, so had Corey's always made her feel special around him.

A few moments later she returned to the living room to find him standing at the window, looking out at the mountains. "Lunch is ready, Dad."

He quickly turned and met her gaze and she understood why. This was the first time she had ever called him "Dad." "Okay, let me wash up. I'll be right back."

She inhaled deeply when he walked toward the back room. She had a feeling that going into the back had more to do with emotions than him needing to wash his hands. She hadn't realized until that moment how calling him Corey instead of Dad had probably bothered him, although he had never mentioned it to her. He had respected her feelings and had given her time to come around on her own time and her own terms, and she appreciated him for doing that.

"So what are we having?"

She turned when he entered the kitchen. "Nothing special, just chicken salad sandwiches and lemonade," she said, sitting down at the table.

"But it's special to me, Casey," he said in an earnest tone. "It's not everyday a man gets to have lunch with his beautiful daughter."

"Especially a daughter he didn't know he had until a few years ago," she said, watching him take the seat across from her.

"It doesn't matter. The moment I found out about you, Clint and Cole, I fell in love immediately. Just knowing the three of you were mine meant the world to me and my love was absolute and unwavering."

She nodded, believing that. "It took me time to come around," she softly admitted. "Mom and I were close and she told me these stories and I believed them. I had a vision of the two of you loving each other and it hurt to know everything she'd said had been lies and you really hadn't loved her at all."

Corey reached out and captured her hand in his. "I did love your mother but in another way. Carolyn *was* special to me, Casey, don't ever think that she wasn't. She came into my life when I was at my lowest and we had some good times together. And because she was a good woman I knew I had to be truthful with her from the start. That's the reason I told her that I could never love her completely—the way a man is supposed to love a woman—because my heart belonged to another."

Casey nodded. "And I'm sure Mom appreciated you being honest with her. Some men wouldn't have and that's probably why whenever she mentioned your name, she could do it in a loving way."

Casey didn't say anything for a long moment and then she said truthfully, "I was prepared not to like Abby, especially when I found out she was the woman you had always loved instead of Mom. But Abby is someone who's hard not to like. She's a special lady, Dad, and you're lucky to have her, and even luckier that she came back into your life after all these years. It's as if the two of you are truly soul mates. You and Abby finally being together is a love story with a happy ending if ever there was one. I can see that now. I can also feel the love each and every time you look at her and she looks at you, and I truly believe that Mom never resented you loving someone else because you gave her something special. You gave her a part of yourself, even if it wasn't your heart."

Casey smiled and tightened her hold on the hand that held hers. She gazed into misty eyes and the thought that what she'd said had touched him truly meant a lot. "You are my father and I love you and I'm proud that I'm your daughter. I find joy being a part of your life like you're a part of mine."

She stood and moved around the table and when he also stood, she went into his outstretched arms thinking it felt good to finally let go of the anger and pain she'd held within her for so long.

She felt her heart thud against her rib cage thinking there was pain still harboring there. But it was pain of the self-inflicted kind. She was in love with McKinnon and was smart enough to know that things couldn't continue between them as they were. In less than a month's time Prince Charming would be fully trained and there would be no reason for her to remain on the ranch. She had gotten lax in looking for a place in town, but she knew she needed to start again. The thought had her heart breaking but deep down she knew it was something she had to do.

She forced the painful thought from her mind that,

like her mother, she would live the rest of her life loving only one man and only have the memories of their love affair to sustain her.

Chapter 12

McKinnon picked up the phone the moment he walked out of the bedroom. He was on his way to town for a business meeting and Henrietta had left to do her weekly grocery shopping. "Hello?"

"Yes, this is Joanne Mills and I'm trying to reach Casey Westmoreland."

McKinnon lifted a brow. He remembered Ms. Mills as the real-estate agent who had shown Casey a couple of places in town. "Ms. Mills, this is McKinnon Quinn. Casey is out in the barn taking care of one of the horses. Is there something I can do for you?"

"Oh, hello, Mr. Quinn. Yes, there's something you can do. You can tell Ms. Westmoreland that after talking with her last week, something has come up on our listing that she might be interested in. The seller is willing to work out a good deal since he wants a quick sale."

McKinnon leaned back against the table. Casey was

considering moving off his ranch? Emotions clogged his throat, making it almost impossible for him to breathe.

"Mr. Quinn, are you still there?"

McKinnon forced himself to speak. "Yes, I'm still here and I'll give her the message."

"Thank you."

McKinnon hung up the phone as a cold chill settled in his gut. He was being forced to admit something he thought could never happen to him again. He had fallen head over heels in love.

"Damn."

He inhaled deeply knowing he had no right to even think about loving Casey. Yet he did. She was everything he could possibly want in a woman or a wife, but he couldn't have her. So maybe it was for the best if she did decide to move on. Things had to eventually end between them anyway.

He quickly headed for the door, pausing briefly to snatch his hat off the rack. If Casey leaving was for the best, why was he feeling so damn bad about it?

Durango glanced across the table at McKinnon. The two of them had just ended their meeting with Mike Farmer, who had made them an offer they couldn't refuse. Not only did Mike want to buy every foal Courtship produced, he also wanted Crown Royal's stud rights at more than half-a-million a coupling. The man was convinced the stallion's offspring would one day become a Triple Crown winner.

"What's wrong with you, McKinnon? Farmer just made us wealthy men and you're sitting there like you've lost your one and only puppy. Forget about that beer you're drinking, man. We should be calling that waiter over to our table with a bottle of champagne to celebrate."

McKinnon leaned back in his chair, remembering the phone call he'd taken right before leaving the ranch. "I don't feel like celebrating, Rango."

Durango sat up in his chair. A frown settled in. "Why not? Hey, what's going on?"

McKinnon met Durango's curious gaze. "That Realtor who's helping Casey find a place in town called and left her a message that she might have found something. With Prince Charming almost trained, Casey really has no reason to stick around, which means she might move into town."

Durango stared at him for a moment before asking brusquely, "And what do you plan to do about it? I won't waste my time asking if you love her because your attitude today has given me my answer. Take my advice about something, McKinnon."

"What?"

"Stop brooding and do what you've always done. Go after what you want."

McKinnon clearly understood what Durango was saying and a hard line formed at his lips when he drew in a deep breath. "This is different. I can't do that."

"Yes, you can."

McKinnon's anger flared and he refused to give in to the surge of emotions that was sweeping through him. "Dammit, Rango, I can't do it *because* I love her. I can't deny her the one thing she might eventually want one day."

"But you don't know for sure that's what you'll be

doing. Casey deserves to know the truth, McKinnon, so tell her."

McKinnon sighed deeply, remembering the night he'd asked her if she wanted children and what her response had been. "Why bother? Things can't be that way between us, Rango. I can't let it. She deserves more," he said grimly.

"Well, I think," Durango said softly, "that you'll be doing the both of you a disservice if you make a decision without giving her a say in the matter. If you want her, McKinnon, don't let anything stand in your way. Tell her the truth and see how things work out. Take it from someone who knows. The love of a woman, a good woman, is the greatest gift a man could ever receive."

Durango took a swallow of his beer before he went on. "If you're so convinced she's going to leave anyway, what do you have to lose?"

Casey glanced across the table at Henrietta as the older woman peeled a bunch of apples for the pie she intended to bake later. There was something Casey wanted to know and was hoping Henrietta would have an answer for her. "Henrietta, who is Lynette?"

The woman stopped what she was doing and glanced over at Casey, her eyes sharp. "Who mentioned Lynette to you? I know it wasn't McKinnon."

Casey nodded. "No, it wasn't McKinnon. Norris let her name slip one day saying that I was nothing like her and he was glad."

Henrietta smiled. "No, you aren't anything like her. And it's not that Lynette was a totally bad person. It's just that she didn't stick by McKinnon when she should have, especially when she claimed she loved him. The woman hurt the boy something awful."

Casey couldn't help but wonder just what Lynette had done. It didn't sound as if she'd been unfaithful to McKinnon. And how should she have stuck by him? Was this Lynette the reason he refused to open his heart to another woman? "Does she still live around these parts?" she asked.

Henrietta shook her head. "No, thank goodness. From what McKinnon told me, Lynette is married now with a child and living somewhere in Great Falls. The last thing McKinnon needs is to see Lynette and her baby."

Casey tilted her head back. Now her mind was flooded with even more questions. Why would seeing Lynette with a baby bother McKinnon? Had he and Lynette lost a baby together or something? She couldn't help but ponder Henrietta's statement. "But why would that bother him?"

Henrietta glanced over at Casey as if she was about to say something, then changed her mind and shrugged wide shoulders. "It's not my place to say, Casey. Maybe one day McKinnon will tell you all about her. About everything."

Casey doubted it. In fact, since waking that morning she'd noticed a change in McKinnon. Usually they ate breakfast together but this morning he had already eaten and left before she'd awoken. He'd been acting strange ever since mentioning Joanne Mills's call. Was he upset that she had resumed looking for a place to live? Did he think she was supposed to just continue to live here with him forever? She really didn't know what to think but she hoped it was her imagination and that McKinnon wasn't trying to put distance between them again.

"Thanks for at least letting me know who she is," Casey finally said to Henrietta.

"No problem," Henrietta said quietly. "Like I said, that woman hurt him but now you've made him happy."

Casey smiled. "You think so?"

Henrietta chuckled. "I know so. He smiles now more and his disposition and moods aren't like they used to be, and you're the reason for it. And I know you love him, too. And I mean really love him." The older woman was silent for a few moments and then she said, "Just promise me one thing."

"What?"

"No matter what happens, follow your heart and you can't go wrong. When it comes to love, there's no way you can turn your back on it and walk away. There's no way."

Casey was waiting for McKinnon later that night when he got in. He hadn't come home for dinner, which only deepened her belief that he was trying to avoid her. She was standing by the fireplace and he looked over at her the moment he opened the door.

"McKinnon," she acknowledged when he didn't say anything. "I looked for you at dinner."

He shrugged, closing the door behind him. "Something came up and I had to stay on the range longer than expected. I'm surprised you're still up."

For some reason she got the impression he'd been hoping that she hadn't been up, and that only strengthened her resolved and made her even more determined to find out just what was going on with him. "Yeah, I'm surprised, too. Especially since we've been going to bed early a lot."

There…she had deliberately made him remember how their nights had been for the past three weeks. He would rush home every day and they would get dinner, take a shower together, go to bed and make love.

"Yeah, well, like I said, I've been busy. Besides, I've been thinking."

She suddenly felt a little queasiness settle in her stomach. "About what?"

"About us. You'll be through training Prince Charming in a few more weeks and will be moving on. I even understand you're looking to buy a place in town and—"

"Is that's what this is about, McKinnon? Are you upset that I resumed looking for a place in town? Because if you are, then—"

"Upset? Why should I be upset about anything? You and I both knew things between us wouldn't last and it's no problem, no big deal. You're doing the right thing by moving on."

She flinched. It sounded as if he hadn't cared, and she refused to believe that. She didn't want to believe it. Yes, she had known the score, but at some point the rules had changed not only for her, but for him, as well. Although she couldn't claim that she thought he had fallen in love with her the same way she had fallen in love with him, she refused to believe she had been nothing more than a willing body to him.

"Is that what you really want, McKinnon?"

He hesitated a moment before answering. "Yes. It will be for the best."

Casey sighed deeply, intent on giving him what he wanted. She had her pride and refused to carry a torch for a man who didn't love her—like her mother had with her father. She'd thought just the memories of what the two of them shared would suffice, but now she knew that they wouldn't. And she had a feeling that at some point her mother discovered that fact, as well.

At that moment she fully understood how her mother must have felt knowing that although she had loved Corey Westmoreland, he did not love her. But he *had* given her babies, which to Carolyn Roberts were all the memories she needed. Casey was certain that each time her mother gazed into her children's faces, which so closely resembled the man she had loved, she was content. And that contentment had lasted until the day she had died. In realizing that, Casey's love and admiration for her mother increased.

Now Casey was faced with a similar decision. During all those times she and McKinnon had made love, they'd never once used protection. The first couple of times had been during the wrong time of the month, but the recent times had not. That meant she could possibly find herself in the same situation her mother had. Single and pregnant by a man who didn't love her. But unlike her mother, who'd kept silent, she intended to let McKinnon know it.

"Fine, I'll leave and find someplace else when my business here is finished, and if I'm pregnant you'll know it. There were a number of times that we engaged in unprotected sex."

For a moment he looked as if she'd slapped him. After a few seconds of silence he finally said, "You aren't pregnant."

She laughed softly to hide her pain. "Oh, so you're a doctor now, McKinnon?"

He leaned back against the closed door and placed his arms across his chest. His face was rigid and stern. "No, but I know you aren't pregnant. There's no way you can be."

Casey frowned as she stared at him. "And what makes you so certain of that?"

Here we go again, McKinnon thought. *Tell her so she can do the same thing Lynette did. Lynette didn't waste any time packing up her stuff and hauling ass because you could never give her the children she wanted. So go ahead and tell Casey the truth and see how fast she leaves.*

He would never forget how he had arrived back at the ranch or his meeting in town with Durango and Mike Farmer. He'd been determined to follow Durango's advice and confront Casey, tell her the truth and let the decision be hers. But when he'd walked in on her in the barn, she'd been talking to Dawn Harvey, the wife of one of his ranch hands who'd had a baby a few months earlier. She had brought the baby by and Casey had been holding it, smiling down at it, teasing the infant by making funny sounds—baby talk. He had known after seeing the glow on her face that he could never deny her from being a mother. He loved her too much to deny her something like that.

He sighed deeply as he lowered his arms and moved away from the door to start crossing the room toward

Casey. When he came to a stop in front of her, he tried to recall the exact moment he'd fallen in love with her and couldn't. Chances were it had been the first time he's seen her at Stone and Corey's weddings. But he *could* recall when he had first accepted that he loved her in his heart. It had been that night they had made love for the first time and she had deliberately seduced the hell out of him. Not only had he surrendered his body to her, but on that night he had surrendered his heart to her, too.

"McKinnon? What makes you so sure that I'm not pregnant?"

He looked down at her, deep into eyes that had the ability to turn him into putty in her arms; eyes that he enjoyed gazing into each and every time he had entered her body. The eyes that would take on a darker shade just seconds before she came.

"The reason I know you aren't pregnant is because I can't get you pregnant." Ignoring the confused look on her face he continued. "About the same time I found out Martin wasn't my natural father, I found out that my real dad had had a rare blood disease that neither he nor my mother knew about. In fact, it was only discovered after he'd been in that car accident that eventually took his life. Although there's no health risks to me, the disease makes me a carrier, which I can pass on to any children I have. I couldn't do that to a child, so I made the decision around eleven years ago to have a vasectomy."

She shook her head, not sure she'd heard him right. "You've had a vasectomy?"

"Yes. So now you know why there can't ever be a future for us."

She looked stunned and then moments later said, "Excuse me. Maybe I'm a little dense or something but I really don't see your point."

"You will eventually and if you'll excuse me I need to take a shower. And I think it will be for the best that you stay at your own place tonight...in fact from now on."

And without giving her a chance to say anything, he turned and walked toward his bedroom, closing the door behind him.

For the longest time, Casey just stood there, seemingly rooted in place as her mind replayed all that Mc-Kinnon had just told her. Was a similar announcement what sent Lynette running? For goodness' sake, if that was true then the woman really hadn't loved McKinnon at all.

A part of Casey, the stubborn Westmoreland part, wanted to follow McKinnon right now, beat on his bedroom door and have it out with him. Surely he didn't think his inability to have children meant she couldn't love him, or didn't love him? But after thinking about it for a few moments she knew he did think that way; mainly because another woman had done that very thing.

Her heart went out to him. Had he and Lynette not discussed other options such as adoption? Had Lynette not wanted to go another route? No wonder Henrietta had said it was a good thing the woman didn't live around these parts since seeing her and her child would probably bother McKinnon. Now Casey understood. Seeing that child would be a reminder of what he hadn't been able to give the woman he'd loved.

He had walked off, letting her know he preferred being alone tonight, and for once she would grant him his wish. Mainly because she needed to think things through to determine what would be the best way to handle McKinnon. How could she make him understand that it didn't matter to her and she would be willing to adopt a child one day, or even consider artificial insemination?

She sighed as she headed toward the back door to return to her own place. Tomorrow she intended to put her plan into motion. Before, it had been seduction. Now, it was all about satisfaction, and she wouldn't be satisfied until McKinnon understood that she was the one woman who would always be by his side, no matter what.

Early the next morning Casey found Norris in the stables and requested a day off work. There was someone she needed to see and talk with immediately. McKinnon's mother.

The moment she pulled into the yard, Morning Star Quinn stepped out of her home wearing a huge smile. Not for the first time Casey thought the woman was absolutely stunning with her huge dark eyes in an angular face, high cheekbones and long, straight black hair that flowed past her back. It was apparent she was Native American and she looked more in her thirties than in her fifties.

"Casey, this is a pleasant surprise," Morning Star said, giving her a hug. "Is everything all right?"

Casey shook her head. "No, but I believe eventually everything will be. First I need to talk to you about something important."

"Sure. Come inside and join me in a cup of coffee."

Casey followed the older woman inside and the moment she stepped foot across the threshold, she felt a special warmth. She followed Morning Star into the kitchen and sat down at the table. "Is Mr. Quinn at home?"

Star glanced up from pouring the coffee, smiled and said, "No, he and your father went hunting today. I don't expect either of them back until later. Do you need to see him, as well?"

"No, you're the person I came to see. I'd like to talk to you about McKinnon."

Morning Star's dark brow lifted as she joined Casey at the table. "What about McKinnon?"

"I'm in love with him," Casey came right out and said, thinking she needed to let Mrs. Quinn know how she felt up front. She began to relax when she saw the huge smile that touched Morning Star's lips.

"I saw it happening," Morning Star said, taking a sip of her coffee.

Surprise lit Casey's face. "You did?"

"Yes. It was there in your eyes whenever you looked at him and I saw the same look in his."

Casey sighed as she took a sip of her tea. If he loved her that was definitely news to her. "We've been together ever since the night of my party," Casey said, pretty sure she didn't have to paint a picture of what she meant by that. "And last night McKinnon sort of broke things off. He told me about his health issue and for some reason he's convinced that—"

"Because of it the two of you couldn't have a future together even if you wanted one," Morning Star finished for her.

Casey met the older woman's eyes. "Yes."

Morning Star didn't say anything for a long moment, but then she met Casey's gaze and said, "We all have Lynette Franklin to thank for that. She took off right after McKinnon confided in her."

Casey nodded. She had figured as much. "But that was her. What does how she reacted have to do with me?"

Morning Star smiled. "Because you are a woman. McKinnon sees you as a person who would probably make some child a wonderful mother, a child he can not give you. He really thinks he's being noble in cutting you loose."

"Well, he's not. Of course I want children, but we can adopt. Giving birth to a child isn't such a big deal to me."

"It is to some women and he knows it." Morning Star sighed deeply before continuing. "Making the decision to have a vasectomy was probably one of the hardest things my son had to do because he loves children and always wanted to settle down one day, marry and have some. He was torn about what to do until one particular day when he had to go to the hospital for his annual tests."

"What happened?"

The older woman stood and walked over to the sink.

Then she turned around and Casey could see the love and pain for her child etched on her face. "While in the waiting room, McKinnon met a man who was also a carrier. The man shared with McKinnon how he'd unknowingly passed the disease on to his six-year-old son, and the rough time his son had had before dying the year before. It's my understanding that from that conversation, McKinnon swore that he wouldn't have any children and risk passing anything on to them."

Casey wiped a tear from her eye, saddened by the stranger's loss and even more saddened that McKinnon's dream for a family had died that day, too. "I refuse to walk away and let him go through life alone with this, Mrs. Quinn."

"He's pretty much made up his mind that he will never let another woman into his life."

Casey stood and met Morning Star's gaze with a defiant look in her eyes. "Well, we'll just see about that. I love McKinnon and I won't let him turn his back on what we can have together. I simply refuse to let him do that."

Morning Star smiled. "And I'm happy to hear it. No matter how difficult he gets, don't let him push you away. Fight him with your love."

Casey nodded. She intended to do that very thing.

McKinnon spotted Casey the moment he turned the corner of the ranch house. She'd sent a message by Norris that she needed to see him, and not knowing if it could wait, he had put his work aside to look for her.

On his way he'd seen Henrietta leaving and wondered why she had ended her workday early. Since it was Friday, chances were she probably had something to do and had forgotten to mention it to him.

He inhaled deeply. Casey was standing in the courtyard by the flower beds, the same place she'd been standing the night they had shared their first kiss. He muttered a curse. That was the last thing he needed to think about now. But hell, how could he not when she looked so beautiful standing there in jeans that cupped her bottom so deliciously and a short silky-looking blouse that showed what nice breasts she had; breasts he had touched and tasted so many times. He let his gaze flick over them one last time before putting his control in place.

"Norris said you wanted to see me, Casey," he said, trying to stop his heart from hammering away in his chest.

She looked up at him. "Yes. I thought we could finish our discussion now." She watched as his body moved into that stance she loved—arms crossed over his broad chest and booted feet braced apart. The man certainly had the body to fill out any pair of jeans he put on. Today his hair was pulled back in a ponytail, making him look very sexy.

He blew out an impatient breath. "We finished our discussion last night. There's nothing to add or subtract."

"I think there is and would like for you to hear me out."

His lips pressed into a firm line and he inhaled deeply. "Okay, say whatever it is you have to say so I can get back to work."

She nodded and slowly crossed the courtyard to him.

He nervously rubbed his hand across the back of his neck when she came to a stop. She was too close for comfort and she smelled too damn good.

"I just want to get a few things straight in my mind, McKinnon. Let's do scenario number one. If I had come to you the other night and told you that I had a female condition that stopped me from ever giving you a son or a daughter, would you have ended things between us for that reason?"

"Of course not!"

"Okay, let's move to scenario number two. If, for any reason, I wanted to adopt a child, would you have had a problem with that?"

McKinnon frowned, wondering where she was going with this. "No, I would not have had a problem with it."

"And what if I wanted to try artificial insemination to get pregnant? Would you have a problem with that?"

"No, I wouldn't have a problem with that, either."

"That's good to know." Then she placed her hands on her hips and glared at him. "Then what the hell is *your* problem," she snapped, all but screaming at him. "What kind of woman do you think I am to expect more from you than I'm willing to give myself? Just like I wouldn't expect you to walk out on me if I couldn't produce a child, I would think you would have the decency not to expect the same thing from me. But do you? Hell, no! You expected me to be like that other woman—who evidently didn't know a good thing when she had it—and run off. There're plenty of babies out there who need a loving home, a home that we can give. I think it's a crying shame that you think so little of me."

"Casey," he said in a low tone, so low it almost

sounded like a whisper. "It's not that I think so little of you. It's because I think so much of you that I want you to have more. I love you. I love you so much it hurts and knowing I can't give you the one thing you might want one day is killing me."

Casey inhaled slowly and deeply, taken aback by his words of love. "If you love me as much as you say you do, then listen for a moment to what I want, McKinnon. I want *you*. The man who tries so hard to hide that easy grin and those kind eyes. The man who showed me just what real love is about, made me see what a wonderful human being my father is and helped me to understand why my mother was willing to live the rest of her life on memories. Well, unlike her I can't be that content, McKinnon. I want you. If I never gave birth to a child it wouldn't matter as long as I had you. I love you and to me, to us, that should be all that matters. We will handle the rest when the time comes."

She reached out, locked her fingers with his, felt the tenseness slowly ebbing away in them. "I want you to be there for me, McKinnon, to hold me close in the middle of the night, to make love to me, to wake up with me. I think these past three weeks have shown us how good we are together, and if it's only just you and me, then that's how things will be. But since you like kids and so do I, I can see a child in our future, a child we will make ours—a child we will watch grow in our love. Martin isn't your biological father but I know you don't love him any less. The same will hold true with our child, our children."

She took a step closer, and after releasing his hand, she lifted hers to cup his chin. Misty eyes stared into his. "Let go, McKinnon. Stop protecting your heart. Place it in my care for safekeeping and I promise it won't ever get broken again."

Before Casey could take her next breath, McKinnon's arms closed around her, brought her to the solidness of his body, and he lowered his mouth to hers. This kiss was like the others, full of passion. It made her world tilt, the ground shake and every bone in her body melt. But then it was different. It was a kiss of love and devotion. Not only was he giving her his heart, he was giving her his body and soul, as well.

He then swung her up into his arms and gazed at her. "Will you marry me?" he asked in a voice filled with emotion.

"Yes!" she said, smiling brightly. "I've gone through seduction, satisfaction and now the next step has to be a wedding—Westmoreland-style. One that will last forever."

He leaned over and placed another kiss on her lips and whispered, "Yes, sweetheart. Forever."

Epilogue

McKinnon glanced over at his fiancée sitting beside him in the church. He knew weddings made some people cry but Casey was taking it to a whole other level. He put the handkerchief back in his pocket, deciding it was useless for dabbing her tears. He knew of only one way to shut her up. So, ignoring the wedding proceedings at the front of the church, his parents and her father and stepmother, who were sitting beside them, he leaned over and kissed her.

And as he'd known she would, she melted right into his arms, so he pulled her from her seat and settled her into his lap. She wrapped her arms around his neck and leaned close into his body. "Thanks, I needed that," she whispered contentedly in his ear.

"Make sure you tell that to your brothers and cousins after the wedding," he whispered back. "They're staring, giving me dirty looks."

Moments later, everyone stood when the preacher presented Ian and Brooke Westmoreland as a married couple. Cheers and applause sounded inside the Lake Tahoe church that had accommodated over three hundred guests.

It had been a beautiful day for a wedding and all the Westmorelands were present. Even Delaney, who looked like she would deliver anytime. Jamal's jet was ready to return them to Tehran immediately after the reception. He was determined that their second child be born in his homeland, as well.

McKinnon and Casey hung back while everyone departed the church for the Rolling Cascade, Ian's casino and resort, where a huge reception would be held. "Okay, why so many tears today?" McKinnon asked, pulling her into his arms.

She glanced up at him with tear-stained eyes. "Because I could feel Ian's and Brooke's love, and because I have so much to be thankful for myself. Next month around this time I'll be the bride and you'll be the groom. For a moment I could picture you standing there, pledging your life to me. And also, the ceremony was beautiful."

McKinnon nodded as he took her hand and led her out of the church. "Yes, it was." They had decided on a November wedding that would take place on Corey's Mountain. Savannah would have delivered her baby by then. Corey was thrilled to be the father of the bride, and to say McKinnon's mother and Abby were excited about planning a wedding was an understatement.

He thought about the party the two women had thrown together last month and shook his head. He and Casey expected their wedding would be on a much larger scale, although they'd let it be known they wanted a small affair. But Morning Star Quinn and Abby Westmoreland didn't know the meaning of small.

"Do we have to stay at the reception for a long time?" Casey asked, stopping on the church step and getting on tiptoe to bring her lips closer to his.

"No, not for long," he said, wrapping his arms around her waist.

Their lips met in a kiss that held promises.

Moments later she stepped away from him and smiled. "I've decided where I want to spend our wedding night, McKinnon."

"You have? Where?"

"Our cave."

He lifted a brow. She looked serious. He smiled, actually liking the idea. "You sure you don't mind finding yourself backed up against a wall?"

She smiled and took his hand as they walked down the church steps. "Not as long as you let me demonstrate my horsemanship to you later."

He chuckled and leaned down and whispered, "Baby, you can ride me anytime."

* * * * *

SPENCER'S
FORBIDDEN PASSION

Prologue

"We've encountered a problem, Spence."

Spencer Westmoreland briefly closed his eyes to blot out two things—the look on his mother's face across the room and the frustrating sound of his attorney's voice on his cell phone.

He opened his eyes to find his mother was still looking at him with that *I-wonder-who's-next* expression. He was in Bozeman, Montana, attending the wedding of his cousin Casey and his childhood friend McKinnon Quinn. The couple was still inside the ranch house taking pictures. Everyone else who hadn't been a member of the wedding party was in the huge barn that had been miraculously transformed into a spacious ballroom for the reception.

He glanced around. Everyone seemed to be having a good time, smiling and happy. Everyone except him now that he'd been interrupted by a phone call from his attorney. Stuart Fulmer was one of the most competent men he knew, known for his precise and expeditious handling of all business matters, which meant if he felt there was a crisis then there definitely was one. "Okay, Stuart, what's the problem?" he asked.

"The Russell Vineyard."

Spencer lifted a dark brow and decided to step back into a corner of the room for privacy, as well as distance from his mother's intense gaze.

A few months ago he had gotten wind that the vineyard, located on over three hundred acres in the Napa Valley, was up for sale. He took the drive to the valley, saw it and fell in love with the area immediately. His research revealed that the owners, the Russells, were having financial difficulties and were struggling to hold on to the land. Spencer had sent his attorney to make the Russells an offer that had been more than generous. His plan for the property, once he became the owner, was to close down the winery and convert the place into a vacation paradise by adding a plush resort hotel and trails for hiking, biking and backpacking. It'd be the perfect tourist getaway.

The last he'd heard, the negotiations were going smoothly and it would merely be a matter of days before the property became his. So what went wrong at this late date?

"What kind of problem are we talking about?" he asked abruptly.

"A young woman by the name of Chardonnay Russell."

He lifted a brow. "Chardonnay Russell? Isn't that the old man's twenty-seven-year-old granddaughter?"

"Yes, that's her. Somehow she has gotten the old man to change his mind."

Spencer frowned, not liking the sound of that. "That's not acceptable. And I thought we pretty much had this deal wrapped up."

"We did."

"I also thought the Russells had a slew of money problems."

"They do."

"Then how can they afford *not* to sell?" he asked. When he noticed a couple of people who were standing around had turned to stare, he became aware that he'd raised his voice.

"They can't. But it's my understanding that she's making one last-ditch effort to get the financing they need to hold on to the place. After all, it's been in the Russell family for over fifty years. I guess she's not ready for the family to throw in the towel just yet."

"That's admirable but too friggin' bad and too damn late. I want that property, Stuart. Do whatever you have to do to get it."

"It's going to be difficult, Spence. Chardonnay Russell isn't making things easy on my end."

Frustrated, Spencer rubbed a hand down his face. This was the first time in the fifteen years he'd known Stuart that he'd heard such aggravation in the man's voice. And all because of one female? Hell, how difficult could a single woman be? He then decided to find out for himself.

"Look, Stuart, let me handle things from here. I'll fly to Napa in the morning and meet with the Russells. Please let them know I'm coming."

He actually heard a sigh of relief in Stuart's voice. "I'm giving you fair warning to prepare yourself, Spence. The granddaughter may have been named after a wine, but there's nothing sparkling at all about her. Believe me when I tell you that she has the distinct sting of a scorpion."

Spencer couldn't help but grin at the words coming from the mouth of one of the most polite and mild-mannered men he knew. Chardonnay Russell must really be a handful. "Thanks for the warning. I'll keep that in mind."

Chapter 1

"That man has arrived, Donnay."

Chardonnay Russell lifted her head and gazed into her mother's worried eyes. She tossed aside the pencil and notebook as she stood up. She hated to see her family agonize over money problems now. The winery had always brought in a substantial profit, but her grandfather's hospital bill earlier that year, and the subsequent cost of his medications had eroded their extra funds. Now they were barely hanging on.

So far every bank they had applied to for a loan had turned them down. Their last hope was the bank she had visited a few days ago in San Francisco. Mr. Gordon, the bank manager, had seemed positive and she had left in a better frame of mind.

"Donnay?"

The nervous tone of her mother's voice cut into her thoughts. A smile played across Chardonnay's face as she crossed the room, not for the first time realizing her mother was a very beautiful woman. Donnay never knew her father. In fact, the only thing she'd been told about him was that her mother had met and fallen in love with him at eighteen. Chad Timberlain was a soldier on extended leave who had worked at the vineyards one summer and then returned to duty before finding out his short stay had produced a child.

"It's okay for him to wait, Mom. I'm sure it won't be the first time."

Or maybe it would be, she silently concluded. Earlier that day she had scanned the internet to read up on Spencer Westmoreland. The thirty-six-year-old had made his first million before his thirtieth birthday. According to what she'd read, the wealthy tycoon had retired last year with more money than he could ever spend. Evidently he had gotten bored and wanted a new toy—her family's winery.

"Where's Gramps and Grammy?" she asked softly. She knew her grandparents were even more worried about their meeting with Mr. Westmoreland than her mother.

"They're in the kitchen. Janice has escorted our visitor to the study and he's there waiting."

Donnay nodded. "All right, then. It's time for us to meet Mr. Westmoreland, and remember the three of you agreed to let me handle him my way."

Spencer paced the room and glanced at the various framed awards on the wall with a wry smile. Timing, he mused, was the reason he was being kept waiting. He hadn't become a successful businessman without knowing how the game was played. He was fully aware that the best way to keep a business opponent on edge was to make them wait. Stall them. Test their patience and their ability to endure.

He shook his head as an even broader smile touched his lips. The tactic was a waste of time with him, but Chardonnay Russell wouldn't know that. She had every reason to believe she was the one calling the shots and no doubt would be surprised to discover she wasn't.

"Sorry that you were kept waiting, Mr. Westmoreland."

Yeah, I bet, he thought, slowly turning toward the sound of the soft, feminine voice. Any further thoughts on his mind died a sudden death the moment his gaze connected to the most gorgeous pair of eyes he'd ever seen. They were silver-gray and he wondered if she was wearing colored contacts lenses, but quickly concluded she wasn't when he noticed the other three persons standing beside her had the same eye coloring. Evidently a family trait.

He quickly gathered his composure and said, "It was no problem."

The truth to the matter was that there was a problem and it came in the form of Chardonnay Russell. The woman was absolutely stunning. In his lifetime he had met and dated numerous beautiful women, but standing before him was definitely a rare beauty.

She was tall, at least five-nine. Slim and curvy in the short-sleeve white blouse and printed gypsy skirt she was wearing. And her facial features were exquisite. Dark, luxurious brown hair flowed around her shoulders. She had long lashes, mocha-colored skin that looked incredibly soft, a perfect nose and kissable lips. The hoop earrings dangling from her ears made her look even sexier. Made him feel hotter.

Never had Spencer's gut clenched so tight or every muscle in his body felt so taut because of a woman. But there was something flagrantly erotic about her, and while looking into her gray eyes all he could think about were satin sheets and entangled bodies.

"I think introductions are in order," she said curtly, slicing into his personal perusal of her and his lusty thoughts. He watched her kissable lips move; however, he wasn't listening. His thoughts were too centered on the alluring package she presented and how he would like opening it up, enjoying it.

"We have you at a disadvantage," she continued saying. "We know who you are, but you don't know us since we dealt with your attorney, Mr. Fulmer, in the past."

His gaze picked up her every movement when she crossed the room, giving him a chance to check out those long legs underneath her skirt as well as her small waistline. And to make matters worse, all it took was one sniff and he picked up her scent. The arousing fragrance only added to his inner frustrations. He had a natural ability when it came to business, but handling such an intense degree of lust was another matter.

"I'm Chardonnay Russell," she said, offering him her hand. "And this is my mother, Ruth Russell, and my grandparents, Daniel and Catherine Russell."

Spencer took Chardonnay's hand in his, and the moment their hands touched, an electrical current raced through him. The sensation annoyed the hell out of him and he tightened his jaw. This was not the time to be reminded that since he'd been extremely busy lately, he hadn't had a woman in over seven months. Unfortunately his increased heart rate was reminding him of that very fact and he was fighting hard to keep his features impassive, his mind sharp.

"Ms. Russell," he said, quickly releasing her hand. He then moved to shake the hands of her mother and grandparents. He noted her grandfather didn't look well and recalled reading in one of the reports that the winery's financial woes were due to the man's escalating medical bills.

"Now that introductions have been made, please, let's sit down."

Chardonnay's voice cut into his thoughts, reminding him of why he was there. "Yes, I suggest that we do," he agreed.

"Like I've told Mr. Fulmer, the vineyard is no longer for sale. And I might as well warn you, Mr. Westmoreland, that if you assume you'll be able to change our minds about that then you are vastly mistaken," she said the moment she took her seat.

Spencer liked her spunk. She was definitely no pushover. "On the contrary, Ms. Russell. In business, one never operates on assumptions—at least not if one intends to be successful in getting what he wants."

He saw the quick frown that appeared around her eyes. Those same eyes he thought looked sexy as hell. "And you think you're going to get what you want, Mr. Westmoreland, even after I've said we no longer want to sell?" she asked, narrowing her gaze at him.

"Yes, I think so," he said rather arrogantly. "Mainly because you haven't seen my new proposal."

He couldn't help cutting her a very cocky grin, one he was certain irritated the hell out of her. But at the moment he didn't give a damn. He was feeling adrenaline of another kind flow through his bloodstream. The one he always felt when pitted against a worthy opponent.

"Now," he said calmly, "I suggest you let me present a new proposal to you."

Donnay's head snapped up from the report she was reading. "What you plan to do with our land is unacceptable."

She saw the look in his eyes was tempered steel, and he didn't blink when he said, "It really shouldn't concern you what I plan to do with the property once I acquire it. All you need to be concerned with is that the price I'm offering is more than fair."

Donnay frowned. He was sitting across from her on the sofa, casually sipping the wine her grandfather had offered him before they got started with business. Some of Russell Vineyards' finest.

"Well, it does concern us, which is why we've decided not to sell. And now after reading this proposal I'm sure my family and I have made the right decision."

"If you think that, then you're wrong. Look at the proposal closely, Ms. Russell," he said in an annoyed tone, sitting up and leaning forward. "I'm willing to pay you a half million more than what I'd authorized my attorney to offer. I think that's more than generous and it's all the increase I'm willing to make. Can you and your family truly turn down the deal I've placed on the table?"

Donnay nervously bit her lip. Truly they couldn't. She didn't want to think about what could happen if the bank didn't approve their request for a loan. She glanced over at her mother and grandparents. They were depending on her to make the right decision for the family, especially her grandfather with his heart problems and diabetes. Still, she refused to let someone like Spencer Westmoreland waltz in and take advantage of their situation.

But then she should have known she was in trouble when she'd entered the room and he stood there, impeccably dressed in an Armani suit and looking like he was ready to buy or sell whatever suited his fancy. Then there were his looks that were sharp, sexy and suave. He had to be over six-three, with coffee-colored skin, short, dark hair, a generous mouth and the darkest pair of eyes she'd ever seen on a man. In fact, they were so intense that each and every time they connected to hers she felt a tingle slowly make its way up her spine.

"I asked you a question, Ms. Russell."

She glared at him, not liking his tone. She drew in an agitated breath as she glanced back over at her family. Her grandfather nodded and a slight smile touched his lips, giving her the encouragement she needed to give Spencer Westmoreland her answer. She had to believe that a miracle would come in the form of that friendly banker in San Francisco, who actually seemed sympathetic to their financial problems.

Taking such a chance might be foolish but, sighing

deeply, she met Spencer Westmoreland's gaze and said, "Yes, we can turn it down and we will turn it down."

She then stood. "We've taken up too much of your time already, Mr. Westmoreland, and we have work to do around here. My family appreciates your interest in the Russell Vineyard but like I said earlier, it's no longer for sale."

Spencer stood and snapped his briefcase closed. He was silent for a long moment then he said, "If you think you've seen the last of me, you are sadly mistaken."

Donnay saw the smile that touched the corners of his lips when he added, "I'm finding you a worthy opponent, Ms. Russell."

She stiffened her spine. "Don't count on being a nuisance, Mr. Westmoreland. Just go find another vineyard to buy. And if you try making trouble for us, you'll be sorry."

His smile widened and the look he gave her sent shivers up her spine. "I promise I won't be the one making any trouble for you, but I can guarantee you that in refusing my offer, you've just made a lot of trouble for yourself. Good day."

Once Spencer had gotten at least a mile from the Russell Vineyard, he pulled the rental car to the shoulder of the road and placed a call on his mobile phone. He couldn't get out of his mind just how beautiful Chardonnay was and the degree of his attraction to her. Never before had he been so aroused by a woman.

He was intuitive enough to know that even with others in the room she had been acutely aware of him, just as he had been aware of her. And she'd been fully conscious of the sexual attraction between them, although in the midst of a business battle they had attempted to stay focused and downplay it.

"Stuart? This is Spence. I want you to find out which bank is leaning toward loaning the Russells the money and let me know immediately."

He clicked the phone shut and sat there for a long moment, focusing on his surroundings. It was a gorgeous day for early December, and the land around him was beautiful. He wanted that land. A thought then flickered across his mind. In addition to the land there was something else he now wanted.

Chardonnay Russell.

His brows knitted together in deep thought. The single Westmorelands were dropping like flies, and from the look on his mother's face at McKinnon and Casey's wedding, she expected the next victim to be another one of her sons. So why should he disappoint her?

After Lynette Marie's betrayal, the thought of ever marrying for love was as foreign to him as a snowstorm in the tropics. He had mourned the loss of his fiancée, who had died in a jet-ski accident over four years ago in Bermuda, only to discover from the coroner's report that she had been six-weeks pregnant. That meant she had gotten pregnant sometime during the two months she had been there on business. That had also meant he had not been the father of her child.

His hand tightened on the steering wheel. A marriage for love was out of the question but he would definitely entertain a marriage for lust. Besides, at thirty-six he had accumulated a lot of wealth, wealth he had worked hard to acquire. It was time to think about his future and make some important changes.

Although he wasn't looking for a love match like three of his brothers, Jared, Durango and Ian, had been blessed with, it was time for him to settle down, marry and secure his future with a child who would one day inherit all of his wealth.

He couldn't help but smile when he thought of all the babies born in the Westmoreland family just this year. His cousin Delaney and her husband, Sheikh Jamal Ari Yasir, had given birth to their second child, a girl, whom they had named Arielle. His cousin Dare and his wife Shelley also had a daughter born in August. Durango and his wife Savannah had been blessed with a daughter in September; and his cousins Thorn and Stone and their wives were expecting new additions to the family, as well. Thorn and Tara's baby was to be born at the end of the month, and Stone and Madison were expecting their firstborn in February.

Spencer restarted the car's engine. As he continued the journey to the Chablis, the resort where he was staying, he knew the next time he and Chardonnay's paths crossed, he would be making her an offer. And this would not be one that she would refuse. He would make damn sure of it. He was now a man on a mission. He was also a man who was known to go after whatever he wanted and didn't let up until he succeeded in getting it.

And what he wanted with Chardonnay was a merger of the most intimate kind.

Chapter 2

"You have a phone call, Donnay."

Busy in the winery doing inventory, Donnay quickly turned and glanced at her mother. "The bank?"

Ruth shook her head, an anxious look on her face, "No, it's not the bank. I believe it's Mr. Westmoreland," she said handing her daughter the phone.

Donnay sighed deeply. Why hadn't her mother told the man she wasn't available? She was well aware that Spencer Westmoreland had gotten on her daughter's last nerve yesterday. "Thanks a lot, Mom," she said sarcastically, taking the phone. "Why didn't you tell him I wasn't here?" she whispered, placing a hand over the mouthpiece.

"But, his call might be important."

She rolled her eyes and gave a little huff under her breath. "I doubt it. The man just wants to harass me some more." She placed the phone to her ear when her mother left the room.

The last thing Donnay wanted to do was talk to the man whose image was still blatantly clear in her mind. Although she hadn't wanted to, she had thought about him after he had left yesterday, and even worse, she had thought about him last night. She had made the mistake of noticing how much of a man he was instead of concentrating on what a forceful, imposing individual he represented. That was one mistake she wouldn't make twice.

"This is Ms. Russell," she said rather gruffly.

"Ms. Russell, this is Spencer Westmoreland. I'm calling to ask if you would have dinner with me tonight."

Arousing sensations automatically flowed through Donnay's body at the seductive tone in his voice. She fought the feelings, not quite sure what to make of the man. She pursed her lips, trying to decide whether to hang up or continue the conversation.

She inwardly sighed before saying, "Mr. Westmoreland, why would I want to have dinner with you?"

"To save your family's winery."

Donnay's arched brow rose a fraction. "I hate to shatter your illusions but Russell Vineyards doesn't need saving."

"Are you absolutely sure about that?"

Donnay leaned back against a wine rack. No, she wasn't absolutely sure; especially since she hadn't heard back from the bank. Mr. Gordon had indicated he would let her know something by noon today. Although she felt fairly confident they would get the loan, she also felt it would be in her best interest to see what Spencer Westmoreland might have up his sleeve.

"I'm willing to listen to what you have to say. However, it doesn't have to be over dinner."

"For me it does. That's the way I conduct most of my business meetings."

Her words were edged with anger when she asked, "And what if I prefer not having dinner with you?"

"Then you don't get to hear what I have to offer."

Donnay tipped her head back. The man had offered a lot of money for the vineyard yesterday, more money than she or her family could have ever expected. "Do you not recall me telling you yesterday that we aren't interested in any offer you make?" she asked bluntly.

She could hear his soft chuckle and liked the sound of it. "I do, but I'm hoping that I can change your mind," he said.

"That's not possible, Mr. Westmoreland. Like I told you, the vineyard is no longer for sale."

"And you're willing to turn your back on my offer on the chance that some banker is going to come through for you?"

An intense degree of uneasiness prickled Donnay's skin. "What do you know about my dealings with any banker?" Her stomach churned as suspicion raised its ugly head.

"I merely assumed as much since a few weeks ago your family was desperate to sell the winery and now you're not. Besides, I make it my business to know the financial position of any potential business partners."

She didn't like the sound of that. "We aren't partners, potential or otherwise."

"If you want to believe that, go ahead. Now back to dinner. We'll go to Sedrick's. I'll be there to pick you up around six. Is that acceptable?"

She wished she could tell him that it was not acceptable, but as she stared out the window at the lush vineyard in the distance, she knew doing so might not be a smart move. She had no intentions of ever parting with the vineyard she was looking at, no matter how confident Spencer Westmoreland seemed to be. She had a feeling he was up to something and there was only one way to find out what. "Yes, six will be fine."

"Wonderful. I'll see you then."

As soon as he clicked off the line Donnay wasted no time contacting Wayne Gordon at the bank. Her stomach settled when he told her he had good news for her. The loan her family had applied for had been approved. Donnay felt happiness all the way to her toes. Spencer Westmoreland hadn't bested them after all. That remark he'd made earlier about her business with the bank had been meant to throw her off, emitting smoke when there really wasn't any fire. Their money worries were now over. She would pull out a bottle of their finest wine and her family would celebrate.

A smile touched her lips. She would take great joy in letting Mr. Westmoreland know she expected him to get out of their lives forever. And she couldn't think of a better opportunity to tell him than that night over dinner.

Spencer smiled as he settled comfortably in the back seat of the limousine he had hired for the night.

The call he had received earlier from Stuart had him

in high spirits. Things were definitely going as he had planned. Thinking about the offer he would make to Chardonnay later tonight sent heat all through him. The thought that he would be the one who made love to her with the full purpose of giving her his child practically had his loins on fire. Of course, not for one minute did he assume she would go along with his proposal.

His lips curved into another smile. There was no doubt in his mind that she would turn him down flat, fight him with every breath she took, which was why he intended to give her no choice in the matter. Not if she really wanted to retain possession of her family's winery.

He glanced out the tinted window, seeing the beauty of the countryside of the Napa Valley. He had fallen in love with California the first time he had visited over twenty years ago after accepting a scholarship to attend Southern California University. As much as he loved Atlanta, California had eventually become his permanent home. After obtaining a bachelor's degree in finance and then a M.B.A., he began a career in banking at one of the most prestigious financial institutions in San Francisco.

He loved going back home to Atlanta for family gatherings, but always looked forward to returning to Sausalito, the charming waterfront community that was located just across the Golden Gate Bridge. The town was often compared to the French Riviera because of its Mediterranean flair and breathtaking views.

His house, a distinguished looking two-story structure, sat on four acres of land with beautiful San Francisco and Bay views. But he had to admit there was something peaceful and charming about Napa Valley. Away from the hustle and bustle of traffic, it was an idyllic setting. The perfect place to settle down and raise a family.

His mind was set, his agenda clear. It was not in his nature to tolerate resistance when it came to meeting any of his goals. And this time would not be an exception.

Chardonnay stared at her reflection in the huge mirror, wondering why she was putting so much effort in looking good tonight, granted Sedrick's was a very elegant and sophisticated restaurant.

She turned slightly and smiled. The strapless, backless black dress made of a sheer material clung to her hips, showing curves she had a tendency to forget she had until she dressed up in a manner such as this. She couldn't remember the last time she had gone out on a real date with a man. After that fiasco with Robert Joseph, her former college professor whom she had fancied herself in love with a few years back, she had a tendency to watch herself around men, especially those who thought they had it all together and expected women to fall in place and cater to their every whim.

She had been twenty-four and in her last year at UCLA, earning a degree in horticulture, when she had met Robert, a divorcé fifteen years her senior. The older man had dazzled her, swept her off her feet and into an affair that had lasted almost a year. A month before she was to graduate, he broke the news to her that he and his ex-wife had worked things out and were getting back together. She had realized then that she had been nothing more to him than a fun pasttime. The pain had taught her a valuable yet hard lesson when it came to men.

She tossed her head, sending her shoulder-length hair forward, framing her face. She grinned at the seductive effect and laughed. The rich sound vibrated in the room and made her realize it had been weeks since she'd had a reason to laugh. Almost losing the only home she'd ever known had taken its toll, but now she had a reason to rejoice.

"You look pretty."

She turned at the sound of her mother's voice and smiled. "Thanks, Mom, and I feel pretty tonight. I can't wait to tell Spencer Westmoreland that we have no reason to sell the vineyard, no matter how much he offers for it."

A worried look touched her mother's features. "Be careful, Donnay. It's my impression that Mr. Westmoreland isn't a man who likes losing."

She chuckled. "That's my impression of him as well, but I can't worry about that. How he handles bad news is no concern of mine."

"I know, but still, Donnay, he's—"

"Mom," she said, reaching out and grabbing her mother's hand. "Don't worry, I can handle Mr. Westmoreland." A smile curved her lips as she glanced at herself in the mirror again, thinking of the sheer arrogance of the man. "The big question of the night is can he handle me?"

Spencer slid out of the backseat of the limo when the chauffeur opened the door. He nodded, thanking the driver before walking briskly toward the huge house. When a cool breeze slid through his leather coat, he slipped his hands into the pockets in defiance of the crisp December air.

Although the sun had set and there was very little light, he could recall vividly the Russells' sprawling country home that seemed to loom out of the hills and sat on over a hundred acres of vintage land. Yesterday he had trekked this same path to the front door. The stone walkway, which seemed a mile long, was bordered with numerous flowering plants that seemed to welcome him.

Anticipation ran through his body with every step he took, and his heart began pounding furiously in his chest when he finally reached the door and pressed the bell. He tried ignoring the rush of excitement, thinking no woman had ever affected him this way, but then he conceded there was a first time for everything. And as long as he didn't let it dull his common sense, he could handle a little bit of craziness on a nippy December night.

The door opened and Chardonnay stood there, a vision of loveliness that practically took his breath away. His mouth pressed in a thin, hard line when he felt his common sense deserting him, and immediately he fought back the feeling. He liked being in control, but at that moment he feared that he was losing it.

She stepped back to let him enter. "It will take me only a minute to grab my wrap," she said, walking off.

His gaze sharpened when he saw her bare back. Her dress seemed perfect for her body and emphasized the svelte lines of her curves and the gracefulness of her long, gorgeous legs. The effect was stunning and he felt it all the way to his groin. He shifted, deciding it best to stay in place by the door, grateful for the full-length leather coat he was wearing.

He watched her grab her wrap off the table, place it around her shoulders and turn. Their gazes locked and at that precise moment, something passed between them. He felt it and was convinced she had felt it, as well. Like him, she stood perfectly still, their gazes leveled, connected.

Then suddenly the sound of a door closing somewhere upstairs in this monstrosity of a house broke the spell, and she tilted her head and frowned at him. A deliberate smile curved his lips.

"Are you ready to leave?" he asked, deciding the sooner he got her out of this house, off this land and into the cozy confines of the limo, the better.

She nodded and he had a feeling that the smile she proceeded to plaster on her lips was just as deliberate as his had been. She crossed the room and, as graceful as a swan, came to a stop in front of him. "Yes, I'm ready."

As Donnay settled into the soft leather cushions of the limo, she inhaled the familiar scent of ripened grapes that drenched the night air. This was wine country. The hills, valleys, fields and meadows bowed to that very proclamation and had done so for years. She had been born here and they had buried a host of other Russells here on this land. This was her legacy. But even more importantly, this was her home.

Through the tinted windows and in the darkness her gaze still scanned the land the car passed. She was grateful she and her family no longer had to worry about losing what was theirs to someone who wouldn't appreciate the valley for what it was. Someone who wanted to destroy the land instead of wanting to cultivate it. Someone intent on turning what would always be a vineyard into a playground for the rich and famous. A vacation spot.

That very someone was sitting a decent distance from her on the seat and hadn't spoken since the limo had left her family's home. She had to admit to surprise once she had walked outside and had seen the limo parked in the driveway. She should not have been. Spencer Westmoreland was a man who evidently enjoyed basking in his wealth.

In the dark interior of the car she allowed her gaze to scan his silhouette, bathed in the moonlight. He wasn't looking at her. In fact his gaze seemed fixed on the objects they passed; although she doubted he was actually seeing anything. That meant he was deep in thought, or just plain ignoring her.

The thought of him doing the latter should not have bothered her but it did. After all, he was the one who had invited her to dinner. She wondered if he'd already detected that this was one deal he'd thought he had wrapped up that he could now kiss goodbye. Not bloody likely. He was probably sitting there thinking of a new strategy to get what he wanted.

Hopefully after tonight she would make it clear as glass that her family would not entertain notions of selling the vineyard. She smiled thinking her mother and grandparents would certainly rest a lot better tonight. But when it came to how well she would sleep, she wasn't as certain. Not with the man sitting beside her on the seat causing all sorts of turbulent emotions to rise within her.

While he was looking elsewhere, she scanned his face. His features were sharp, as sharp as his arrogant tongue, a tongue he was holding tonight, thank goodness. But everything else about him was out there, in the open. He was handsome. That fact was a given. Every single detail about his features—the rounded chin, the short dark hair, the full lips—contributed to a face that would make any woman take a second look. Then there was the way he fit his clothes. Yesterday she hadn't failed to notice he was a sharp dresser. No doubt beneath his leather coat was a designer suit.

"Have you been to Sedrick's before?"

She blinked, realizing he had spoken. He had shifted positions in the seat and was staring at her. When had he done that? While she had been admiring his clothes? If that was the case, he hadn't missed her studying him.

Deciding she needed to answer his question, she said, "Yes, several times. Have you?"

"Once. I was impressed with both the service and the food."

"The food is wonderful," she said, suddenly wondering if they needed more space between them. For some reason it seemed the distance separating them had decreased.

"And that will give us a chance to talk."

She lifted a brow. "About what?" she asked, wanting him to get specific.

"A number of things." With a move that was so premeditated that it caught her unawares, he eased closer to her on the seat. Her heart rate escalating at an alarming rate, she glanced up at his face and fought back the panic she felt rising in her throat. She had made light of her mother's warning, however, when it came to experience, she was no match for Spencer. He had a sensuality about him that made the pulse in her throat twitch. Robert had been an older, handsome man who had impressed her with his intellect. But when it came to style, sophistication and fashion, he'd been slightly unkempt. He was a professor, and in his social circles and profession, one wasn't supposed to look like he belonged on the cover of GQ.

But it was a whole different story for Spencer Westmoreland. He was a businessman, suave, debonair, handsome…arrogant. Even now his presence was dominating the interior of the car. There was no doubt in her mind that in his world, his word ruled supreme. She doubted very few opposed him. And those who did probably paid the price. One didn't make it to where he was in life, and at such a young age, without being ruthless to some degree. Donnay shuddered at the thought. He wanted Russell Vineyards. She wondered how he would handle knowing it was no longer within his grasp?

She drew in a deep breath when he stretched his arms across the back of the seat. "I really wasn't sure you would go out with me tonight," he said in a throaty tone.

Her senses became focused fully on him when she said, "I'm a woman full of surprises, Mr. Westmoreland, and there's one I intend to share with you later."

"Is there?"

"Yes."

She saw his gaze study hers intently before he said, "You have beautiful eyes."

She could respond by echoing the compliment, but instead she decided to play it safe. "Thank you."

"You're welcome. You're also a gorgeous woman."

She slanted him a cool glance. It was on the tip of her tongue to tell him she was too levelheaded to fall for sweet talk. She wondered why he was wasting his time and couldn't imagine what he hoped to gain by using such flattery. It might work on other women but not on her.

"I must thank you for a second time, Mr. Westmoreland."

"Let's dispense with the formality. Call me Spencer."

She nodded. "All right, and I'm Donnay."

He smiled. "I like Chardonnay better."

She mentally shook aside the sexiness in his voice when he said her name. The scent of grapes, she noticed, had been replaced with the scent of man. Whatever cologne he was wearing was manly, robust and sexy. She knew for some woman he would probably be the perfect lover since there was no doubt he would be good at anything he attempted.

"Chardonnay."

She glanced up and saw his gaze was focused exclusively on her. She wondered what he was staring at so intently. Then she realized her lips had captured his attention and were holding it. She drew in a quick breath and felt a stirring begin in her stomach and slowly spread to all parts of her. And then there had been the way he'd said her name. Placing emphasis on certain syllables in a way no other man ever had, giving it an undeniably sensuous sound.

She parted her lips to draw in a much needed breath, and in a daring move he leaned closer and darted out his tongue to moisten her lips, before capturing her mouth with his. The contact had been so unexpected, so sudden, that instead of pulling away she felt every cell in her body vibrate under the onslaught of a combustible combination of overzealous hormones and much-deprived lust.

It was too late to revamp her senses. Too late to think about resisting. The moment his tongue touched hers she was a goner and she had a feeling that with his arrogant, utterly confident self, he very well knew it. What other reason could there be for him deepening the kiss and pulling her closer to him in such a way that had her moaning sounds she'd never heard before.

No man had ever kissed her this way. So completely, so totally, so downright absolutely. The kiss aroused her, stimulated her like none before. She responded to his actions on instinct and not experience. Her tongue had never participated in a kiss the way it was doing now, emanating a need within her that she didn't understand. But evidently he did, because the more she greedily demanded from him, the more he gave.

Suddenly he pulled back, and disappointment poured through her like cold water on overly heated skin. She noted she was draped over him, practically in his lap. And he was staring at her with an intensity that held both longing and possession. She knew at that moment, as she tried pulling herself back together and away from him, that she was out of her league. And to think she'd actually thought she could handle him.

"Your taste is one I'll never forget, Chardonnay."

She focused her full attention on him when he added, "And one I intend to indulge in time and time again."

His words were filled with confidence, as if barring any opposition or debate. By the same token, her reaction to them was immediate and instinctual. "I disagree."

He shook his head and smiled at her. It was a smile that touched his lips, corner to corner. "That's your prerogative. But the way I see things, your loyalty will be your downfall, but then at the same time it's what sets you apart from all others. It's what I admire most about you."

She frowned, not understanding what he was saying or what he meant. Before she could ask, he glanced out the car window and said, "We've arrived at our destination and I prefer resuming this discussion over dinner."

Chapter 3

Spencer knew he had selected the right restaurant the moment he led Chardonnay through the doors. The ambiance alone deserved the establishment's five-star rating.

Situated on a grassy slope in the heart of the Napa Valley, the huge European-style structure boasted elaborate stone and brickwork. The interior glistened with holiday decorations. Even on a Tuesday night the place was packed, and he couldn't help but note that more than a few males looked his way with envy in their eyes. More on instinct than anything else, he entwined his arm with Chardonnay's. When she gave him a questioning look, he smiled and said, "I made reservations so we shouldn't have long to wait."

No sooner had he said the words then the maître d' appeared to escort them through the throng of well-dressed patrons to a private room in the back of the restaurant. Brick walls with dark wooden beams and cast-iron chandeliers that hung overhead created a romantic setting.

After being seated at the only table in the room they were given a wine list and their menus. They were informed that a waiter would arrive shortly to take their wine selection and dinner order.

Moments later he was alone with Chardonnay. Spencer glanced up at her face, trying to read her expression as well as guess her thoughts. He knew he had surprised her when he had touched her arm with such possessiveness. Hell, he had surprised himself. Never had he been jealous of another male's attention to any woman he was with. It wasn't in his makeup to do such a thing.

Giving himself a few moments to clear his rattled mind, he followed her gaze around the room. It was quaint and cozy, almost completely surrounded in tinted glass, and it provided a beautiful illuminated view of an outdoor gazebo that was surrounded by thick shrubs, blossoming flowers and running vines.

"The room is lovely."

Chardonnay's comment caught his attention and he met her gaze. It was on the tip of his tongue to say that the room had nothing on her. "Yes, it is," he said instead. The taste of her was still on his lips and he doubted even the strongest drink would be able to remove it. He had enjoyed kissing her, sliding his arms around her and holding her close to him while he mated with her mouth at will. And when her arms had wrapped around him, and he'd heard the soft moans from her throat, he had done what had come naturally. Deepened the kiss even more.

Not that he was complaining, but the intimate exchange had lasted longer than he had intended. All sense of time and place had flown from his mind in the awakening lust that had consumed his body. And when she had stretched up against him, he had effortlessly pulled her into his lap without disengaging their mouths.

His thoughts came to an abrupt end when the waiter brought in glasses of water and then took the time to take their wine and dinner order. They both agreed on a veal dish and a bottle of Russell Chianti.

"Have you ever tasted our wine before?" Chardonnay asked after the waiter had left, leaving them alone again.

He shook his head. "No, but I understand it's delicious."

She frowned. "It's more than delicious. It's superb. The best in the land."

He chuckled. "You would say that but I'll see for myself in a minute." He then leaned back in his chair. "What exactly do you do at the winery?"

She shrugged. "A little bit of everything, depending on the season. I handle PR during the winter months—spring and summer I work the vineyard, pruning, planting and I even know how to operate the equipment to crush and ferment the grapes. In the fall I take on the role of wine taster. So I guess you can say I enjoy wearing several different hats."

After taking a sip of her water, she asked, "Why are you interested in what I do?"

He smiled, wondering if she was always so suspicious of people or just him. Then again, she had good reason to be. "Um, just curious."

She placed her glass down and met his gaze. "And I'm just as curious, Spencer," she said, leaning forward and saying his given name for the first time. "What is tonight all about? Why did you invite me to dinner?"

He leaned forward as well and countered by asking in a low, husky voice, "Why did you accept?"

She slowly drew back and lifted her chin. "Because there was something I wanted to tell you."

"What?"

She inclined her head toward the closed door. "I prefer we wait for our food, especially the wine, since what I have to say is a cause to celebrate."

He lifted a brow. "Is it?"

"Yes, I think so."

"All right, then. In the meantime tell me about yourself."

He immediately saw defiance light her gray eyes before she said. "I already have. It's your turn."

Spencer started to say she was wrong. She hadn't told him everything about herself. Since she would eventually become his wife, he had an urge to know a whole lot more. However, he said, "I'm a Westmoreland."

The smile that touched her lips stirred something deep in the pit of his stomach. "And that's supposed to mean something?" she asked, seemingly amused.

He shared her smile and felt rather comfortable in doing so. "In Atlanta it does. Just like your family has deep roots here, mine has deep roots in Atlanta. My cousin Dare is sheriff of College Park, a suburb of Atlanta. And my cousin Thorn Westmoreland is—"

"The man who builds motorcycles and races them, as well," she finished for him, smiling brightly. "I didn't make the name connection until now. I used to have a poster of him on my bedroom wall when I was sixteen. Boy was he hot."

Spencer chuckled. "I understand there are some women who think he still is. He's happily married, and he and his wife, Tara, are expecting their first baby later this month. It's going to be a boy."

"That's wonderful. And what about siblings? Do you have any?"

"Yes, I have an older brother, Jared, and four younger brothers—Durango, Ian, Quade and Reggie."

"They all live in Atlanta?"

"Jared and Reggie do. Ian lives in Lake Tahoe and Quade works for the government in D.C."

"Really, what sort of work does he do?"

"Quade works in security at the White House. Because of the high level of security entailed, we're not really sure what he does and he's never divulged any details." And so she wouldn't ask any more questions about Quade's job, he asked a question of his own. "What about you? Is it just you, your mother and grandparents?" he asked.

"Yes, and the four of us are very close."

"And your father?"

She shrugged. "I never knew him and he never knew me. End of story."

Spencer knew it was the end of the story only because she deemed it to be. At that moment the waiter returned with their wine. After he filled their glasses and left the room, a smiling Chardonnay held hers up for a toast. "To Russell Vineyards, may we last forever, and with the loan we got approved today from the bank, we are well on our way of doing just that."

She glanced at him over the rim of the glass as she then took a sip, smiling. Spencer knew she was feeling really good right now, thinking she had just burst his bubble.

She lifted a brow as she put her glass down, evidently disappointed that she had failed to get a rise out of him. "Well?"

He lifted his own brow. "Well, what?"

"Don't you have anything to say?"

He smiled and then replied, "Yes, I have quite a lot to say, but I prefer to do so after we enjoy our meal. I wouldn't want any words we might exchange to ruin our dinner."

Apparently thinking she *had* succeeded in getting him riled after all, she leaned back in her chair and said smugly, "You'll get over it."

"And if I don't?"

He watched as she drew her breath, saw how her lips curved in a frown. She leaned forward again. "It will be a waste of your time since there is nothing you can do about it."

The waiter entered with their food. Spencer smiled at her and said, "Our dinner has arrived, Chardonnay. Please hold your thoughts until after our meal. Then I will tell you why you're wrong."

Donnay declined dessert, thinking she was tired of this cat-and-mouse game she and Spencer were playing. During the drive over, she had felt elated, confident, thrilled at the prospect that he would be experiencing a letdown like he hadn't felt in a while, given what she had read about him. He should be totally disappointed, frustrated and probably more than a little upset to learn Russell Vineyards was completely out of his reach. Instead it didn't appear that the news had affected him at all, which made her wonder if perhaps he knew something that she didn't.

And then there was the kiss she couldn't get out of her mind. The one that still had her insides sizzling. His lips had connected to hers in a way that immediately set off a rush of heat within her. And the chemistry that had been stirred between them was as potent as anything she'd ever felt before. His taste had literally zapped her of her senses and it was taking everything she had to get her entire body back on track.

Not able to handle the tension or curiosity any longer, she tilted her head up and looked into his face. "Tell me why you think I'm wrong, Spencer."

She watched him set aside his wineglass. He then eased his wallet out of his jacket pocket and withdrew a business card. He offered it to her.

Donnay took it, studied the information that was printed on it before looking back at him with a questioning look. "What am I supposed to be looking at?"

"My profession."

She glanced at the card again before raising her head to meet his gaze. "Financial management investor?"

"Yes. Like you, I enjoy wearing several different hats," he said, putting his wallet back in his pocket.

Donnay sat straighter in the chair. Their gazes held for a long time when she finally asked, "Meaning what?"

Spencer continued to hold Chardonnay's gaze. There was no doubt in his mind that she wouldn't like what he was about to say. She would probably like even less the proposal he intended to offer her. For a fleeting instant he thought of undoing all he'd done; let her and her family keep the land and just walk away. He knew that although he could walk away from the land, he could not walk away from her. Spending time with her tonight had only solidified his interest, attraction and desire. He wanted her with a passion unlike anything he'd ever known.

He met her eyes as intently and said, "Earlier you said your family had managed to secure a loan."

"Yes, it's been approved."

"I know it has."

"And how would you know that?"

When he didn't answer her right away, she repeated the question. "How would you know that, Spencer?"

He leaned back in his chair. "Banks offer loans to individuals that sometimes have to be underwritten by a third party because of their risky nature."

He gave it a few moments and then he saw the light that came on in her eyes, letting him know she was finally getting the picture. That same light suddenly flared with fury when she asked. "Are you saying you're the one who underwrote the loan?"

He answered her, deciding to speak slowly and deliberately, making sure she understood completely. "Yes. The bank couldn't find any other investor to do it. So basically, once you sign the loan papers I'll be the one holding the mortgage to the vineyard."

His words had the effect he knew they would. Her

eyes hardened and began shooting fire at him. "You want our land that much?" she asked in a tone he knew she was trying to control.

He decided to be completely honest. "Yes, but there's something else I want, Chardonnay, and it has become even more important to me than Russell Vineyards."

"And what is that?"

He only paused a second before saying, "You."

It took Chardonnay a few moments to gather her composure. And she couldn't help inhaling a deep breath several times before asking what may have been a relatively stupid question. "For what purpose?"

He took his time in answering her. "I want to marry you and give you my child. In fact, several of them."

She gasped first in surprise, then in outrage. "Do you honestly think I will go along with a notion as crazy as that?"

"Yes. You will if you want to keep your family winery," he said, looking her straight in the eye. "Evidently you don't fully understand your family's predicament, Chardonnay. Without the backing of a third party, no bank will agree to loan you the amount of money your family needs. You've depleted a lot of the business assets, not to mention you continue to be a mom-and-pop operation that has been operating in the red most of this year. However," he continued, "I'm willing to guarantee the loan for whatever amount you need. And to show what a generous person I am, I'm giving you two options. You can take out the loan but it will have to be paid back in full within six months."

"Six months!"

"Yes. If you default on the loan, everything will be mine. Or you can consider the second option. Agree to marry me and have my child and I will let you continue to run and operate the winery as you see fit. In fact I will put a lot of my money behind you to expand the winery to an international one."

Anger swept through her. Neither were acceptable options. She leaned over and glared at him. "Forget both options."

He gave a small nonchalant shrug. "If that's what you really want. But either way, Chardonnay, I will own your land one day and will do whatever it takes to do so. I suggest you take the second option. It's less risky. And if you do, I will even forgo my dream to build the vacation resort on the land. Instead I will devote my time and attention, when I'm not trying to get you pregnant, to building up Russell Vineyards' reputation and standings."

"I will not be your brood mare!" Donnay stood, amazed at just how much anger she could feel toward one single individual. "You have to be the vilest man I know to suggest something so despicable. The last thing I'd want is to marry you. And as far as having your baby, I can't imagine the two of us ever sharing a bed to do such a thing."

"Are you saying that you're willing to walk away from everything I'm offering knowing the outcome?" he asked in a calm voice.

"Walk away and not look back. Take note, Spencer Westmoreland, because that's just what I'm doing. And don't worry about taking me back home. I'll call a cab."

And then she did just what she'd said she would do.

With her head held high she turned and left the room. And she did so without looking back.

When Spencer caught up with Donnay outside the restaurant, she was thanking one of the valet's for calling her a cab. "I'm taking you home, Chardonnay," he said, coming up behind her.

She swiveled and the look she gave him would have turned lesser men to stone. "No, you're not. I refuse to have anything to do with you, and if you try forcing me to do anything against my will, I will let out a scream the likes of which you've never heard before."

He believed her. "Very well, then," he said quietly, taking a step back. "But there is one thing I'd like to ask."

"What?" she all but snapped.

"Forget about the vineyard for a moment and all the things my proposal entails. I want to know what is there about me that rubs you the wrong way."

Donnay shook her head. The man really didn't have a clue. Did he not know how degrading his offer was to her? He wanted to marry her and use her to have his child. What could possibly be romantic about that? The sad thing about it was that she wanted the very things he was proposing—marriage, babies, a way to take the winery to an international scale. But not this way and definitely not on his terms. What he was proposing only showed just how ruthless he could be and how far he would go to get anything he wanted.

She tilted her head up and looked him dead in the eye when she said, "The reason I can't conceive the two of us ever coming together romantically, Spencer, is that personally, you are *not* my type."

"Miss, your cab has arrived."

The attendant's words claimed Donnay's attention. She hurried over to the parked cab, leaving Spencer standing there alone.

"How was dinner with Mr. Westmoreland?"

Donnay glanced up at the stairs at the sound of her mother's soft voice. She could not tell her mother or grandparents the true nature of her evening with Spencer. The last thing she wanted was for them to worry about anything.

"Dinner was okay," she said as she watched her mother descend the stairs.

When her mother reached the bottom stair, Ruth smiled at her and said, "It was just okay? I've never known a time that I went to Sedrick's that the evening ended up being just okay."

Donnay smiled back at her mother. "Well, considering the company, it was just okay."

"And?" Ruth probed.

Donnay lifted a brow. "And what?"

"And how did he handle the news that we had secured a loan?"

"Better than I wished he had, giving me the feeling that he won't give up," Donnay said, admitting that much.

"Well, considering everything, how much ruckus can he stir? Getting the loan puts him totally out of the picture now since we won't need his money."

"Let's hope so," she said guiltily in response to her

mother's words. She wished she could be completely honest and tell her mother that Spencer and the loan were tied together as one. The first thing she would do tomorrow would be to visit with Glenn Forbes, their attorney. She was certain Spencer had done something unethical in the handling of the loan. If fighting him legally was the only way then she would do so.

Needing to change the subject, she glanced at what her mother was wearing. It didn't take much to tell that her mother, who rarely went out, had gone somewhere tonight. "And where have you been?" Donnay asked, curious. Years ago, she had stopped encouraging her mother to get out more, meet a nice man, have fun and date, since her mother claimed there would never be another man in her life she could possibly love more than she had Donnay's father.

"McClintock Café," her mother answered. "After you left I got a call from a friend I hadn't seen in ages who was passing through. We got together for coffee and to catch up on old times."

Donnay nodded. It was good seeing her mother taking interest in something other than the winery. "Well, I'm glad. You look nice."

Yawning, her mother said. "Thanks. And I believe we're both up later than usual and need to go up to bed. The next few weeks will be busy ones for everybody."

The winter months were usually less hectic. Except for winter pruning, there wasn't much to do but take precautions to assure that the sometimes harsh weather didn't cripple or destroy the crop. It was also a time for staff members to discuss how to increase productivity and retain quality.

But a couple of weekends from now, downtown Napa would be hosting the annual Taste Napa Downtown event, which for wine lovers was the most popular wine tasting event in the world. Russell Vineyards would be represented again this year.

"Yes, and I can't wait. The excitement is spreading already," Donnay said, giving her mom a hug. "Good night, Mom."

"Good night, Donnay."

Donnay was halfway up the stairs when her mother called out to her "Donnay?"

She turned. "Yes?"

Her mother stared at her for a moment then shook her head and smiled. "Nothing, sweetheart. At least it's not anything that we can't talk about later."

"You're sure?" she asked, studying her mother's features to detect if something was wrong. When she couldn't identify anything, she relaxed her brow.

"Yes, I'm sure. Go on to bed and get a good night's rest."

Donnay smiled. "I will and you do the same."

Chapter 4

You are not my type...

Irritation lined Spencer's brow as he took a sip of coffee. He couldn't imagine any woman saying such a thing to a Westmoreland. And if Chardonnay thought from one minute her words would stop him for acquiring the single most important thing he wanted—namely her—then she needed to think again. But still, what she'd said had irritated him, although he didn't have to speculate on the reason she'd said it.

He took another sip of coffee. He didn't care what she claimed, especially when her lips had said differently. He might not be her type but she had enjoyed the kiss they had shared. There was no way she could convince him otherwise. And he couldn't help wondering if memories of being in his arms had kept her awake last night as they had him. In addition to her beauty, there was something so beguiling about her that he hadn't been able to take his mind off her, even when he'd slept.

And that wasn't good.

With a frustrated sigh he pushed away from the table and stood. How could he have become so mesmerized by one woman? And so quickly. Even now the scent of her still lingered with him. It was such an arousing fragrance, one he couldn't let go of. He had left his cousin's wedding with the intent of coming to California to turn a deal around. Instead he was the one getting turned around. The woman was having just that kind of effect on him. He wanted to marry her. He wanted her to have his children. He wanted it all, and as far as he was concerned, no one else would do. On the other hand, he didn't expect this to be any sort of love match. Everything was strictly a business affair.

However, she had made it pretty clear, business or otherwise, she wasn't interested. He would turn up the heat a little, because in the end, he very much intended to have every single thing that he wanted, especially her. And he wasn't someone who wasted time once he'd made up his mind. He glanced at his watch. It was almost noon and time for him and Chardonnay to have another talk.

Less than an hour later he was strolling up the walkway toward the Russells' front door. He refused to entertain the notion that considering how they'd parted the night before, Chardonnay would refuse to see him. Whatever it took, he would get her alone so they could talk.

He was halfway to the door when suddenly it was flung wide open and Chardonnay's mother appeared, frantic, almost hysterical with tears streaming down her face. "Mr. Westmoreland, please come quickly! Help us. It's my father. He's collapsed and is unconscious."

"Are you saying there's nothing that we can do, Glenn?"

Glenn Forbes had been the attorney for Russell Vineyards for years and Donnay was trying hard not to let the man see her frustration.

"Unfortunately that's exactly what I'm saying," the sixty-something year-old man answered. "It will be Westmoreland's money that he's loaning out so he can set up any terms and restrictions that he wants. And chances are, he will be giving you stiff ones since the bottom line is that he wants your land."

"How stiff?"

"He will probably call in the loan during a time he knows you can't possibly pay it back, or hike your interest rates up so high that you'll have difficulty making the loan payments, which will ultimately push you into defaulting. On the other hand, if you don't take the loan and he's the only one interested in buying the property or if he keeps the same offer on the table that he made a few days ago, then you and your family will make a lot of money."

"But we'll lose our home." She sighed deeply, knowing Spencer had backed them into a catch-22 situation. Either way he stood to gain and they could lose everything that truly mattered to them. "Thanks for the information, Glenn."

"No problem. How's your grandfather's health?"

Donnay smiled. "It's been good. His medication is expensive but we've been able to handle it so far. He's a little disappointed that we've had to put aside our plans for expansion for a while. Right now our main focus is surviving."

For years her grandfather, who was the master wine-maker in the family, had worked hard to improve the quality of the wines they made. Although Russell wines had a great reputation in the United States, the next stage in their plan had been to start doing business in the overseas market. That meant hiring more employees, some with specialized winemaking skills. That was one of the reasons Spencer's offer to transform the winery from a mom-and-pop operation to an international one had merit. It was the same plan her grandfather had been dreaming of for years. But the price Spencer demanded was too high.

She stood. "Well, I need to be going, Glenn. I've taken up too much of your time already."

"Nonsense," the older man said, also standing. "Just be careful with those city slickers like Westmoreland. He'll take advantage of any mistake you make. If he wants that land bad enough he'll do just about anything to get it."

Donnay didn't need to be warned. She already knew how far he'd go. She gave Glenn a small smile and was about to make a comment when her cell phone went off. Pulling it from her purse she checked caller ID. "Excuse me, Glenn, it's Mom calling." She answered her phone. "Yes, Mom?"

Seconds later she grabbed the edge of Glenn's desk

for support when a lump of panic swelled within her throat. "What! How is he?"

She nodded anxiously. "I'm on my way."

"Is anything wrong, Donnay?"

She glanced up and met Glenn's concerned expression right before she quickly headed for the door. "Yes, it's my grandfather," she said to him over her shoulder. "He collapsed and had to be rushed to the hospital."

Donnay rushed through the E.R. doors and looked around frantically for her mother and grandmother. Relief washed over her when she saw them, but tension and anger quickly consumed her when she saw who was with them.

What was Spencer Westmoreland doing here? Was he responsible for whatever was happening to her grandfather? Had he said something to upset him? Her grandfather had been perfectly fine when she had eaten breakfast with him that morning, long before her mother and grandmother had awakened. And now he was here in the hospital.

Inhaling deeply and trying to consume the anger she felt, she crossed to where the three individuals sat. Spencer was the first to see her and stood after whispering something to her mother and grandmother. They glanced up and rushed over to her.

"How's Gramps?" she quickly asked.

"We don't know," her mother responded softly. "The doctor hasn't come to talk to us yet. Everything happened so fast. We were all in the kitchen. He was fine one minute and the next thing we knew he was clutching his chest and then he collapsed."

"There's a possibility he had a heart attack," Spencer said when he joined them.

Donnay's eyes locked with his. Rage consumed her. "And what do you know about any of this?"

Her mother answered. "He was there to—"

"He was there!" Donnay broke in as her anger escalated even more. "What did you say to my grandfather? You had no right to upset him. If anything happens to him I will never forgive you."

"Donnay, you're wrong. Mr. Westmoreland—"

"Sorry your opinion of me is so low, Chardonnay," Spencer cut into her mother's words. "And since my being here has upset you, I'll leave." He turned and quietly headed toward the exit.

Ruth grabbed her daughter's arm, highly disturbed. "What is wrong with you, Donnay? Why would you talk to Mr. Westmoreland that way?"

"I can't stand the man. You know that, Mom."

"Yes, but it was a blessing that he showed up when he did today or your grandfather might not be alive."

Donnay was too stunned to speak. After a moment she asked in an unsteady voice. "What do you mean?"

"After your grandfather collapsed, I was rushing out of the house to get one of the workers when I saw Mr. Westmoreland coming up the walkway. He ran in and administered CPR to your grandfather until the paramedics arrived. He was not responsible for what happened to your grandfather. Instead of sending that man away, you should have thanked him. What you just did was incredibly inconsiderate."

Donnay knew she looked as totally embarrassed as she felt. The floor could open up and swallow her whole and she would deserve it. "Mom, I didn't know. I truly thought he was responsible."

"I don't know why you would think such a thing. You owe him an apology."

Before she could respond, they turned when the doctor walked into the waiting room. Donnay rushed over to him. "How is he, Dr. Miller?"

The older man, who had been her grandfather's doctor ever since it was discovered that he had a heart condition earlier that year, gave them a small smile. "He's resting and, yes, he did have a heart attack. One that could have taken him out of here had it not been for the quick thinking to use CPR. As soon as he's stable we want to run more tests. That surgical procedure we discussed a few months ago would help tremendously although most insurance companies won't pay for it since it's still considered experimental in nature."

"Can we see him?" her grandmother asked softly.

"Yes, but one at a time and for no more than five minutes. It's important that he continues to rest."

It was only after her grandmother's and mother's visits with her grandfather that Donnay entered his room. She had seen him like this before, hooked up to various machines and monitors, but seeing him now profoundly affected her. In her eyes he had always been strong, robust and bigger than life. Now he appeared tired and weak.

She walked quietly across the room to stand beside his bed. She gazed down at him, remembering years when he represented the only father figure in her life. She couldn't think of losing him, like she had refused to let him consider losing the one thing that meant everything to him, other than her grandmother—the vineyard.

When the family hadn't been able to see through their financial situation, he had been willing to part with the one thing that had been in the Russell family for generations, although she'd known doing so was killing him inside. She'd known then that it would be up to her to make sure he'd never have to do that. That burden was still on her shoulders.

"Donnay."

She blinked back tears when he opened his eyes, met her gaze and said her name, barely murmured under his breath. "Yes, Gramps, I'm here."

"Pretty."

She smiled. He'd always told her she was pretty. She watched as he tried moving his gaze around the room and knew why. "Grammy and Mom were here earlier. They will only let us see you one at a time."

He nodded, letting her know he understood. "I'm nothing but trouble."

She frowned upon hearing his words. "No, you're not, so don't even think that. Everything is going to be all right."

He looked up into her face. "The winery?"

She felt a thick lump in her throat as she nodded and brushed moisture off his forehead. "The winery is going to stay with us. We got approved for the loan, remember?"

He nodded again and a slight smile formed on his lips. "We're going to keep it."

She blinked back more tears. "Yes, we're going to keep it."

"For your kids."

A smile touched her lips. Even in his condition, he was again dropping hints about her personal life. "Yes, one day for my kids."

"My great-grands."

"Yes, Gramps, your great-grands." She watched as his eyes closed. He was dozing off again, apparently being tired out from talking to her.

"Miss, I hate to interrupt but your five minutes are up," a nurse stuck her head in the door and said, smiling apologetically.

"Thanks, I'm leaving." Leaning over she placed a kiss on her grandfather's cheek, then clutched the shoulder strap of her purse as she left the room.

Spencer stared down into the dark red depth of his wine before swirling it around in the glass. Russell Vineyards' finest. Last night Chardonnay had referred to it as superb and he had to admit she was right. He'd never had a reason to taste the wine before last night but now he was mildly surprised. He hadn't expected such a fruity, yet tartly smooth taste. He found it incredibly pleasing to his palate.

Instead of sipping he put the glass to his lips and thought, what the hell. He had ordered it. Room service had delivered it. And at the moment, he needed it. He took a rather large gulp and then licked his lips while the warmth of the liquid flowed straight through his body to settle in a part of him right below the belt.

Seemingly sensual. Definitely erotic.

It was then, and only then, that he took the time to fully recall every vivid moment of the scene that had played out at the hospital with Chardonnay. A hard muscle twitched in his cheek. She had wrongly accused him, but instead of defending himself, he had walked away. He had discovered last night that once Chardonnay became upset about something, the woman was downright hard to deal with…even when her facts were wrong.

But unlike his attorney, Stuart, he had no intentions of letting her test the level of his endurance or get on his last nerve. After all he still intended, whether she liked it or not, to marry her. She just wasn't making things easy for him, which meant he would continue to make things hard for her.

He crossed the room to gaze out the window in an attempt to calm his frustrated mind. The abundance of land his eyes touched was incredible, amazing, simply beautiful. The sun was sending golden highlights across the valley in a way that was astounding and peaceful.

As if to break that peace, his mind went back to Chardonnay. He loathed the very idea that she thought he would intentionally bring her grandfather harm. If she knew how much he had cherished and loved his own grandfather, she would know how totally wrong she was. Scott Westmoreland had made an impact on all of his grandchildren's lives, making them believe that they could fulfill their dreams, no matter what they were. Like Chardonnay's grandfather, he had been a master, not at wine but at food. His reputation as a cook and restaurant owner was legendary. And Spencer had loved him as deeply as Chardonnay loved her grandfather.

He turned away from the window when his cell phone rang. Thinking it was Stuart or one of his brothers, he answered. "Yes?"

"I owe you an apology."

Spencer felt a deep tingling in the pit of his stomach the moment he heard Chardonnay's voice. There was just something incredibly sexy about it. However, the effect it had on him was too intense for his frame of mind, and resentment set in. For a moment he didn't know what to say since he never expected her to call to apologize. "Do you?" he finally replied in a clipped tone.

"Yes."

"I'm sure it's something you don't do often. Do you really know how it's done?"

There was a slight hesitation on her part and then she said in an irritated tone, "Look, I don't need this."

He'd gotten her mad. Good. "And neither do I, Chardonnay. I don't like being falsely accused of anything."

"I told you I was sorry. What else do you want?"

"Have you decided to indulge me in the things I want?" he retorted coolly, waiting for her response, knowing it would probably be just as biting and sharp as his had been.

"You have got to be the most—"

"Be careful what you say, Chardonnay, or you might very well be apologizing for a second time." He was taunting her and he knew it. She had pushed a number of buttons that no other woman had pushed before and he didn't like it.

"I think we need to end this conversation," she said brusquely.

"I don't. The reason I was at your home earlier today was that I felt we needed to talk. I still feel that way," he said.

"Maybe some other time."

"No. Tonight."

For a moment she didn't say anything and then asked, "And if I refuse?"

"Then either way, you can kiss the winery goodbye." He had said the words calmly, but Spencer was fully aware she knew he meant them.

"One day you'll regret what you're doing."

She was probably right but as long as that day wasn't today he was fine. "We'll do dinner at seven, here at the resort. I'm staying at the Chablis." He also knew his words probably sounded like an order.

An incredulous smile touched his lips when he heard the sound of the phone clicking in his ear. That wasn't a dropped call. She had deliberately hung up on him.

Hours later, Donnay murmured not so nice things about Spencer under her breath when she headed down the stairs. Spending time with him again was not something she wanted to do. The less she saw of the infuriating man the better. However, she had to admit that they did need to talk. She just didn't want to do it tonight.

"There you are," her grandmother said, smiling. "I was just about to come up and get you. The car has arrived."

Donnay lifted a brow. "What car?"

"The one Mr. Westmoreland sent for you. It's parked outside."

As soon as her feet stepped off the bottom stair Donnay walked over to the window and looked out. That same limo from the night before was parked outside. Why had he sent a car for her? Spencer said they would be dining at the Chablis, the luxury resort on two hundred acres of land that overlooked the May-acamas Mountains and provided a stunning view of Napa Valley.

She turned to her grandmother wondering if she knew what was going on.

"Is Spencer outside waiting in the parked car, Grammy?"

"No, he sent his driver for you. The man came to the door to let us know he was here, and said he'd been instructed to take you to Mr. Westmoreland at the Chablis."

Donnay looked outside again at the limo and shook her head. The man really did have a lot of nerve. She turned back to her grandmother. "I'm using my own car."

She walked across the room and gave her grandmother a peck on the cheek. "I'll have my cell phone on if you need me."

They had already checked with the hospital and her grandfather was still resting peacefully. Her grandmother had wanted to spend the night with him but they had talked her out of it.

Donnay glanced around. "Where's Mom?"

"She went out."

Again? Donnay lifted a brow. Evidently that friend her mother had met for coffee last night was still in town. "Will you be okay here alone, Grammy?" she asked with concern.

Her grandmother waved off her worries. "Of course. Go on and enjoy the evening with your young man."

Donnay frowned, doubting that she would. "Well, if

you're sure you'll be okay, I'll go and let the limo driver know I'm taking my own car."

"All right, dear."

Grabbing her purse off the table Donnay quickly walked out the door. She strolled down the long walkway to the chauffeur and smiled up at him. "Hello, I'm Chardonnay Russell, and I won't need your services since I'm driving my own car."

The man's face remained expressionless when he said, "Mr. Westmoreland instructed me that if you were to refuse my services, madam, to give you this," he said, presenting a sealed envelope to her.

Frowning, she took it from the man, quickly opened it up and pulled out the note.

I prefer that you do things my way, Chardonnay. For your safety, comfort and convenience, I have sent the car for you and I expect you to use it. Failure to do so means all talks are off, including my backing that loan. Spencer.

A part of her wanted to say good riddance, but she knew she couldn't do that, especially after she had assured her grandfather today that all was well with the vineyard.

Keeping her irritation in check, she glanced at the driver and gave him a small smile. "It seems I'll be using your services tonight, after all."

Chapter 5

His dinner guest had arrived.

A semblance of a smile danced across Spencer's lips as he reached for his jacket on the back of the sofa and put it on. He'd figured that Chardonnay would refuse to ride in the limo so he had taken the necessary steps to deny her a choice. It might have appeared underhanded on his part but he could not entertain thoughts of her driving back home alone late at night.

The moment the limo came to a stop, he walked out the front door of the two-story cottage he was occupying. Standing in the doorway he watched the driver walk around the front of the impressive shining black automobile to open the rear door. The windows were tinted so Spencer couldn't see Chardonnay, which he figured was just as well since chances were she wasn't too happy with him about now. She was a woman who didn't like being told what to do, especially when he was the one doing the telling.

He continued to watch as the chauffeur presented her his hand and she stepped out of the car. Tonight she was wearing her hair up and several strands had escaped confinement and were curling around her face. To his disappointment she was wearing a pair of slacks, which meant he wouldn't be ogling her legs tonight. Too bad, they were such a stunning pair, too gorgeous to be hidden.

His senses remained locked on her every movement and when she glanced his way, a frown settled on her features. He was tempted to cover the distance separating them and kiss that frown right off her face. Instead he continued to stand there, portraying an expression of nonchalance when he felt anything but.

Seeing her again was having one hell of an effect on him, an effect he was struggling to control. Lust in itself was a killer, a yearning of the worst kind. But when you mixed it with obsession, especially one that kept you from thinking straight, you were in deep trouble. The bottom line was that he wanted her. At almost any price. However, she would be the last person to know since that kind of information in her hands would be tantamount to lethal.

"Glad to see you arrive in the car I sent, Chardonnay," he said when she began walking toward him. He tried deciphering her mood and quickly reached the conclusion that she was definitely not a happy camper.

"Did I have a choice?" she asked curtly when she stopped in front of him, tilting her head back to look directly into his eyes.

"No," he said simply, truthfully, before moving aside to let her enter. It was either that or be done in by the turbulent depths of the stormy gray gaze that narrowed at him. His restraint not to reach out and pull her into his arms to smooth her ruffled feathers was weak.

"I thought we were having dinner."

She was standing in the middle of the living room, glancing around. Evidently she had expected to see a table set for two and had noted there wasn't one. He moved toward her, deliberately slow, fighting back the urge to let his gaze slide over her from head to toe. She looked good in her black slacks and a turquoise top. The shade, he thought, complemented her coloring. Since the evenings and nights in the valley could get rather chilly, she had brought a tweed jacket, which was slung over her arms.

"We *are* having dinner," he said. "But I didn't want the food to get cold before you arrived. It won't take long for room service to set things up, and I hope you enjoy the entrée I ordered for us."

She glared at him. "And if I don't?"

She was itching for a fight and he sure as hell had no intentions of obliging her. He was getting used to her moods. Besides, he would be calming whatever storm was brewing inside of her soon enough. Therefore, he responded to her question with a dispassionate shrug and said, "Then I suggest you don't eat it."

He saw the way her lips tightened into an even deeper frown. "Do you always manage to have things your way?" she asked coolly.

"On the contrary," he replied, thinking if that was true she would be in his bed this very moment.

"There are some things I find myself doing without," he added, sliding his hands into his pockets so he wouldn't be tempted to reach out and pull her into his arms, capture her mouth beneath his, and touch her all over. The thought of doing any of those things had his heartbeat accelerating.

To counteract the effect, he nodded toward the huge window and said. "So, what do you think of the view?"

She followed his gaze and an unexpected smile touched her lips, making his guts clench. "It's beautiful," she said with something akin to spellbinding awe in her voice. "But then this is home for me and I've always thought the valley was the most exquisite place to live."

"I'm beginning to believe that, although I love my home in Sausalito."

She turned back around, and met his gaze with an arched brow. "You live in Sausalito?"

"Yes. You sound surprised."

"I am. I thought you would prefer the fast pace of San Francisco instead of the quietness of a small town."

He chuckled. "I grew up in a fast-paced town— Atlanta. I always wanted to live someplace peaceful and serene."

"I'm surprised such a thing doesn't bore you."

"I'm sure there's a lot about me that would surprise you, Chardonnay."

Her expression was one of indifference, and a part of him was determined to change that. "Make yourself comfortable while I call for dinner."

She didn't verbally acknowledge what he said. Instead she moved toward the sofa and sat down. He felt

perspiration form on his brow while watching her graceful movement, appreciating the way her hips swayed,
the slender curves of her body.

Deciding he needed to do something with his hands,
he picked up the residence phone. "This is Spencer
Westmoreland. You can deliver dinner now."

"When will we talk, Spencer?"

She asked the question the moment he'd hung up the
phone. He met her gaze, saw the gray glint that was still
ready for combat. His pure male persona was fighting
an inner war not to put his plan of seduction in place
before it was time. "We'll talk after dinner," he replied.

She reluctantly nodded and he knew that he would
need as much strength as possible, because in dealing with Chardonnay Russell, only the strongest would
survive.

Donnay drew a long, deep breath as she tried to keep
her eyes off Spencer. It was hard. He had received a
phone call and she'd been glad for the slight reprieve.
Now she had time to study him without him being
aware that she was doing so. He was rich, powerful
and suave, and dressed in a pair of expensive trousers,
a white designer shirt and a smooth-cut suede blazer.
He definitely looked the part of a millionaire.

In addition to all that, he was magnificently built:
tall, strong and masculine. The perfect male specimen.
His very presence was causing emotions to flood her
that were better left alone. The man was a predator. He
was ruthless and lethal all rolled into one, but at that
moment she thought he was the most desirable man
she had ever come close to knowing. With a snap of

his fingers he could destroy her and her family's livelihood. And she couldn't let that happen. What she wanted, what she needed to know was why he wanted to marry her. Why he wanted her to have his children. The man was as rich as he was good-looking, so finding a woman to fulfill his every need shouldn't be a problem. So why her?

"I just received good news from home," he said, hanging up his cell phone and reclaiming her thoughts.

She mentally shook off seeing the smile on his lips, the one that sent blood rushing through her veins. "And what is the good news?"

"Thorn and Tara's son came three weeks early."

"Is he okay?"

Spencer chuckled. "The baby and Tara are doing fine. However, I'm not sure about Thorn. I just finished talking to him and I think he's still in a daze. He was there with Tara during the delivery and said it was an awesome experience."

"I'm sure it was."

He didn't say anything for a moment, but his features held a pensive look. And then, as if he'd made his mind up about something, he crossed the room and halted directly in front of where she sat on the sofa. "That's what I want, Chardonnay."

Donnay met his gaze. As far as she was concerned the man wanted a lot of things and it was hard to keep up. "And what is it that you want?"

He stared at her for a moment and then said, "I want to be there when my wife gives birth to our child."

To her surprise, his voice was gentle. Her senses registered his sincerity. And the look in his eyes was intense. Too intense. It was actually sizzling her insides. She hadn't expected that and lifted her head, narrowing her eyes. "Then I suggest you let the woman you intend to marry know that."

"That's precisely what I'm doing."

His gaze had her entire body feeling hot. "Don't fool yourself about that," she tried saying in a calm voice. "I am *not* the woman you're going to marry."

"Can you afford not to be?" he asked smoothly, cool and controlled.

She refused to let him back her against the wall any further. Her back stiffened. "You would use my family's land to force me into marriage with you?"

She watched his mouth hardened around the edges. "Yes, and I wouldn't hesitate doing so."

"And you would marry me, knowing I would despise you for it?"

He nodded. "Yes, because I'll put forth an extra effort each and every day to make sure you would eventually get over it."

She opened her mouth to give him the blasting retort she felt he rightly deserved when there was a knock at the door, indicating their dinner had arrived.

Chardonnay's fragrance was getting to Spencer. It was an arousing scent that made him think of everything other than the half-eaten steak on his plate. The food had been delicious. But then, he figured, so was the woman sitting across from him. He wanted Chardonnay with a passion that, until now, had been foreign to him. During his lifetime he'd never allowed himself to be swept away by passion, infatuation or obsession.

He hadn't done that with Lynette Marie and he'd been quite taken with her. At least he'd thought so at the time. They had met and dated in college, and after graduating they had gone their separate ways, each wanting to devote time to their chosen careers.

Hers had been in broadcasting and she had immediately landed a job at CNN as a television journalist. They had renewed their relationship almost ten years later after bumping into each other while both had been in New York on business. Afterward, they began a long-distance romance, which had worked for the both of them, lasting a couple of years. When he'd felt the time was right, he had asked her to marry him and she had accepted.

A few months after announcing their engagement, she had gone to Bermuda on a three-month assignment. Unfortunately, with his busy work schedule, he never got a chance to visit with her while she was there. Then one morning while shaving, he'd gotten a phone call from her parents informing him of her accidental death.

The coroner's report had indicated that at the time of her death she was six weeks pregnant. Spencer had known the child wasn't his since they hadn't made love in over four months. Her betrayal left him determined to never share his emotions with a woman again. And he had sufficiently heeded that decision…until now.

Inwardly frowning, he lifted his gaze and looked over at Chardonnay from across the table. Other than inquiring about her grandfather's health and other mundane small talk, they hadn't said much during dinner; however, she seemed to be enjoying her meal.

Deciding they had put off the reason she was there

long enough, he said, "Now we'll talk, Chardonnay. But keep in mind we need to stick to the important issues, and I want your decision in forty-eight hours."

She narrowed her gaze at him. "You can't expect me to make up my mind that soon."

"Yes, I can and I do. And I won't change my mind about it. I refuse to give you time to drum up alternatives that I won't go along with. All you'll be doing is wasting both of our time. I presented the two options to you last night. Do you have anything you want to ask me about them?"

"Yes," she said, setting down her wineglass. "If we agree on the loan, what limits and restrictions will you be placing? And what happens if we miss a payment?"

He leaned back in his chair. "The interest rate will be higher than the present market and if you miss a payment, I'll begin foreclosure proceedings before you can bat an eye."

He had been brutally honest and from the look on her face she hadn't liked his answer. He was intentionally making the loan unattractive and blatantly risky.

He watched her hesitate a moment, fiddling with the food on her plate before lifting her head. Her stony-gray eyes met his dark ones when she asked in a curt tone, "This marriage of convenience you want. Just what would you expect of me?"

A smile touched his lips when vivid visions flooded his mind, some so blatantly sexual they made him ache. "I would expect of you what any man would expect of his wife. I want to sleep with you every night, make love to you, get you pregnant—several times—and provide a home for you and our family."

She hesitated again, and then asked, "And after I've ceased being of any value to you?"

He mused, surprised by the question. "Why would you think a time would come when you'd cease being of value to me?"

From the expression on her face he could tell his question confused her, so he decided to ask another. "Just how long did you assume I wanted our marriage to last, Chardonnay?"

She shrugged her shoulders. "Until I had given you all the children you wanted."

He threw his head back and laughed. "Then what was I supposed to do with you after that?"

"Divorce me."

He arched an eyebrow upon realizing she was serious. "There hasn't been a divorce in the Westmoreland family since before I was born. In our eyes, marriage is sacred."

Donnay frowned. "Are you implying that you expect us to stay together *forever?*" she asked with disbelief in her voice.

"Yes, till death do us part. Why wouldn't that be the case?"

He could tell his question caught her off guard. "Because most marriages of convenience are for a set period of time, and usually a rather short one."

"Ours won't be. But I need to make sure you understand that love will not be a factor in our relationship mainly because it won't have a place in our marriage. I don't need it and personally I don't want it."

He paused, wanting to make sure she understood what he was saying. When he continued speaking, his voice was slow and his words were chosen carefully. "If you agree to marry me, you'll be agreeing to a loveless marriage, basically a business arrangement between us. I will treat you with respect and bestow upon you everything that comes with being my wife."

"Except love," she interjected.

He nodded. "Yes, except love."

She didn't say anything for a brief moment. "And if I go along with marrying you, what guarantee do I have that you will give up the idea of turning the winery into some vacation resort?"

"There aren't any guarantees other than my word. And I will give it to you now. If you agree to marry me, Chardonnay, you and your family's financial worries will be over. I will turn my attention toward three things. Getting married, getting you pregnant and doing whatever it takes to escalate the winery to an international scale. I agree that Russell wine is superb and I will put my money into making sure the entire world knows it, as well. I will help build the vineyard into something that we can one day pass on to our children."

"Why?" she asked quietly. "Why is getting married and having children important to you all of a sudden?"

He lifted a brow. "What makes you think my wanting those things is a sudden urge?"

She met his gaze. "Because you would have them already, if you truly wanted them."

He wouldn't admit to her that he'd always wanted children. In fact, that was the main reason he had asked Lynette Marie to marry him. But after her death he had eradicated a family from his agenda...until the moment he had seen Chardonnay. Even now the thought of spending time with her in bed, getting her pregnant with his child, made him hard.

"I'll be thirty-seven in less than six months and over the years I've accumulated a lot of wealth. It's wealth I want to pass on to my offspring and I need a wife to do it," he said.

"No, you don't," she argued. "Men get women pregnant without marriage on their minds all the time." He couldn't help but wonder if she was thinking about her own father since he obviously wasn't in the picture.

"That's another Westmoreland rule," he said with strong conviction. "We take responsibility for our actions, no matter what they are. The only woman I ever intend to bear my child is the woman I'm married to."

His heart began beating like an insistent drum when he watched her push her plate away, signifying that dinner was officially over. He stood and walked over to the phone and called room service to come clear away their plates and to bring them another bottle of wine from Russell Vineyards. After that was done he leaned against the counter and said, "Now I have a question for you."

Her gray eyes flickered his way.

"I know about your involvement with that professor a few years back. Are you involved with anyone now?"

He watched as a dark color stained her cheeks and he could tell that once again she had been caught off guard by one of his questions. She probably felt outrage in knowing he had dug into her past, knew her personal business. "Don't be bothered by the question, Chardonnay. Like I told you before, I make it my business to know everything there is to know about any business partner, and that's exactly what you and I will be if we choose to marry. Partners. There won't be any secrets between us."

"Would it matter?" she all but snapped. "It appears I don't have any secrets you don't know about anyway."

"No, you probably don't," he agreed quietly, thinking he'd let one woman do him in with her secrets and blatantly refused to let such a thing happen again. "You never did answer my question as to whether you're involved with anyone now."

She glared at him. "You seem to know everything there is about me. What do you think?"

He slowly strode over to the table to stand in front of her. "It doesn't matter what I think, Chardonnay. It's what I want to know, what I want you to tell me, what I want to hear from your own lips. And if I ever find out you've deceived me, there will be hell to pay and the Westmorelands will have the first divorce in the family in over fifty years."

A sudden knock on the door announced the arrival of room service. Deciding to let her sit while his words sank in, he moved away toward the door. Minutes later, after the hotel staff had cleared the table and left, they were alone once more and he had no intention of letting her not answer the question he had asked earlier.

Seconds turned into minutes before she finally gave him an answer, after releasing what he considered a frustrated sigh.

"No, I'm not involved with anyone."

He took a step back, satisfied. A smile touched the corners of his lips. "That's good to know, especially considering what I'm about to do," he said, removing his jacket.

She frowned. "And just what are you about to do?"

He glanced at her. "Prove you wrong. I intend to show you that I am most definitely your type."

Chapter 6

Donnay quickly got to her feet. "You will do no such thing!"

She stared at Spencer, wondering if he had lost his mind…and at the same time wondering if she had lost hers, when desire began heating her entire being. She gritted her teeth, refusing to give in to what she was feeling, what was trying to take control of her impeccable good sense.

"Why shouldn't I get the chance to prove I am your type?" he asked, taking off the cuff links to his shirt. "However, if you want to go ahead and concede that you're wrong—"

"I am not wrong!"

"Then prove it," he countered. "Or rather let me prove otherwise."

She held her ground, though she could feel herself

start to tremble. With fear…or desire? "I don't intend to let you prove anything, Spencer."

"That means you either don't know your own mind or you're afraid of what I'm capable of doing to that mind."

The latter was true and in acknowledging that fact, a sensuous shiver rippled down Donnay's spine. Their kiss last night had done things to her she hadn't expected. It had literally blasted her world into another hemisphere. Another kiss might be even more lethal than the last and she had no intentions of playing with fire. Seeing him now, standing there, staring at her with his intense dark eyes, was making her entire body flush with some sort of feminine heat she'd never encountered before. The room suddenly felt hot and she felt hot right along with it and wondered if she was running a temperature. The Spencer Westmoreland kind.

"Do you know what I think? What I truly believe?" he asked in a deep, husky voice that set her body throbbing.

She met his gaze. He was standing in the middle of the room, his legs braced apart in a sexy stance, with his hands in the pockets of his trousers, staring at her with an intensity that nearly made her weak.

"No, and I couldn't care less what you think or believe, but I'm sure you're going to tell me anyway," she said curtly, just as angry with herself as she was with him. Why was he the one man who could cause such conflicting emotions to rip through her?

"I think you're a very passionate woman."

Passionate? Her? He had to be kidding. If he was basing his opinion on what had happened the other night he was way off. Although Robert had never complained, to be quite honest, she never found sex to her liking. It was all right, but definitely nothing she couldn't do without. In her mind it was a process intended to make bodies sweat and give your muscles a fairly good work-out. Nothing more, nothing less, and she was okay with that. But then, she couldn't explain what was happening to her now. She didn't think what she was experiencing had anything to do with passion. It was more akin to lust.

"I think you have me mixed up with someone else," she decided to say. "Either that or you've drunk too much wine and it's screwed up your brain."

He didn't respond and she eyed him as he bent over to remove his shoes and socks. "May I ask what you're doing?" she inquired. He straightened up and kicked his shoes aside.

Another smile touched his lips. "I told you what I'm doing. I intend to prove to you that I'm your type."

She placed her hands on her hips. "Evidently you didn't hear me when I said that you're not doing any such thing, and I don't take you as the type of man who would force himself on a woman."

He smiled. "I'm not, but if a woman begs, then—"

"Beg? The only thing I'll beg is your pardon. Do I look like a woman who would beg a man for anything?"

"Not yet."

He slowly began walking over to her, like a hunter cornering his prey. But she refused to back up. He intended to prove her wrong and she intended to show him she was right. He was cocky, ruthless, domineering...

all the things she never liked in a man. Therefore, he wasn't her type. Men like him turned her off.

Usually.

So why not now? Why was the hard glint in his eyes daring her to look away, making certain parts of her body feel hot, wet and amazingly charged? And why was she suddenly remembering the kiss they had shared last night? The one that had had her purring, had made her want to press closer to him, feel every inch of him against her. The one that compelled her to drape herself over him, find her way into his lap while he claimed her mouth in a way no man had done before.

He came to a stop in front of her and then stood there, almost body to body, face-to-face. "You're remembering last night, aren't you?" he asked, breathing the words against her mouth in a way that nearly moistened her lips.

"No, I'm not remembering last night," she denied.

"Then how about letting me jog your memory?" he said. At the same time he reached up and tenderly caressed her cheek with his fingers.

She forced the lump back down in her throat, the one that was almost responsible for the soft purr that threatened to come out. She was beginning to forget everything, especially just how much she didn't like Spencer. Instead she stood there and stared into his eyes in heated fascination while intense sensations flooded her stomach.

"Do you know I could actually taste you in my mouth all day?"

She licked her lips nervously, thinking Robert had never told her anything like that the day after they'd kissed. And when Spencer's fingers left her cheek to caress the underside of her right ear, she couldn't think at all. She swallowed and forced herself to speak, although the voice that came forth didn't really sound like her own. "Can we talk about something else?"

He chuckled, and she watched how the smile lines spread from one corner of his lips to the other. "Sweetheart, to be quite honest, we really don't have to talk at all. In fact I prefer that we didn't."

Donnay knew what was coming next and tried taking a deep breath to prepare for it, but nothing could have prepared any woman for the mouth that suddenly swept down on hers, taking it, capturing it while at the same time a sweet and delicious tongue danced inside.

Instead of resisting, she met him and let him lead. She thought he had the flavor of peppermint, but the tang of man. A part of her felt a deep need to savor both. Her mind wasn't prepared for this, although it seemed her body was. When she felt his arms wrap around her, pulling her body closer to the fit of his, she became aware of the way the hard, toned muscles of his abdomen complemented the lower part of her body, further stimulating its feminine heat.

In some part of her mind it registered that his hands had moved from her waist and had begun a journey, exploring every inch of her body within their reach. But she was too preoccupied to get caught up in what Spencer's hands were doing. She was too busy drowning in the warm scent of his cologne, and the way his tongue was melding to hers.

Suddenly, however, she did become aware of his hands again when they inched down the back zipper of her slacks and slowly went inside the waistband to touch bare flesh. Her skin sizzled beneath his caress; her entire insides began throbbing. His hands were made for a woman's pleasure. They were manly, yet soft to the touch.

A part of her couldn't believe this was happening or that she was letting it happen. It was as if she'd given up any willpower she had, giving him the liberty to latch on to her mouth, to taste her senseless, to touch her in a way that had a rush of heat flooding her body. Never had she experienced a kiss so intimate, pleasurable, one that had her insides tingling all the way down to her toes. Beneath the onslaught of his mouth she felt breathless, weak in the knees, consumed with desire.

She suddenly realized Spencer had slid her slacks down to her knees and was gripping the bare flesh of her behind that the thong she was wearing didn't cover.

She felt herself slowly falling, then realized that wasn't the case, it was Spencer easing her down onto the sofa. And, as if it had a mind of its own, her body became supple, receptive and nonresistant in his arms. When she felt the soft cushions at her back she opened her eyes and looked up into his at the same time he pulled his mouth away to slip a hand beneath her head. His face hovered above hers as he shifted their bodies to a more comfortable position and lay half propped over her.

Her heart began beating at an alarming rate and the urgency she felt within her couldn't be held at bay. Their faces were close and their gazes were locked. She detected his change in breathing the same moment she detected her own.

Slowly he leaned forward, softly whispered her name

before capturing her lips, playfully nibbling, licking and sensuously torturing them with his tongue and teeth. What he was doing elicited a fierce reaction from her and she closed her eyes against the sensations ripping through her, fearful of losing her sanity.

And then he was kissing her again, even more intensely than before, sweeping her away on a turbulent storm that made a guttural moan escape her lips. And just like before, she kissed him back, needing the taste of him, wanting to be physically close to him. She would probably regret all of this later, but for now, she accepted what she wanted and what she needed.

Drugged by desire, she returned his kiss with a passion and hunger she hadn't known till now. In his arms she turned brazen, wanton. Only Spencer had the ability to rob her of common sense and replace it with something so addictive she couldn't think straight.

The moment she felt cool air hit her skin, she realized he had lifted her blouse, and before she could give a moan of protest, he moved his lips from her mouth to undo the front clasp of her bra with his teeth. The moment her bra fell open and her breasts escaped confinement, he was there, greedily taking one into his mouth, his tongue lavishing pleasure of the most erotic kind.

Then she felt his hand ease inside her thong and possessively clutch her feminine mound just seconds before his fingers stroked her, making her wetter than she was before. She moaned out his name although she tried holding it back.

What he was doing to her down south, coupled with his mouth on her breasts up north was having one tremendous effect and she felt herself floating on a sensuous wave. Nothing she and Robert had done had ever escalated her to this degree of passion. This was foreplay at its finest and experiencing this kind of intimacy nearly shattered her brain cells. She closed her eyes, thinking she'd been dead wrong. He was her type in more ways than one. He was sharing with her the kind of passion she hadn't known she possessed. Forbidden passion. Hidden passion. He was exposing it and making her aware that not only did it exist but it was his for the taking.

And then he shifted his attention to her other breast while his fingers remained between her legs relentlessly stroking her. She opened her eyes, willing her strength back, but she felt as though she was drowning in delicious waves that were completely overwhelming her, possessing her, forcing her to acknowledge his power over her.

He finally let go of her breast and before she could say anything, he captured her mouth again. He interwove his tongue with hers, mated thoroughly, extensively, completely.

Suddenly he pulled back, rested his forehead against hers, breathing in deeply. She had a feeling that, like her, he was fighting hard to reclaim a normal heartbeat, which wasn't easy. Moments later he looked down at her, and she felt herself falling deeper into the intensity of his gaze.

"Tell me," he whispered hotly against her lips. "Tell me you were wrong and that I am your type, your perfect match in every way."

After the way he had made her feel, Donnay felt weak enough to say anything he wanted to hear, but another part of her knew if she did what he asked then he would always consider her putty in his hands. With the strength and willpower that had deserted her earlier, she refused to give in to what he wanted and stubbornly shook her head and said in as firm and absolute a voice as she could, "What I just experienced meant nothing. I still say you aren't my type and we are far from being a perfect match."

"Meant nothing?" He gazed down at her, narrowed his eyes for a fraction of a second and then, to her surprise, moments later smile lines replaced the frown. "Then I will have to work at changing your mind about that, Chardonnay. I hope you're prepared because I love a challenge."

She glared at him. "You can try."

A smile spread from one corner of his lips to the other, and he said, "Don't think for one minute that I won't."

After Spencer opened the rear door to the limousine for Donnay, she hung back. "You aren't riding in the limo to take me home, are you?" she asked with a serious frown on her face.

He met her gaze. "That's my plan."

She narrowed her eyes at him. "Then change it, because it's really not necessary."

"I believe that it is. Your mother and grandmother have enough to worry about with your grandfather's illness. They shouldn't have to worry about you, too."

"They won't, since they know I can take care of myself," she threw over her shoulder as she slid into the back seat of the car.

"Can you?" he asked, easing into the seat beside her. She scooted over, putting distance between them.

He laughed. "If I wanted to bite, Chardonnay, I would have done so earlier tonight when I had the chance."

His words reminded her of one of the places his teeth had been and the hardened tips of her nipples began throbbing in response to the memory. As much as she wanted to, she couldn't forget the skill of his fingers. She immediately glanced out the window so he wouldn't see her blush. The man had a tendency to say whatever it was that pleased him.

Sensing that his eyes were glued to her, she continued looking out the window as the driver pulled away from his cottage. A part of her was mortified at all the things she had allowed Spencer to do to her tonight, but then another part had been deliciously pleased, although she would never admit such to him.

"Don't forget you only have forty-eight hours to give me your decision, Chardonnay."

That statement made her turn toward him. Then she wished she hadn't. In the dimly lit backseat of the car they were separated from the driver's vision by a deeply tinted glass plate. They could see the driver but he couldn't see them. Spencer was lounging casually against the seat in what she assumed he thought was a comfortable position. Personally she thought it was a thoroughly sexy position and, to make matters even worse, his gaze was fixed on her.

Tension, as well as desire, began swelling up within and she dragged in a deep breath to force both back down. She knew at that moment that he was someone she should not get involved with, let alone contemplate marrying. Somehow, she would get out of this mess she had gotten both her and her family in. The last thing she wanted was to be under Spencer's control, because whether she admitted it to him or not, the man had proven tonight that he was more than just her type. He had shown just how easy it would be to lose control and give in to him during a weak moment—and she could see herself having plenty of those types of moments with him.

"I need more time than forty-eight hours."

"I'm truly sorry you think that, but that's all the time you're getting. You'd have to agree that the plans I have to improve and expand the winery are pretty good ones."

"That isn't the only thing that concerns me," she said, breaking eye contact with him to glance back outside the car's window.

"It should be. Whether you want to admit it or not, I've already proven we're compatible."

She turned back and glared at him. "You've proven no such thing. It was simply a kiss and a little fondling that got out of hand."

He started to speak again, stopped and then chuckled before saying, "Think whatever you want. I'm sure the decisions you have to make are rather hard for you, and it's obvious your family depends on you to make the right ones for them. But consider this one thing, Chardonnay. Will you be worse off with me...or without me?"

Conversation between them had stopped several minutes ago and Spencer assumed she was huddled in her corner of the limo angrily sulking. But he should have known that a woman as tough and stubborn as Chardonnay didn't sulk. She had fallen asleep.

He could take that two ways. Either she had gotten bored with him or he had tired her out earlier. And she wanted him to believe she'd merely considered it to be a kiss and a little fondling.

He leaned back against the seat as he continued to watch her, thinking she was definitely a sleeping beauty. His stomach knotted when he was assailed by a wave of memories of what had transpired between them earlier that night. Unfamiliar emotions filled him. He wanted more times like that with her, and he wanted the opportunity to take it further without any thoughts of stopping. He wanted her in his bed.

A shudder suddenly raced through him with that obsession. He'd never been so taken with a woman before. He had given her forty-eight hours, but in his mind she was already his, and what she didn't know was that he would move heaven or hell to have her. When they had lain together on the sofa, her lithe body had seemed the perfect fit for his and they hadn't even connected intimately yet. Just the thought of being inside her sent previously checked emotions flooding all through him. Everything he was feeling was new to him. New, as well as troubling.

He sighed deeply as he continued to watch her sleep, trying to remember the last time he'd done such a thing. With Lynette Marie perhaps? He truly didn't think so. And if he had, it hadn't been with such intensity and concentration as he was doing at this precise moment. Nor with such longing. She evoked a desire and need within him so strong that even now he was tempted to pull her into his arms and wake her in one rather delicious way. And when the chauffeur turned down the mile-long, scenic lane that would carry them to her home, he thought, *Why the hell not?*

He slid across the seat closer to her, gently caressed the side of her face with his fingertips. "Chardonnay, you're home."

He watched as her eyes slowly opened. She stared at him, seeing how close his face was to hers. "Let's kiss good-night before we get out of the car," he urged in a voice that sounded deep and throaty to his ears.

She continued to stare at him and for a minute he thought she would tell him where he could shove his kiss. Instead he noted the exact moment her breathing became labored. The exact moment her eyes became dilated with a need that mirrored his own.

And when she eased her lips closer to his, the warmth of her breath touched him. He decided at that moment that this kiss would be slow and easy but filled with a fervor he wasn't used to giving or sharing. Deciding he needed to hold her in his arms, hold the body he had possessed and claimed as his earlier, he shifted slightly and pulled her into his lap at the same time he reached out and ran his fingers through her hair before lowering his mouth hungrily to hers.

The moment their mouths touched, connected, locked hard, a hot tide of sensations surged through him. When he felt his insides start to burn, he pulled her closer, and the degree of desire and his ravenous need nearly undid him. She had a taste that was more fulfilling than any meal he could ever eat. Unique, rich and overpowering, it soothed a throbbing ache within him on one hand, and started an agonizing one on the other. He tried dragging his common sense to the forefront, forcing his body to get a grip. But the only grip he wanted was a tighter hold on her. The moment her tongue began dueling with his, pure exhilaration invaded his already fevered body.

He shifted his hips and her right along with them, determined to stroke her bottom. Even through her slacks, cupping her in such a personal way had heat blazing through his veins, groans sounding deep in his chest. The next time they were together this way, he wanted her to wear a dress. It would make it easier when he undressed her. And he intended to undress her and touch her all over. He wanted to make love to every part of her body. Just thinking about all he wanted to do had him wound up tight as a coil.

It was only times like this, when they were seeking mutual satisfaction, that they were on one accord and in tune with each other's wants and needs, willing to give in to their desires. Whether she wanted to accept it or not, she was giving herself to him, had given herself to him earlier that evening. Her actions spoke louder than any words could have, so she might as well make up her mind to become his wife. Besides, he wasn't going to listen to her refusal. He wanted to see that heat in her eyes again, hear her labored breath that signified she was as filled with desire as he was. He wanted to make her wet to his touch, sharing every kind of intimacy with her. He wanted to make her come while embedded deep within her.

Deeply engrossed in the kiss, he hadn't been aware

the driver had brought the car to a complete stop until the man thumped on the top of the car. Spencer reluctantly broke off the kiss and pulled back and gazed down at her. There was nothing she could say. No denials, no accusations, no crying foul play. Not this time.

She had wanted the kiss, had enjoyed it as much as he had and they both knew it. Besides, over the next forty-eight hours they both had a lot to think about. He needed to understand why he was swamped by emotions he hadn't known he had. How this young wisp of a woman could overwhelm him the way she had, so quickly and deeply.

"Forty-eight hours," he whispered softly against her moist lips.

Instead of the flaming retort he expected, she nodded and then pulled herself out of his arms, straightening her clothes. He watched her draw in a huge breath before glancing over at him. She exhaled slowly and said, "Are you sure you want me as a wife? I really don't think you know what you're asking for."

He thought about all the satisfaction he'd gotten from what they'd shared back at his place and the limo ride home, all the satisfaction and fulfillment a future with her would bring, and countered by saying, "Yes, I want you as my wife, and I know exactly what I'm asking for."

Chapter 7

Forty-eight hours.

She had only ten of those left and she'd yet to make a decision.

Donnay sighed as she stepped out of the shower and grabbed a towel to dry her body. She reassessed the predicament that she and her family were now facing, and although she didn't want to admit it, marriage to Spencer was the only solution, especially after talking to her grandfather's doctor yesterday. His condition was improving; however, sooner or later he would need the surgery, and the insurance company would deny paying for it since it was considered experimental treatment. That meant even if she opted for the loan, they would run the risk of not being able to keep up the mortgage payments.

She then thought, as she finished dressing for the day, about the pros and cons of marrying Spencer. She would have to endure a loveless marriage, which was the main thing she couldn't get past just yet. She would have to willingly subject herself to spending the rest of her life with a man who didn't love her and would never love her. Given his attitude toward love, she wondered about the woman responsible for breaking his heart.

On the flip side, if she agreed to marry him, her family's financial worries would be over. And the added plus was that he had agreed to take the winery to the next level. Staying a regional mom-and-pop operation had served its usefulness. In order to compete in a broader market and bring in a higher profit, changes needed to be made, and they were changes that could only come about with Spencer's financial support.

She sighed deeply, feeling like the sacrificial lamb. If she were to tell her mother and grandparents about Spencer's outlandish proposal they would be outraged. On the other hand, if she were to waltz in and tell them she had fallen in love with him and planned to marry him, they would become suspicious anyway, since she had made it pretty clear that she detested the man.

The good thing was that she hadn't heard from Spencer since that night he had brought her home in the limo. She considered his absence a blessing. The last thing she needed was for him to further mess with her already muddled mind. With his hands she had been on the brink of her first real orgasm and just thinking about it had hot streaks of sensations rushing through all parts of her. One thing their marriage wouldn't lack was passion. He had more in his mouth and fingers than most men had in their entire body. He wanted kids and she didn't doubt he would have her pregnant within the first year. But then she had longed for kids, and a husband who would love her. Getting one out of two wasn't so bad, she told herself.

Her mind then went back to the passion. Spencer had touched her in ways she had never before been touched, making her feel things she'd never before felt. What happened to her whenever she was around him? Why was it so easy for him to entice her to indulge in things that she really didn't want to do? And why was the thought of being married to him turning her on instead of turning her off?

She knew one thing that was for certain, he was wiggling his way into her family's affections. According to her grandmother and mother, he had visited with her grandfather at the hospital yesterday, and of course everyone thought it had been extremely kind of him to do so.

She glanced around when she heard the knock at the door. "Yes?"

"I have a delivery for you, Ms. Russell."

Donnay felt relieved it was Janice, their housekeeper, and not her mother or grandmother. No doubt they would have questions about the loan. It had been three days since she'd told them they had been approved and she had yet to act on it and they had to be wondering why. As far as they were concerned the loan was the only hope for the winery's survival.

"Come on in, Janice."

Janice walked in carrying a huge vase of red roses that was almost larger than she was. In her late fifties, she was a tiny thing, barely five feet, weighing a little over a hundred pounds. She and her family had worked in one capacity or another at Russell Vineyards for years.

"What on earth," Donnay exclaimed, immediately crossing the room to relieve Janice of the megasize delivery.

The older woman smiled. "They just arrived for you. Aren't they gorgeous?"

Donnay smiled. Yes, they were, and it wasn't hard to figure out who had sent them. "Yes, they are nice," she said, pulling off the card and then making space for the vase on the table that faced the window.

"Well, I need to get back downstairs and prepare Ms. Ruth's and Ms. Catherine's breakfast."

As soon as the door closed behind Janice, Donnay pulled open the card that simply read: *Thinking of you. Spencer.*

Donnay rolled her eyes. In other words, he was sending her a reminder that her time was running out and he expected her decision in the time frame he had given. But when she glanced over at the roses, she had to admit he'd given her a very beautiful reminder.

She remembered the words Spencer had spoken two nights ago, and he was right. She had to decide, in ten hours or less, if she would be worse off with him in her life than she would be without him in it.

Spencer pulled his BlackBerry out of his jacket to check stock market results after noticing Daniel Russell had drifted off to sleep. He could vividly recall sitting at his own grandfather's hospital bedside years ago.

Scott Westmoreland's death from lung cancer had been hard on the Westmorelands since he had been the rock of the family. All of his grandsons, and at the time the one lone granddaughter, Delaney, had learned something from him that would carry them through life to face the many challenges and hardships.

As he placed the BlackBerry back in his jacket, he glanced back over at Chardonnay's grandfather. Yesterday, the two had talked and Daniel had asked if he would return today to shave him and he had. Also yesterday, the man had been a lot more talkative. He had shared with him all his hopes and dreams for the winery and had apologetically told Spencer that he regretted they wouldn't be selling the vineyard to him after all, but that they felt strongly that it should remain in the Russell family. His words had let Spencer know Chardonnay had yet to tell her family about his offer. He didn't know if that was a good sign or a bad one. But a part of him was confident she would end up doing the right thing—which would be to marry him.

Suddenly he became aware that someone was watching him. He glanced up and felt a tantalizing throb in his gut when he saw it was Chardonnay. At that very instant it seemed that he couldn't breathe. She was standing in the doorway to the hospital room staring at him. Her eyes weren't glaring or shooting daggers at him. They were just staring. He was certain she was wondering why he was there, and before she could ask, he stood and beckoned her to follow him into the hall so they could speak privately and not disturb her grandfather.

"I dropped by this morning to shave him," Spencer said as soon as they had stepped into the hall.

She nodded. "I know. Mom told me that he asked you to do it yesterday. Any one of us could have done it for him but I guess it's a man's thing." She then smiled sheepishly and said, "Or it could be that the last time we shaved him we left him with quite a few cuts and nicks."

"Ouch." His response made her laugh and Spencer found himself relaxing somewhat…as well as taking the time to notice her outfit. She was wearing a pair of jeans and a light blue pullover sweater. Both looked good on her and the light blue brought out the color of her eyes in a pretty way.

"Thanks for the flowers. They're beautiful," she said.

"You're welcome."

When a moment passed and they didn't say anything, she said, "We need to talk, Spencer. I've made my decision but I don't want to go into it here."

He met her gaze. "Okay. Let's have dinner tonight."

"All right, but not at your place again."

He started to argue, to tell her she was in no position to make decisions, but then thought better of it. Dinner tonight would be about decisions—hers—and he wanted to know which ones she had made no matter where they dined.

"And I prefer meeting you someplace. Don't waste your time sending a car for me because I won't get in it," she added curtly.

He nodded. "Okay, I won't be sending a car for you. I'm coming to pick you up myself and I do expect you to get in."

He saw her stiffen, her jaw set tight. "I'll be there to pick you up at five," he said.

She glanced down at the floor where she was tapping her foot. Probably counting to ten to hold back her anger, he thought. She had a tendency to dislike him giving her orders. "Are we on this evening for dinner at five, Chardonnay?" he asked, deciding to make sure they were on the same page.

She glanced back up at him. Her gaze was made of stone. "Do I have a choice?"

"No."

He said it quickly and unerringly.

"I have a request to make of you," she said, and from the look in her eyes he knew he wouldn't like it.

"What?"

"Promise me that you'll keep your hands and lips to yourself tonight."

He couldn't help but smile at that one. "Does that mean I can't kiss you…or touch you anywhere I want?" he asked as calmly as he could.

"Yes, that's exactly what it means."

He shrugged broad shoulders. "In that case I won't make such a promise because I plan to kiss you, Chardonnay. I like kissing you, and as long as you kiss me back, letting me know you're enjoying the kiss as much as I am, I see no reason to stop. And need I remind you that you initiated the last kiss we shared? I might have had my mouth in the right place at the right time, but it was you who made the first move."

He hated reminding her of that, but she needed to hear it. She needed to know that he was fully aware each and every time she participated in their kiss. "But as far as touching you like I did before, unless you give me a reason to think you want me to touch you there, I won't, since I've accomplished what I intended to do."

She frowned. "Which was?"

"Claim it as mine." Before she could open her mouth

to deny his words, he said, "When your grandfather wakes, let him know I'll be stopping by again tomorrow."

"Why?" she asked when he was about to turn and leave.

He smiled. "Mainly because I like him. He reminds me a lot of my own grandfather and I was close to him. All his grandchildren were. He left a huge void in our lives when he died. He was a good man, and I believe your grandfather is a good man, as well."

Deciding not to say anything else, he walked off toward the bank of elevators.

"Did your grandfather wake up and ask about me?"

Donnay turned from gazing out the car window to find Spencer looking over at her when he'd stopped at a traffic light. Just like he'd said, he had arrived exactly at five. She had been ready.

"Yes, and he seemed pleased that you would be returning tomorrow," she said, not liking it but being totally honest. She could tell her grandfather liked Spencer. So did her mother and grandmother. "You never said where we're going," she decided to say when the car began moving again.

"Into San Francisco. There's a nice restaurant I want to take you to. I think you're going to like it."

She was sure she would since it seemed that Spencer Westmoreland didn't do anything half-measure.

"Tell me about this surgery the doctor wants your grandfather to have."

She glanced over at him. "Who told you about it?"

she asked, annoyed. It was family business and he wasn't family.

"Your mother and grandmother. They seemed worried that it wouldn't be covered by the insurance."

She wished her family hadn't taken Spencer into their confidence. But they didn't know how he could use such information to his benefit. However, since they had done so, she figured she might as well level with him. "There's a good chance it won't be since it's considered experimental."

"And if they don't, what's your next option?"

She sighed deeply. Did he look at all solutions by way of options? "If the insurance company denies payment then we'll pay for it out of our pockets. Either way, if Gramps needs that surgery then he's going to have it."

She knew Spencer was probably taking this all in and in doing so figured she had only one option open to her. The one he wanted her to take. He must be feeling pretty good knowing he had her family stuck between a rock and a hard place.

"You're right," he said, breaking into her thoughts. "Either way if your grandfather needs that surgery then he's going to get it. I'll take care of the cost, no matter what option you've decided to take."

Donnay snatched her head around, thinking she had definitely not heard him correctly. He'd come to another traffic light and was looking at her. "Why would you do that?" she asked, barely getting the words out and staring at him wide-eyed.

"Would you believe because I'm a nice guy?" he asked.

"No. I think that you can be a nice guy but that usually you aren't."

He chuckled. "My family would be the first to disagree with you. The personal side of me is nice all the time, but oftentimes, I have to take on another persona when I'm negotiating business. It comes with the territory. In that arena, nice guys finish last, and I like being first."

She believed him. "I don't want you to think the Russells are a charity case that need your handout, Spencer."

"I appreciate you telling me that, Chardonnay," he said, and she easily picked up the edge in his voice. "But the truth remains, charity case or not, your family needs my financial assistance and I'm willing to give it either way. Do you have a problem with that?"

Saying she did would, in essence, be the same as biting off her nose to spite her face, and she was too smart to do that. There was such a thing as family pride, but then there was also such a thing as knowing when to exercise good common sense. "No, I don't have a problem with it. Thank you for making the offer."

"You're welcome. And now it seems that we've arrived at our destination."

A frown darkened Spencer's brow as he watched Chardonnay finish the last of her dessert. What he'd told her in the car was true in most circumstances, but he was finding himself being a rather nice guy in his business dealings with her. Case in point, he hadn't immediately asked for her decision the moment the two of them had sat down to dinner. Nor had he inquired as to what it was over dinner. Instead he had engaged her in conversation about other things, things he normally didn't give a damn about, like who was messing around with whom in Hollywood or which rapper had offended Bill O'Reilly or vice versa.

Now he couldn't put off asking any longer, nor did he intend to. "So what have you decided, Chardonnay?"

He watched as she lifted her head and her gray eyes stared at him. She placed her fork down then took a napkin and wiped her lips. They were lips he had thought about kissing all evening. Suddenly the room seemed to get silent as he tuned everything out to concentrate on one thing. Her decision.

She continued to look at him directly and he knew whatever she'd decided that he hadn't made things easy for her. That had been deliberate on his part. But now, if her decision went the way he wanted, she wouldn't have to think of anything hard again. He would guarantee it… Almost. There was still that question regarding her degree of loyalty. That was important to him and it was something he had to be certain that he had from her, no matter what.

"I've decided to marry you, Spencer."

Her statement seared through him, made his heart squeeze tight and had blood pulsing rapidly through his veins. She bowed her head to resume eating and a frown gathered between his brows. Had she really meant it? His jaw tightened at the thought that she was playing with him.

"Chardonnay?"

"Yes?" She lifted her head again and for a long moment his eyes stared into hers. A deep desire to have her slowly replaced any irritating thought he'd had. She had been serious. She would marry him. For better or for worse. And she was accepting her fate of a loveless marriage. He gave a mental shrug, refusing to feel guilty. It was her decision.

"We need to make plans. I want the wedding to take place before Christmas."

Her eyes widened. "That's impossible. Christmas is less than three weeks from now."

"I know. We had a Christmas wedding in the family last year when my cousin Chase married. In fact it was on Christmas Day. Everyone had to make arrangements to be away from their homes during the holidays to attend. At this late date some people may have already made other plans this year. I prefer having a private ceremony before Christmas, here in the valley with just our families."

She narrowed her eyes at him. "What's the rush?"

"I'm surprised you would ask me that, Chardonnay." He knew she could read between the lines quite clearly and she proved it when her cheeks darkened.

"I guess you wouldn't entertain the thought of us waiting to get to know each other a lot better before engaging in something so intimate," she said softly.

"No, I wouldn't," he said quickly, deciding to once again make his position clear. "I want you, Chardonnay. I've never hidden that fact. And I want babies. Marrying you will give me all the things I want and you will benefit from the marriage, as well."

A frown formed on her face. "And what will you tell your family about us? What am I supposed to tell mine?"

He picked up his wineglass to take a sip. "We'll tell them we met and fell in love immediately. It will be a lie of course, but considering…"

She raised a brow. "And they're supposed to believe it? Just like that?" she asked, snapping her fingers.

He leaned forward. "Yes, just like that," he said, snapping his own fingers. He chuckled. "My mother won't have a problem believing it since she's a true romantic."

He then straightened in his chair and said, "I'm flying out to L.A. for a few days to attend several prescheduled business meetings. When I get back I plan to move into your home, so make room."

"What?" She looked incredulous.

"Now that you've given me your decision—one I will trust you to keep—work will begin on the winery immediately after I get back and I need to be around for that. If there's not room for me at the main house, I'll settle with living in one of the guest cottages. I'll remain there until we marry."

From her expression he could tell he was moving too fast for her, but he had no intentions of slowing down.

Donnay stood outside her mother's bedroom door, trying to get a grip on her nerves. She had exchanged very few words with Spencer during the drive back home from the restaurant. Instead they preferred the silence since there had been very little left to be said.

Now she was to convince her family that she had miraculously fallen in love with him. Her grandparents might fall for that story but her mother would see through it. Taking in a deep breath, Donnay knocked on the door.

"Come in."

Donnay opened the door, stepped into the room and paused. Her mother was dressed to go out and she looked absolutely stunning. She couldn't recall the last time her mother wore something out other than slacks and a blouse. Tonight she was wearing a dress Donnay had never seen before. The soft tobacco-brown fabric slithered down her mother's curves.

"You're going out, Mom?" Donnay asked, although the answer was obvious.

Her mother gave her an easy smile. "Yes. How do I look?"

"Beautiful."

"That's good. That friend I told you about who's passing through, we're meeting for dinner tonight."

Donnay continued to look at her mom. "In that case I think you look too beautiful to be going out with an old girlfriend. You should be going on a date with a man."

Her mother chuckled. "Haven't we had this discussion before?"

"Yes, several times," Donnay agreed, leaning against the closed door.

"And what have I always told you?" her mother asked.

She'd always told her that she could never love another man the way she'd loved her father and that she was content and didn't need another man in her life, a man she could never love. Donnay wondered if that was the same for Spencer. Was there a woman out there whom he loved and that was the reason he could not love another?

"You're worried about something, Donnay," her mother said, breaking into her thoughts. "Come. Let's sit and talk." Her mother sat down on the bed.

With a deep sigh, Donnay crossed the room to take a seat beside her mother.

"Okay, tell me what's bothering you."

Donnay let out a breath, not sure how she was going to say it. Then she decided to just get it out. She turned toward her mother. "Mom, it's about Spencer Westmoreland."

Ruth raised a brow. "What about Mr. Westmoreland? Did you know he came back to visit your grandfather today?"

"Yes, I know."

"I think your grandfather likes him."

"I can believe that."

Ruth studied her daughter. "So what's bothering you about Mr. Westmoreland?"

Donnay felt her stomach tighten into knots. "He's asked me to marry him, Mom, and he wants to have a private ceremony here in the valley before Christmas."

Ruth looked stunned. "You're kidding, aren't you, sweetheart?"

Donnay shook her head. "No, Mom, I'm not kidding and it's the only way."

Ruth frowned. "The only way for what?"

Donnay took the next twenty minutes to tell her mother everything, including the details of the loan as well as Spencer's proposal.

Her mother didn't say anything for a moment then

said in a relatively calm voice, "You must have misunderstood Mr. Westmoreland."

Donnay rolled her eyes. Spencer had her mother and grandparents convinced that he was Mr. Nice Guy. "Trust me, Mom, I understood Spencer perfectly."

Ruth shook her head. "If what you say is true, Donnay, then how can you even think your grandparents and I would let you go ahead with such a marriage? You mean more to us than the winery."

Instinctively Donnay reached out and took her mother's hand in hers. "I know, Mom, but it's something I must do."

Ruth studied her daughter. "And could it be something that you *want* to do, as well?"

Donnay couldn't believe that her mother would ask such a thing. "Of course not. You of all people know how I feel about that man."

Ruth patted her daughter's hand a few times before asking, "Did I ever tell you that I disliked your father at first, too?"

Donnay looked back at her mother, surprised. "No, you never mentioned that. I assumed, considering how much you loved him, that it was love at first sight."

Ruth chuckled. "Far from it. I saw him as a threat."

Donnay lifted her brow. "A threat? To what?"

"To my relationship with Dad. Dad hired him on and the two of them quickly became close. I saw Chad as the son Dad never had, and I began thinking that Dad would regret I was born a girl and not a boy who would carry on the Russell name."

Donnay thought about what her mother had said for

a moment then asked, "Did my father know how you felt?"

"Yes, I wasn't the easiest person to get along with and at times I deliberately made things hard for him. At least I tried to. But he saw through it all. And for some reason he understood."

Her mother got quiet and Donnay knew she was remembering those times, and recapturing those moments. It had to be hard for her mother. Donnay wished there was a way she could convince her to leave the valley for a while to find the man she loved and had allowed to walk out of her life. There had been times while in college when Donnay had been tempted to look up Chad Timberlain, get to meet the father she never knew and who didn't know she existed. But she never did.

For all she knew, and what her mother suspected, he was now married with other children. Children who were her half siblings. She never got the courage to find him because she hadn't ever wanted to be the one to verify her mother's assumptions that the man she loved and had let get away had another life that included a wife and children.

"Mom, I appreciate you sharing that with me about you and Dad, but the situation with me and Spencer is totally different. I appreciate what he did for Gramps, but he's not the man you and Grammy think that he is."

Her mother touched her arm. "And considering everything, I have a feeling he's not the man you think that he is, either, Donnay."

Chapter 8

An aura of intense longing swept over Spencer the moment he rounded the corner of the building where he was told he would find Chardonnay doing a wine tasting. It had been almost a week since he'd seen her and he'd been stunned as to just how much he'd missed her, to the point that once his plane had landed in San Francisco, he had driven straight to the Russell Vineyard.

He followed the sound of voices and stepped into the crowded tasting room. Chardonnay was to taste the first wine to be bottled and packaged from this season's pruned crop. If the wine passed her inspection, it would continue to age.

Shivers of awareness passed through him when he saw her. She was standing on a platform facing the crowd—a Russell who was about to place verdict on a Russell wine. She stood before a table that held four glasses filled with wine. Sun shining through the huge windows slanted glints of gold on her head, adding highlights to her hair. Emotion gripped his gut at the sight of her. She was the most strikingly beautiful woman he knew, the woman who would become his wife and the mother of his children. She had been on his mind constantly since he'd left the valley, but no memory could compare with the woman in the flesh.

He watched as she rotated the glass a few times on the table. According to what he knew about wine tasting, she was swirling the wine around in the glass to mix it with air. The motion would cause the aromatic compound in the wine to vaporize and get that unique smell.

Moments later she picked up the glass and brought it to her face, sticking her nose into the airspace of the glass where the aromas were captured. Tempting visions, erotic in nature, filled his mind and fueled his imagination. While she was concentrating on the wine's scent, he was remembering hers, the one he considered sharply seductive, the one that could send sensations racing through him the moment it filled his nostrils.

Trying to get a grip, he watched as her eyes closed before she took a sip. He remembered another time he had watched her close her eyes like that. That night she had been at his place. The same night he had decided that no matter what it took, he had to make Chardonnay Russell his.

She opened her eyes and the smile that touched her lips was priceless. He knew the wine she had just tasted had successfully passed her inspection. Of course it would go through other tasters, but everyone knew her opinion counted most. Nodding her approval, she moved on to the next glass.

He leaned back against a solid wall. He had a clear view of her but doubted she had seen him yet, which was just fine. She would know his presence in all things, especially her life, soon enough.

His trip to Los Angles had been very productive. He had met with Steve Carr, the man whose construction company would be responsible for the expansions he wanted made to the winery. Work would begin rather quickly and he was getting excited about it and couldn't wait to tell Chardonnay so she could share his excitement.

When he heard everyone around him clapping, his concentration went back to Chardonnay. She had tasted all four glasses and evidently had approved all of them. Then, as her gaze spanned the crowd, she saw him. The moment their eyes connected, even if only for a brief second, he felt it as well as saw it. He saw the darkening of her eyes at the same moment he felt deep need pass through him.

She broke eye contact to speak with the people who had begun gathering around her. After she thanked them for upholding the Russell tradition in producing superb wine, she excused herself from the group and began walking his way. He hadn't moved an inch and his gaze flicked across her from head to toe as she made her way toward him.

He was mesmerized, utterly captivated. And not for the first time he was asking himself how one woman could snag a man's emotions so thoroughly and completely.

"You're back," she said in a tone of voice that didn't give away whether she was delighted or disappointed.

"Yes, I'm back. Have you set a date for the wedding?" he decided to ask, thinking there was no reason not to.

She gave a resigned shrug of her shoulders and her voice was very cool when she said, "Did I have a choice?"

If she expected a softening of his heart, she wasn't getting it today. "That depends on what you want and what's important to you," he replied in a voice that was painstakingly clear. "And I thought we'd gotten beyond all of that, Chardonnay. No need to whine about it now."

She narrowed her gaze. "Is that what you think I'm doing?"

"Sounds like it. What I was really hoping for was a nice welcome-home kiss."

"Sorry to disappoint you," she said sarcastically.

She had disappointed him but not surprised him. He smiled, thinking he would make doubly sure she made up for it later. However, he definitely wouldn't tell her that. Instead he decided to change the subject. "I spoke with your grandfather yesterday. He sounds good."

She smiled and he could tell it was genuine and sincere. "Yes, we're all pleased with his progress. If it continues he'll be able to come home at the end of the week. The doctor wants to give him time to build up his strength before planning the next phase of his treatment."

"The surgery?"

"Yes. They want to schedule it sometime after the holidays, providing his health continues to improve.

I'm going to visit with him later. Would you like to come with me?"

He was surprised by the invitation and had no intentions of turning it down. "Yes, I'd like that, but first I need to make arrangements to have my things moved here from the Chablis."

He watched her mouth tighten. "You're still planning on living here?"

"Yes, nothing has changed," he said in an even tone. "All my plans are still the same. The ones I have for the winery as well as the ones I have for us. And speaking of which, your mother said you would be the one to show me to the guest villa."

"Yes, I guess I am," she said, her voice trailing off as she turned around and noticed everyone had begun to leave.

"Yes, sweetheart, you definitely are," he said softly.

Donnay turned back to Spencer, trying not to let the throaty tone of his voice take over her senses and make her forget how he had succeeded in turning her entire life upside down. And then there was the term of endearment he'd just used. *Sweetheart.* It had a nice ring to it, but was actually meaningless in their situation.

The shutting of the door claimed her attention and she was grateful for the distraction until she saw that everyone had gone and she and Spencer were left alone. Definitely not a good thing. Especially when simply standing close to him was making all sorts of wanton thoughts flow through her head. Those boundaries she had set the last time they'd been together were fading away and she couldn't let that happen.

"If you're ready, I can walk you over to the guest villa. It's not far from here," she heard herself saying, as she took a step back, away from him.

In a surprised move, one she hadn't been prepared for, he reached out, snagged her arm and pulled her back closer. "Not yet. There's something I need to do first."

His touch had every nerve in her body tingling and as usual she had immediately drawn to him. From the look in his eyes she knew he wanted to kiss her, was going to kiss her, and as much as she didn't want to, she felt the anticipation of his kiss all the way down to the bone. She refused to play coy. She wanted this.

"Do you know how many nights I lay awake thinking about you?" he whispered, leaning closer to let his mouth brush her cheek. She could feel the warmth of his breath on the underside of her ear. Not waiting for her response, he answered his own question by saying in a husky voice, "Way too many nights."

And then unerringly, his mouth found hers, locked on to it, claimed it and successfully obliterated any and all coherent thoughts from her mind. Instead she concentrated on only one thing—his tongue and the way it was stroking hers, tangling with it in a deeply intimate way, sending sensuous chills up her spine, making goose bumps form on her arms and leaving no doubt in her mind that he had succeeded in touching something deep inside of her once again. He moved her in a way no other man could and she doubted ever would. A part of her knew she should reclaim her senses, put on the brakes. But she couldn't, nor did she want to. The way he was kissing her, so deep, sensual and intimate, he was making it plainly difficult, absolutely impossible, not to respond in kind. So she did.

She knew the exact moment her arms voluntarily reached around his neck to hold his mouth to hers, as well as when she felt his warm, hard fingers entwine in her hair. She also felt the heat of his body pressed intimately to hers, every hard plane and indentation, and she sank helplessly deeper into his strength, while he sank deeper into her mouth. His kiss was filling her with a physical yearning she only encountered with him.

When their lips finally parted, he pulled her closer into his arms, holding her, and they remained that way, silent for the moment.

Knowing she couldn't afford to give in to any sort of weakness or throw away good common sense, she pulled out of his arms. "I think we need to make some ground rules," she said in a shaky breath.

"I don't" was his response, as he brushed a stray curl back from her face. "Every time I kiss you that way, I want to proceed and strip you naked."

Like he'd come close to doing that other night, she thought. "I'd rather keep my clothes on around you. I think it's safer."

"Safer but not as satisfying. I think you should stop trying to fight me, Chardonnay, and give in to your wants and desires."

She shook her head. "I can't."

He held her gaze. "Yes, you can and eventually you will. We are perfect for each other."

She inhaled deeply as her mind absorbed his words. He might think the two of them were perfect but she did not. She refused to become too enthralled with any man again, let him take over her mind and thoughts. Besides that, Spencer was a man who could wiggle his way into a woman's heart if she wasn't careful. He would have her falling in love with him even though she knew he would never love her back.

"I would have to disagree with that," she said with conviction. "Now I suggest that I show you to the guest villa."

She hoped they were back to square one. No matter how much she might respond to his kiss and intimate caresses, she had to prove that nothing had changed. She still considered him a threat to her happiness.

As they walked along the path, Donnay was surprised at how relaxed she suddenly felt in Spencer's presence. It was as if the torrid kiss they'd shared moments ago had been what she needed to ease the tension.

"How many guesthouses do you have?" Spencer asked, breaking into the silence surrounding them. They were strolling a path very familiar to her, one she had always enjoyed as a child because the area surrounding it was always manicured, while the land beyond was overgrown with blackberry, raspberry and tomato vines.

"We have four guest villas, and a gardener's cottage that's located at the edge of the vineyard," she said, remembering the day she had planted her very first grapevine nearby. Her grandfather had given her the space to grow her own to keep her from picking and eating the ones to be used for the wines.

"The guest villa you'll be staying in is actually where I was going to live when I returned from college. I never moved in since I preferred staying at the big house with my mother and grandparents. I felt it would be lonely living there and too far away from things."

"But you will be living there with me, once we're married."

She glanced over at him. He hadn't asked a question but had made a statement he expected her to obey. A part of her wanted to rebel but she knew there was no use. In the end he would get what he wanted. "Yes, I'll be living there with you."

He smiled, seemingly satisfied with her acceptance of her fate. "Will you help me move in today?" he then asked.

Considering they seemed to be drawn together like magnets whenever they were alone, she didn't think that was a good idea. "There are some things I need to do before visiting Gramps at the hospital."

He nodded. "I understand and that's fine. But I'm counting on you to help me later since I'm sure I'll still have a few things that will need unpacking when we get back from the hospital."

She knew he was letting her know that he wouldn't allow her to put distance between them. Whether she liked it or not, they would be spending time together later tonight. "We had the phone service and electricity turned on a few days ago so you're all set," she said.

"Okay."

When they didn't say anything for several moments, he broke the silence by asking, "So you said you'd decided on a date?"

"Yes, I thought two weeks from this Saturday would do it. What do you think?"

He chuckled. "I think it's time to give my family a call and tell them about you. Of course they would want to attend the wedding ceremony. Wild horses won't be able to keep Mom away." He tilted his head and looked at her. "I see you've already told yours since your grandmother and mother congratulated me and welcomed me to the family when I arrived today."

She shrugged. "I saw no reason not to go ahead and tell them. I basically told my mother the truth regarding our relationship. However, I led Grammy to believe we miraculously fell in love."

"And your grandfather?"

She stopped walking and gazed up at him. "I haven't told him anything yet, and Mom and Grammy promised they wouldn't, either. I thought it was best to wait until you returned so we could tell him together."

Spencer nodded. "And how do you think he'll take the news?"

Donnay couldn't help the wry smile that touched her lips. "Oh, he'll handle it quite nicely since your plans fall so neatly in with his. He's been after me for some time about finding a man, settling down and giving him great-grandkids. So in essence, you'll be giving him something he truly wants."

"And it's something I truly want, as well," he said, smiling over at her. "And I'm more than happy to oblige."

They began walking again and she was glad moments later when they came to the private path that led to the guest villa where he would be staying. As soon as she got him there she planned to hightail it to the nearest shower to cool off. The man had a way of heating her body with a touch or a mere look. Resisting him was becoming a challenge.

"This path leads to the villa, the one you'll be using," she said, turning to walk a few steps ahead of him down the trail. "It's surrounded by a wrought-iron fence and is secluded enough to assure complete privacy. It's like your own little world inside a bigger universe."

He smiled. "It reminds me of a French château and I like it already," he said when he reached the gate and he saw the huge two-story structure. From his expression she could tell it was more than he had expected. "Who was this place built for?" he asked when she opened the gate for them to enter.

"No one in particular. The other villas are relatively small compared to this one and Gramps wanted to construct one that was larger and roomier. Like I said earlier, I think it was meant for me, although he would never admit he would do anything to persuade me to stay if I ever decided to leave. He felt pretty bad about what happened between my mother and father."

Spencer lifted a brow. "What happened between your parents?"

Donnay glanced over at him as they strolled up the walkway toward the front door. "They met when my father took a summer job here. He was in the army and was working at the winery while waiting to be deployed. He met and fell in love with my mother and she fell in love with him, too. He tried convincing her to marry him and travel the world with him since he planned on making the military a career. Although she loved him, she turned down his marriage proposal and sent him away because she didn't want to leave my grandparents alone. She felt her place was here with them at the vineyard. It was only after he left that she discovered she was pregnant with me."

Spencer paused, his hand on the doorknob. "So he never knew about you?"

"No. She tried writing him but the letter came back. Evidently he moved around a lot in the military."

"And you never tried finding him?"

She shook her head. "No. It's not that I never wanted to know Chad Timberlain—it's just that I knew developing a relationship with him would be a constant reminder to my mother of the love she gave away. That would be painful for her, especially if he had eventually married someone else over the years. My grandfather has always felt he and Grammy were unintentionally responsible for Mom turning her back on her true love, although they tried convincing her they would be fine here and that she should follow her heart."

When he opened the door she took a step back. "You don't really need me to give you a tour of the place so I'll leave you alone now."

He leaned in the open doorway, his stance nearly overpowering. "What time do you want to leave for the hospital?"

"Anytime after five will be okay. Grammy is spending the night with Gramps tonight. We prefer that she didn't because she'll be sleeping on a cot they bring into the hospital room, which won't be all that comfortable. However, no matter what Mom and I say she's determined to do so. After fifty years of marriage, I think she misses him."

He nodded. "I understand. Although my parents

haven't been married quite that long, they have a strong marriage, as well."

"Do they?"

"Yes. Like I told you, strong and long-lasting marriages run in the Westmoreland family."

Yes, he had told her that. "Well, I'll see you later," she said backing up to leave. If you'd like, you're welcome at lunch. Grammy usually has it on the table around one. If you want to get back to the main house just follow the path and you won't get lost."

"All right, and thanks for the invitation. I might take you up on it."

"You're welcome," she said, forcing a cheerful smile before turning and quickly walking away.

"I appreciate you offering to help," Spencer said, ignoring Chardonnay's raised brow as he opened the door to the villa later that night. He knew she was thinking she hadn't offered. He really hadn't given her a choice in the matter.

She hesitated before stepping over the threshold and he strolled in behind her, closing and locking the door. He watched her glance around for a few minutes, and then she turned to him with a bemused expression. "I expected to see boxes all over the place."

He smiled in a perfectly calm way. "Did you?"

"Yes. You said you needed my help putting things away."

"I do. But everything didn't arrive today, so I have time."

The suspicion he saw in her eyes then became more pronounced. "In that case why am I here?" she asked, placing her hands on her hips "Why did you lead me to believe that you needed me tonight?"

She would have to ask, he thought as he leaned against the closed door and stared at her. And since she had, he would be completely honest when he gave her an answer. "Because I *do* need you tonight."

Donnay inhaled sharply. The tone of his voice, the intent of his words both were a soft caress across her skin. Their gazes held and she felt it, unquestionably. His eyes were so dark she actually felt their intensity, could see the desire lining their depths. An instant passed, and then another and she felt herself getting breathless beneath the depth of their attraction for each other. Regardless of wanting to deny it, she couldn't.

She opened her lips to say whatever he needed tonight was his problem and not hers, but closed them when shivers raced up her spine. He was doing that to her and hadn't even touched her, hadn't even moved away from the door. His concentrated stare was making crazy things happen to her.

Sensations began gripping her and she felt the tips of her breasts grow hard as she remembered his mouth, tongue and teeth on them. She also remembered the place his fingers had been and felt a sudden ferocious ache right between her legs. She shook her head, trying to clear her mind of such memories and found it was no use. She then concluded that what she had deemed as *his* problem was now *her* problem, as well.

She watched as he came toward her and she had the mind to take a step back and couldn't. Every fiber in her being was attuned to him, attracted to him, aroused by him. She couldn't resist him any longer. Nor did she want to.

"I want you and I need you, Chardonnay," he whispered huskily when he came to a stop in front of her.

She tilted her head back and looked at him, felt the heat coming from his gaze. And when he reached out and slipped his hands around her waist, bringing her body against the solid hardness of him, she inhaled when she felt his rock-hard erection press against the juncture of her thighs. Even the denim of her skirt couldn't downplay just how firm he was.

For moments he held her close against him, as if he needed the contact as much as she did. It then became crystal clear that her life and her future were going to be tied to him. He said he wanted a long-term marriage and a bunch of kids and she believed him; so why not accept how things were destined to be for her and move on? Why continue to fight what she couldn't change? Her grandfather was happy about their pending marriage, so was her grandmother. However, she could tell her mother was more worried than elated.

"Chardonnay?"

She tilted up her head to stare into his face. "Yes?" He was a strikingly handsome man. The thought of having a son or daughter who shared his features pulled on her heartstrings.

"I've told you what I want and need. Now it's your turn. Tell me what I can do for you tonight. If you say there's nothing you want or need from me then I will accept that and walk you back home. But if you have desires, I will not let you leave here unsatisfied."

Donnay swallowed because that's what she was

afraid of. Spencer had unraveled her emotions in a way that Robert never had. What she should do was tell him good night and leave. Instead she found herself asking in a soft, curious voice, after remembering her intimate times with Robert, "What makes you think you can?"

He raised a dark brow. "Can what?"

"Satisfy me."

She watched as a slow, confident smile touched both corners of his lips. "Why would you think I can't?"

Since they would be getting married soon and he was determined that they would share a bed, she decided to be honest with him. She might be one of those women a man couldn't completely satisfy. "Robert didn't."

His brow arched higher. "The professor?"

"Yes, the one and only guy I've slept with."

"I can't imagine any man making love to you and not making you feel like an explosion hit and that every part of you has been shot to the stars and beyond."

Donnay couldn't imagine anyone making her feel that way. "And how will you accomplish that?"

The look in his eyes indicated that he couldn't believe she really had to ask. But he answered anyway. "First, I'll undress you, kissing every part of you that I expose, lingering on some areas a lot longer than others. Next I'll take you into the bedroom and engage in foreplay of the most intense kind. So intense that I'll have you begging."

She shook her head. He'd made that claim before and she recalled how close she'd come to doing just that the night when he'd invited her to his place at the Chablis. "Is that what you think, that you'll make me beg?"

"No, sweetheart, that's what I know. In addition to

long marriages, there's something else Westmorelands are known for."

She was almost afraid to ask but did so anyway. "And what's that?"

"Satisfying their mates. We are extremely physical beings who enjoy making love. Our sexual needs are sometimes inexhaustible."

Donnay felt a frantic tug between her thighs. "Thanks for the warning."

"It's the decent thing to do since I plan to keep you in bed with me quite a lot after we get married."

She wondered if he was joking, although the look in his eyes said otherwise. "Do I have a choice in the matter?"

His smile was amusing. "I guess you could always claim a headache, but I doubt that you would want to."

For some reason she doubted it as well, although she would never admit it to him. He was too sure of himself already.

"You know what?" he asked, breaking into her thoughts.

She heard the serious tone in his voice. "What?"

"I'm tired of talking."

A lump formed in Donnay's throat. She'd figured that sooner or later he would be.

"And if you plan on leaving, now is the time to do so because I told you what happens if you stay," he added.

She didn't move. She didn't say anything. She just stood there and stared at him. The more she stared, the more his gaze was touching her all over, making her feel hot and bothered, pushing her over the edge of her control.

And then he tipped the scales when he said in a voice too sexy for words, "Chardonnay Russell, soon to become Chardonnay Westmoreland, welcome to my world of forbidden passion."

He extended his hand out to her while locking his gaze on hers. She thought of everything he said he would do to her if she stayed and knew once she gave her hand to him, she would become his. For some reason that thought didn't bother her as it once had.

Inhaling deeply she placed her hand in his and watched his eyes darken even more before taking her hand and lifting it to his lips to kiss her fingers. And then he was slowly pulling her into his arms and taking her mouth with an intensity that would have brought her to her knees had his hands not wrapped around her waist.

His strength became the overt force that sustained her, the given power that was unconcealed and unrestrained. A shiver raced through her entire being when his tongue mated with hers in a way different from before. This was one of care, custody and control. He was placing ownership all over her mouth, claiming every breath she took and making the moans erupting forth from her throat totally his. The effect was enthralling, sensuously spellbinding and shockingly blazing.

Then she felt his hand working at the zipper at her waist, and moments later when he stepped back slightly without breaking the kiss, she felt her skirt slide down her hips to pool at her ankles. She was left in her blouse, a half-slip and a thong. And as she very well knew, this man had amazing fingers and definitely knew how to use them. He could strip a woman naked before she realized he was doing so. She then felt him slide his hand beneath the waistband of her slip to palm her almost bare bottom.

The moment he touched her, she moaned into his mouth and instinctively her body melded to his, felt his hardness, his erection, and the center of his arousal. He was taking more than she had been prepared to give, was priming her for what was yet to come and fanning a need within her to flashpoint. So she did the only thing she could. She let go.

Then suddenly he pulled back and swept her into his arms. Taking the stairs two at a time he entered the bedroom and placed her on the king-size bed. Her heart began beating faster, almost out of control, when he quickly worked at the buttons of his shirt.

Watching him, studying his eyes, she detected a hunger he was holding in check for now. Her mind began twirling with questions as to what could or would happen if he were to ever let go. She didn't want to think how he would overwhelm her if that were to happen.

He removed his shirt and tossed it on the other side of the room and her breath caught. His chest was so beautifully carved that she felt a moment of intense pride. This was the naked chest that would touch her own each time they made love, skin to skin; the chest she would rub her face in whenever she wanted to inhale the essence of his scent. And his shoulders, broad and firm, were the ones she would cling to when that explosion happened. And for a reason she didn't understand, she had believed him when he'd said it would.

A shiver racked Donnay's body when Spencer's hand went to the zipper of his pants. She held her breath as he eased it down, felt a lump form in her throat when he lowered his pants down his legs and stepped out of them. She finally released her breath and stared at him, her gaze more concentrated than before. It swept past his shoulders and chest to the area hidden by the black silk boxer shorts. The impression showed a very well-endowed man, a man who had everything to back up all the talk, and she believed he knew how to use everything he was packing.

She focused on that part of him that would soon connect their bodies, their minds, their entire beings. In the short time she knew him, she had come to realize that he didn't take too many things lightly. He was intense, demanding, a highly unmanageable person. But on the other hand, she believed he was fiercely dedicated. He would not deceive her like Robert had done.

"What are you thinking?"

His words broke the silence and she looked up to his face. She decided to be only half truthful. "I was wondering how I would handle you. Handle *it*."

He smiled at that. "You see both as a challenge?"

She blew out a breath. If only he knew. "Yes."

"Don't."

Evidently changing his mind about removing his briefs just yet, he moved back to the bed and pulled her up on her knees toward him and then bent down and captured her mouth in one smooth sweep. Something stirred the air surrounding them. She felt it as his tongue began mating with hers again. She felt it when his hands went to her blouse, when he broke the kiss just long enough to pull it over her head. And then he was easing her back into the bed, into the soft, thick cushions of the bedcovers, and straddling her body.

He pulled back and with a quick flick of his wrist and ready fingers, he removed her slip, thong and bra. Before she could inhale a deep breath, his lips were trailing a path down her body, continuing without pause until he reached the twin globes of her breasts. He began kissing them, devouring them, taunting them with his tongue, lips and teeth until she was moaning from deep within her throat. Desire set her ablaze when moments later his mouth began moving again, downward past her ribs and toward her navel. There he discovered her one moment of liberation during her first year in college. A belly ring.

He lifted his head, met her gaze and a broad smile touched his lips. She couldn't help but return his smile and at that moment something significant had passed between them. Acceptance of each other's likes, dislikes and values.

He lowered his head and her stomach tensed when he formed a ring on her belly with his tongue, a hot, wet one that seemed to brand her skin. And then he angled his head as his mouth began moving lower. She stiffened when he kissed the undersides of both her thighs while he reached down to let his fingertips trace a path along her calf.

She heard him murmur words that sounded foreign to her befuddled mind just seconds before he placed the other hand between her thighs to open her legs to him. And then she felt him there, his tongue touching her intimately in a way that lifted her hips off the bed. Her action only seemed to serve his purpose when he took the liberty to lift those same hips closer to his mouth and plunge his tongue inside her, even going so far to raise her legs over his shoulders for deeper penetration.

What he was doing was shooting sensation through her so intensely she felt every part of her shattering. With every flick of his tongue she felt a tug at her insides, as he deliberately pulled everything out of her, every single resistance, every rebellious thought. The feeling was excruciating, intense, unbelievably erotic. She reached out and gripped his shoulders, powerful and strong, and held on for dear life when he demanded anything and everything she was holding back from him.

And then she felt it. A wild, uninhibited dive into waters she had never been in before. But instead of drowning she was caught up on a wave so electrifying, she groaned deep within her throat before screaming out his name.

"Spencer!"

He refused to let up. His tongue went on in a frenzy, as out of control as she was, and she arched her back as an explosion ripped through her. She felt every muscle in her body take a hit as she moved relentlessly against his mouth, unable to remain still.

She experienced a sense of loss when he pulled back and watched through glazed eyes when he shifted to pull off his boxers. And then he was there, straddling her, and in one swift, smooth move he entered her. Her body's reaction to his invasion was spontaneous. Flesh against flesh, he moved and she moved with him, every thrust as potent, deep and overpowering as the one before. Skin against skin, he slid against her, interlocking their limbs in a hold that was meant to go unbroken, uninterrupted and unremitting. Any boundaries she'd established were shattered, totally demolished under the powers of his torrid lovemaking.

And then it happened again, another explosion tearing through her. She called out his name a second time, at the same moment he called out hers. And again she felt her body explode, shoot to the stars and beyond. Before she could gather her wits, Spencer's mouth covered hers in a long, slow and drugging kiss that erased all logical thought from her mind.

And she became caught up in Spencer's forbidden passion once again.

What woke Donnay was the feel of a masculine hand running along the side of her thigh, a slow and gentle caress. She slowly opened her eyes. And if she had any doubt just where she was, the hardness of the naked body pressed up against her own was a stark reminder.

She lay there knowing Spencer's hand was intent on serving a very sensuous purpose; one she had come to expect since last night. He had warned her that when it came to making love he had inexhaustible energy, and over the past three hours he had proven that to be true. The man was so disturbingly virile she hadn't been sure she would be able to keep up. Surprisingly she had. There hadn't been a time when he had reached out for her that she hadn't willingly gone into his arms, knowing the pleasures that awaited her there. And at no time had she been disappointed. Each and every lovemaking session with him had left her totally and completely satisfied.

When she felt his hand ease between her legs and his efficient fingers went to work, she softly moaned his name.

"I see you're awake," he whispered, rising up on an elbow to gaze down at her.

She looked up at his naked chest, broad and muscular with a spray of dark hair. She remembered burying her face in that chest, taking her tongue and tracing a trail over it when he had been making love to her in one hell of a unique position. The man not only had an infinite amount of energy, he was also very creative. "Did you really expect me to sleep?" she asked, switching her gaze to his face and almost drowning in the depths of his dark eyes.

He smiled and that single smile, sexy to the bone, sent tingles through her body. "I didn't want you to get into any trouble."

She raised a brow. "Trouble?"

"Yes, it's rather late. And as much as I would love for you to stay here with me all night, I don't want to get on your grandmother's and mother's bad side by not returning you home at a decent hour."

She glanced over at the clock on the nightstand. It was already close to two in the morning. She couldn't help but chuckle. "Just what do you consider decent?"

His own voice was slightly amused when he said, "Anytime before daybreak."

Donnay inwardly shivered when his fingers began caressing her womanly core, making her hot and wet again. "Um, you don't have anything to worry about. Grammy is spending the night at the hospital and Mom is meeting a girlfriend in San Francisco and staying overnight. So I would have been home alone anyway."

His fingers went still, and he leaned in closer to her. "Are you saying that you can stay all night?"

She met his gaze and saw the intensity in it as well as the deep-rooted desire. It did something to her to know that even after making love several times tonight he still hadn't gotten enough of her. Robert was always eager to send her away from his apartment afterward. Of course she later found out why. She nodded. "Yes, that's exactly what I'm saying."

His expression indicated her words had pleased him and he had no intention of letting her leave his bed now…which was fine with her.

When he lowered his head she was ready and parted her lips the moment he touched them, immediately becoming caught up in the throes of the passion he could generate so effortlessly.

From somewhere deep inside, she was suddenly struck with a terrifying realization. If she wasn't careful and protective of her heart, she could very easily fall in love with Spencer Westmoreland.

Chapter 9

The following morning, Donnay awakened to the loud sound of some sort of heavy machinery. She got out of bed, grabbed Spencer's shirt and slipped it on while quickly walking over to the window to peek out. The sun was just coming up over the horizon, and from a distance across the wide expanse of the vineyard she could see huge construction trucks making their way down the road toward the winery.

"I see Steve's men are on time as usual."

She swung around to see Spencer coming out of the bathroom. It was obvious that he had taken a shower. A towel was tied at his waist, and there were beads of water on his shoulders and chest. She narrowed her eyes and tried not to recall the role his shoulders and chest had played in their lovemaking during the night. There were more important matters to be concerned with right now. "What are those trucks doing here, Spencer?"

He walked over to the dresser, pulled a few items of clothing out of the drawer before dropping the towel. "I think it's obvious what they're doing here, Chardonnay."

She inhaled sharply the moment the towel hit the floor. He was standing before her stark naked and she was trying hard not to stare as he casually slipped into a pair of briefs. She had seen his nude body all last night and during the predawn hours, but seeing it in the bright sunlight was another thing altogether. The memory of all the things that body had done to her, shared with her, made sensations flood her insides. She shook her head and tried to clear her mind of such wanton thoughts and shift it back to what he'd said. "Well, it's not obvious, so tell me," she said.

He glanced over at her. "Those trucks belong to the company I hired to do the expansion to the vineyard."

She became livid. "How dare you!"

He raised a dark brow questioningly and leaned back against the dresser. "How dare I what?"

"How dare you take over. What gives you the right to make such a move without discussing it with any member of my family? We aren't married yet and already you're—"

"I discussed it with your grandfather."

Donnay locked her mouth shut but only for a second. "My grandfather?" she asked in a voice that had suddenly gone soft.

"Yes."

"Are you telling me that you told my grandfather everything about our arrangement?"

"Of course not. During our visits, he talked and I listened, which is a good thing because he shared his dreams with me for the winery. I took in all that he said. He was giving me the big picture—his hopes and dreams. I took it and consulted the best architect I know, and decided to try to make your grandfather's wants viable. Tonight, after telling him we would be getting married, I told him I would make his dream come true."

Donnay stared and then frowned. She didn't recall him saying anything like that to her grandfather. "When did you tell him this?"

"After you left the room to get him a blanket from the nurses' station."

She paused, tilted her head to one side as she considered his words and then asked softly. "And what did he say?"

"Thank you."

Every fiber in Donnay's body wanted to cry. She of all people knew just how long her grandfather had dreamed of expanding the winery, and how depressed he'd been the first time he had become ill and had seen those dreams slip through his fingers when the money for them was needed elsewhere. No one had to tell her that Spencer was giving her grandfather his life back, a reason to get better, a reason to want the surgery he'd been hesitant about having.

She met Spencer's gaze. "It seems I owe you an apology."

"Another one?"

He was standing in nothing but a pair of black briefs, in a sexy stance with his legs braced apart and his arms folded across his chest. From his expression it was obvious he was pretty annoyed with her for jumping to conclusions again. "Well, what was I supposed to think?" she asked in her own defense.

"I can tell you what you weren't supposed to think. The worst about me."

Okay, maybe she shouldn't have, but she had. What did he expect considering the reason he was in their lives? Their marriage would be nothing but a business deal.

As if reading her mind, he said, "I'm a man of my word, Chardonnay."

She slowly crossed the room to him. "And I'm a woman who doesn't have a problem admitting when she's wrong."

"And you're admitting it?" he asked when she came to a stop in front of him.

"Yes, on some things about you," she said, steadily holding his gaze.

He lifted a dark brow. "And the others?"

She shrugged her shoulders. "The jury's still out. But from now on you're innocent until proven guilty."

He caught her wrist and brought it to his lips and kissed it. "It's a good thing for you that I'm a very forgiving man."

"Are you?" she asked in a low tone, feeling heat travel all over her the moment his lips touched her flesh.

"Yes, on some things."

"And the others?"

"The jury is still out. But I don't have a problem with tampering with the jury if it will serve my purpose," he said, reaching out and slipping his shirt off her shoulders to fall in a heap at her feet. She stood before him naked but she had no intention of covering herself. From the look in his eyes, he evidently liked what he saw.

And he wanted what he saw. Again.

"You're very smooth," she said silkily, taking a step closer to wrap her arms around his neck and to bring her body close to his. "And you have one hell of an appetite."

"Don't say I didn't warn you," he said, sweeping her off her feet and into his arms to carry her over to the bed.

"I won't," she murmured into his strong, masculine chest.

Hours later after a long and lazy morning of love-making, Donnay and Spencer got dressed and he walked her home. Both her mother and grandmother were there but neither seemed inclined to ask where she had been.

Spencer then went to talk to Ray Stokes, the foreman for Carr Construction Company. Fred Akron, the architect he had paid, would be presenting his plans for the expansion of the winery by the end of the week. In the meantime, Ray and his crew's job was to clear land to extend the boundaries of the vineyard. Come spring they would be planting more grapevines for more wines to market.

It was way past noon when Spencer returned to the villa, and the moment he opened the door, memories of the night before assailed his mind when he picked up Chardonnay's lingering scent. It seemed to be all over the place. And he liked it. He had drunk chardonnay numerous times but never had he got the taste like he had last night. Good wine was supposed to have a lingering effect, get absorbed into your tongue, your mouth, your flavor palates. He licked his lips, still able to savor her taste on his tongue. Delicious.

He heard his cell phone ring and immediately pulled it out of his pocket. He glanced at the number. It was his brother Ian. Ian was the fraternal twin to his brother Quade and had gotten married that past June. Spencer fondly referred to his brother, who was six years his junior, as the gambler, since he had this unique ability to beat the odds, whether it was poker, a slot machine or blackjack. No one liked playing against Ian since he was known to walk away with everybody's money. He owned a casino and resort in Lake Tahoe, but if you were to ask Ian, his most prized possession was his wife, Brooke.

"And to what do I owe this honor?" Spencer asked teasingly. Since getting married Ian seldom called, saying his time was spent doing more important things. Spencer could just imagine what those other things were.

"Just checking to see if you're still living. Stuart was here at the resort last week and said something about how bad he felt about sending you to face a scorpion."

Spencer chuckled, wondered how Stuart would handle it when he found out that he would be marrying Chardonnay. "It's not that bad," he said and decided Ian would be the first family member he broke his news to. "In fact, it's pretty good. Her name is Chardonnay and I'm marrying her."

There was a pause and then, "You're joking, right?"

"No."

"You're marrying a woman name Chardonnay? Who would name their child after a wine?"

Spencer smiled. "Someone who owns a winery I would imagine."

"You're serious about getting married?"

"Yes. I'm giving the family a call later today. Your call was perfect timing and as a result, you're the first to know."

"When did you meet her?"

"A few weeks ago."

"Um, love at first sight?"

"No." The answer was simple, straightforward and true. "You know me better than that."

"Well, I'm one who knows that love can make you do foolish things."

"Possibly. But I'm not in love," Spencer said, being completely honest with his brother.

"Then why are you getting married? She can't be pregnant already."

Ian's words reminded Spencer that they hadn't used protection any of the times he and Chardonnay had made love last night. That thought didn't bother him since he wanted babies, plenty of them. "I'm getting married because I want to be married. Why let you, Jared and Durango have all the fun? Besides, Mom gets to put another smile on her face."

"But that won't stop her from going after Reggie and Quade," Ian advised.

"No," Spencer agreed. "But they're big boys. They'll have to handle Sarah Westmoreland as they see fit."

He glanced at his watch and saw it was almost two in the afternoon. He wanted to visit Chardonnay's grandfather and give him a report on today's activities. "Look, Ian, there's somewhere I need to be in about an hour. Keep your lips sealed about my upcoming marriage. I want to be the one to tell everyone."

"Okay, my lips are sealed...until such time as I use them to kiss my beautiful wife."

Spencer rolled his eyes heavenward. "Whatever." He then clicked off the phone.

"The two of you are marrying within two weeks? Why the rush?"

Donnay's looked at Spencer sitting beside her at the dinner table, wondering how he would respond to her mother's question. Not surprisingly, he met her mother's eyes and in a clear voice he said, "Because I don't want to wait."

She expected her grandmother or mother to ask, "Wait for what?" Instead both nodded their heads as if they understood his meaning.

She rolled her eyes. If they did she certainly didn't. It couldn't be that he couldn't wait for them to sleep together since they'd already done that. So the only thing she could figure was that he was anxious to get her pregnant since he was so gung ho on starting a family.

"I think it's romantic."

Donnay's lips pressed together as she ignored her grandmother's words. Did she really think that or was she just in an extremely good mood because Donnay's grandfather would be coming home from the hospital at the end of the week? She felt Spencer's eyes on her and turned her head to meet his gaze. Fire immediately shot through her veins at the look he was giving her.

She figured he was wondering why she had deliberately made herself scarce over the past couple of days. She'd had no choice because otherwise, she would fall deeper and deeper under his spell. And what was more pathetic than for a woman to fall for man who had no intention of ever falling for her?

"Daniel is going to be very pleased with all the work those men are doing on the vineyard," Donnay heard her grandmother say.

Spencer dropped his gaze from hers to look across the table at Catherine Russell. "I hope that he will be. I tried to follow his exact specifications."

Donnay would be the first to admit that he had. She knew that Spencer visited her grandfather daily and always kept him abreast of what was going on with the vineyard. One day she had walked into the hospital room to find her grandfather sitting up in bed with a bunch of architectural plans across his lap while he and Spencer had their heads together, making additional plans.

They'd been so absorbed in their discussion that they hadn't noticed her presence. For a moment she had felt the closeness of the two men and suddenly knew how her mother had felt all those years ago. It was as if Spencer had become the grandson Daniel never had. Not knowing how she felt about that, as well as the other emotions she'd begun feeling around Spencer, she'd decided the best thing to do was to stay clear of him while she screwed her head back on right.

After dinner while clearing the table, Spencer approached her when her mother and grandmother had left to take an evening walk. She'd been hoping that he'd accompanied them and soon discovered he hadn't.

"Okay, what's wrong, Chardonnay?" he asked, his voice low, strained and concerned.

For a moment she couldn't reply. What could she say? *I'm falling in love with you and I refuse to do so and will do whatever it takes to make sure it doesn't happen?* Instead she shrugged. "What makes you think something is wrong?"

"You've been avoiding me."

She decided to pretend she didn't know what he was talking about. "Avoiding you in what way?"

"You haven't been back to the villa."

Did the man expect her to seek him out and tumble in his bed every chance she got? Her stomach knotted upon remembering his ferocious sexual appetite and concluded that yes, he probably did.

"I've been busy," she responded, both angry and frustrated. They hadn't been alone but a few minutes and already she could feel heated tension sizzle in the very air they were breathing.

"Come to me at midnight," he whispered in a voice tinged with throaty sexuality. He moved closer and drew her to him.

She didn't think of pulling back and although she was trembling inside, she did manage to say, "No."

"Yes," he countered hotly. And then his mouth swooped down on hers before any further protest could come from her lips. The moment his tongue entered her mouth, she remembered, she relented and she surrendered. Every nerve in her body began quivering under Spencer's skillful tongue. The hand he had placed at her waist wasn't helping matters. It only pulled her closer, making her more aware of his powerful heat.

When he finally lifted his head, he had to tighten his hold to keep her from falling. "I won't go to sleep until you get there," he whispered hotly against her lips.

She gazed at him thinking that he wouldn't be going to sleep after she got there, either. There was no doubt in her mind that he intended to keep her awake and busy.

He leaned down and took her lips in his again and then she wasn't thinking at all.

Donnay couldn't sleep.

She had tossed and turned most of the night. Her body felt hot. It was sensitive. It was experiencing a need to get physical. She kicked back the bedcovers, got out of bed and began pacing the floor. Spencer Westmoreland had gotten under her skin and as much as she tried she couldn't get him out. As a result, she was torn between what she wanted to do and what she knew she should. She had underestimated Spencer.

The man was turning out to be the exact opposite of what she'd assumed he would be. Of course there was a brashness about him she wouldn't even try to discount. But there was also a sense of caring. Her grandfather was proof of that. It wasn't just the time he'd spent with him, but also the fact that he had shared plans of the expansion with her grandfather when he really didn't have to. And then he'd gone further by giving him peace of mind that the vineyard would remain in the Russell family. She had begun seeing another side of Spencer, and with it she felt a grudging respect for him and everything he was doing to be fair to her family.

And she felt something else, something she could no longer deny. Love. She loved him. She sighed. She would marry him, bear his children and make him a good wife. And she hoped and prayed that one day he would grow to reciprocate her love.

A glance at the clock on the nightstand told her that midnight was approaching. She wondered what Spencer was doing. Was he in his bed thinking about her? Waiting on her? Wanting her?

That thought triggered chills that traveled down her spine. She took a few steps over to her closet and moments later she was slipping out of her nightgown and pulling a skirt and blouse over her head, not bothering with a bra and panties. The outfit was simple, easy to get out of and even a bit sexy. A few moments later, after easing her feet into a pair of loafers, she opened her bedroom door and quietly slipped out.

Spencer refused to sleep.

He was feeling restless and positively filled with a need that only Chardonnay could quench. He glanced over at the clock on the wall. It was getting close to midnight. What if he'd pushed too hard and she didn't come? He breathed in deeply, refusing to consider that possibility.

He had spoken to his mother earlier and had given her his news. As expected, she had asked questions, but nothing had stopped her from being elated. Another one of her sons was getting married and she was tickled pink. He knew by tomorrow morning the entire Westmoreland clan would hear about it. He would get calls, probably more questions—especially from his brothers and cousins who knew how his mind operated—but that thought didn't bother him. Like he'd told his mother, Chardonnay was the woman he wanted and the woman he intended to marry here in the vineyard in two weeks.

A sense of accomplishment rolled over him as he thought of having the things that were most important to him. The most significant one at the moment was Chardonnay. He thought of her often, even times when he didn't want to. What he'd told her mother at dinner was the truth. The reason he wanted to rush into marriage was that he didn't want to wait…mainly to make her his.

Deciding if she were to come to him he preferred her not making the trip from the main house through the vineyard alone, he slid out of bed and slipped into the jeans and shirt he had on earlier. His skin felt hot to the touch and he wondered if the same heat consuming his body was consuming hers. When he'd kissed her earlier that night, he had felt her response, had tasted her desire, inhaled her heat.

He wanted it.

He needed it.

His mind was becoming mentally shaken, his body physically addicted. They had made love one night, numerous times over, and that was all it had taken to reduce him to a man who stayed royally aroused around her. A man who spent most of his day dealing with frustrated lust. As he left the bedroom and began walking down the stairs his mind was filled with one thing and one thing only. Making love to Chardonnay.

Moments later he was closing the front door behind

him as he made his way down the path. It was dark and the only light was from the moon overhead. The night air was cool and he wished he had thought to grab a jacket. It had rained earlier, right after he had returned home. It hadn't rained a lot, but enough to dampen the earth, supplying a distinctive aroma of wet grass, blooming plants, thickening vines and the earthy fragrance of freshly turned soil.

Feeling his fingers go cold, he hooked them in the pockets of his jeans. He suddenly sharpened his gaze when he heard a rustling sound. Thinking it was Chardonnay, he was about to call out to her then stopped after seeing it was her mother instead. Then before he could blink, another figure—that of a tall, muscular man—stepped out of the shadows and into the moonlight in front of her.

Spencer's protective instincts kicked in and his senses immediately went on full alert. Then he watched as the man pulled Ruth Russell into his arms and kissed her, and it was quite obvious she was kissing him back.

Spencer lowered his head, not wanting to intrude on such a passionate moment between the couple who, like him, were meeting for a midnight rendezvous. Moments later he glanced up in time to see them disappear into the shadows heading in the direction of the empty gardener's cottage.

Not that it was any of his business, but he wondered if Chardonnay knew that her mother was involved in an affair. If she didn't, she definitely wouldn't hear about it from him. When it came to secrets, he was the king of discreet. Still, he couldn't help but wonder about the man's identity. Was he one of the workers at the winery?

Fairly certain the couple was halfway to their chosen destination by now, he began walking again. The night was quiet so he easily picked up the sound of footsteps coming his way. He stopped and focused his gaze. And then he saw her.

She hadn't seen him yet so he leaned back against an oak tree to study her features in the moonlight. Beautiful. And then his body began thrumming at the realization that although he was fairly certain she hadn't wanted to come, desire had driven her to seek him out.

Something gave him away. Possibly the sudden intake of his breath when he saw her outfit. It was one of those fit-and-flare skirts and a jersey-knit top with billowy sleeves. The way they clung to her body sent a surge of adrenaline pumping through his veins. She stopped walking and stared at him and he pushed away from the tree and strolled toward her.

He had spent the last three hours wondering if she would show up, and now that she was here, his already hot blood was boiling even more at the thought of how they would spend the rest of their time together. He wasn't used to a woman taking control of his thoughts like she was doing.

"You came," were the only words he could fix his mouth to say at that moment, he was so filled with unleashed passion.

"Yes, I came," she whispered, and the sound sent his insides to quivering. He battled the urge to take her then and there, to let their naked bodies roll in the damp earth, get tangled in the vines and—

"It's cool out."

He saw her rubbing her arms and quickly realized

that like him she hadn't worn a jacket. He smiled a tight, restrained smile. Anything else would cause the erection to burst in his crotch. "Then let's go to my place where I can warm you. But that's not all I plan to do to you tonight, Chardonnay."

Her incredible gray eyes gazed deeply at him when she asked in a soft, sexy voice, "What else do you plan to do to me?"

She had a right to ask. She had a right to know. "Taste every single inch of you. Let my fingers stroke you. Let my body make love to you in all kinds of ways and various positions."

He took a step closer to her. "Will you let me do all those things to you again?"

"Yes."

Pleased she hadn't hesitated with her answer, he dipped his head and tasted her lips, savoring his own special brand of Chardonnay. He lifted his mouth, deciding he needed to take her to a place more private before he lost control. The last thing he wanted was for her mother to come upon them like he had on her earlier.

"When you leave my bed tonight I want you to be totally and thoroughly convinced that I am the only man you'll ever want and need." And then he swung her up into his arms and began walking back toward his villa.

He had gotten halfway there and couldn't go anymore. The feel of her in his arms, the way her breasts were pressed against chest, the scent of her in his nostrils, the way she had tucked her hands beneath his shirt to keep them warm, all of them increased his sexual craze. He couldn't move another inch without the threat of his aroused body exploding then and there.

Inhaling deeply, he placed her on her feet. She gazed at him for a moment and then as if understanding what he couldn't put into words, she took his hand and said, "Come with me. I want to show you something."

She led him through a thicket of low-hanging branches, parting several grapevines that blocked their way, to guide him to a grassy path. There at the end of it was a glass-enclosed summerhouse, sitting amidst vines, ferns, a cluster of oak trees and palms. She glanced at his expression. He didn't even try to hide his smile.

"Gramps had it built years ago for my grandmother, a place where she could get away, sew, read and rest. She hasn't used it much over the years. It's climate controlled and should be nice and warm inside," she said, opening the door. He followed her inside and then she locked it behind them. It was nice and warm on the inside and the window blinds assured complete privacy.

After she turned on a lamp, he glanced around but only for a second. His gaze immediately returned to her when he saw the frown bunching her brow. "What is it?" he asked.

"Um, nothing, I guess. It's just that no one ever comes out here but me to read and take a nap on occasion. However, it seems the bedcovers have been changed since the last time I was here."

Spencer had an idea who had changed the bedcovers but kept his thoughts to himself. "Does it matter?"

She met his gaze and shook her head. "No. Nothing matters but this moment. With you."

Something tugged deep inside of him. He could not deny the sensation even if he wanted to. Even if he didn't fully understand it. He opened his arms to her and she took the few steps to walk into them. Instinctively she lifted her head and at the same time he lowered his, covering her lips.

A ferocious ache overtook him and he whispered words against her lips, not sure what he was saying and at the moment not caring. The only thing that mattered to him was the ravenous desire running rampant through his entire body. She arched against him and his senses went into overdrive.

Like a man with no control, he stepped back and tugged her blouse over her head. The moment he saw her braless, he closed his hand over her breasts, reveling in their shape, their firmness and how right they felt in his hands. He then leaned down and kissed them, satisfying his hungry need to taste her.

But he soon discovered it wasn't enough for him.

He dropped to his knees in front of her and tugged her skirt down her thighs and almost swallowed his tongue when he stared her feminine mound smack in the face. She hadn't worn panties.

He leaned forward to do his own taste test as his nose nuzzled the curls at the apex of her thighs, taking in her scent, letting his nostrils absorb her aroma just seconds before his tongue thrust deep inside her while grabbing hold of her bottom, pulling her closer to the fit of his mouth. He became lost in heavenly bliss while his tongue stroked, caressed and probed, refusing to let up or let go. He heard her moans, felt the torture on his shoulders when her fingernails dug into them, but he refused to release her from his grip.

This was his Chardonnay and he intended to enjoy

it to the fullest. Even when he felt her body explode beneath his mouth he held tight, needing to fully taste the very essence of her.

It was only after the last tremor had left her body that he drew back from the intimate kiss. He glanced up at her, met the dazed gray of her eyes and a smile curved his mouth as he licked his lips. "Best Chardonnay I've ever had the pleasure of tasting," he whispered before standing and sweeping her naked body off her feet and into his arms.

He carried her over to the daybed and placed her on it and then quickly began removing his clothes. It had started raining again, a downpour that beat against the rooftop and glass walls. The air seemed to thicken with the fragrance of flowers, grapes and sex. He inhaled it. He licked his lips and could still taste it. He was suddenly filled with a sexual rush, a need to mate to an extreme he never thought possible. He wanted her. Damn, how he wanted her.

He moved back toward the bed. Instead of wrapping her arms around his neck like he assumed she would do, she grabbed hold of his shaft and stroked the head of his erection with soft fingers. In his already sexually glazed mind that was the last thing he needed but exactly what he wanted. Her touch was eliciting sounds from his throat, and he felt himself weaken, giving in to the demands of his body. The demands of her hands.

He felt her touch all the way to his bones, felt himself harden even more beneath her fingertips. She mentally fractured any thoughts he had, igniting a fuse within him that could explode any minute. And when she pushed him back on the bed and took him into her mouth, he clenched his jaw to keep from hollering. He gripped the bedcovers as her mouth began ravaging him, sapping him of any strength while at the same time seizing the air in his lungs. Sensations swamped him and he gave himself up to them, and to her.

Good God! What was she doing to him? He had to stop her before he was stripped of everything within him. A deep moan escaped his lips when he shifted and pushed her on her back, locking his thighs over hers, trapping her beneath him. Before she could mutter a single word of protest, he entered her and they both released moans of pleasure at the same time, just seconds before they began spiraling out of control.

He reached under her and lifted her hips as he thrust in and out of her, and with each stroke she arched her body to meet him, creating a sensuous blend of perfect harmony.

"Incredible," he murmured, just seconds before dipping his head to her mouth, laving her lips with his tongue from corner to corner before inserting his tongue into her mouth. Below he felt her inner muscles clench him, milk him, attempt to pull everything out him, and she succeeded.

"Chardonnay!"

His body seemed to explode in tiny pieces as his seed spilled deep inside her, overflowing within her and overwhelming him. Never before had he given so much to any woman and with no regrets and no restraints. That thought became logged in his brain but he refused to dwell on it now. The only thing he wanted to think about was how he felt inside her and how his body was still throbbing from the effects of the most intense orgasm he'd ever experienced.

Their gazes connected and he felt like he was sinking in quicksand. He clung to her, afraid if he let go that would be the end of it…of them.

As he pulled her shaking body closer to him, more sensations shot through him and at that moment, he couldn't fathom a life without the woman in his arms.

Donnay came awake to discover Spencer gazing down at her. She blinked, wondering how long she'd slept. The last thing she remembered was coming apart in his arms while he was buried deep inside of her, feeling the heated essence of him shooting to all parts of her.

"I have something for you," he whispered huskily.

His words made her study his features. "What?"

"This."

And then she felt him slip something onto her finger, and she knew what it was. Her engagement ring. The huge diamond shone brightly in the moonlight and Donnay's breath caught. It was exquisite, the most beautiful ring she'd ever seen.

Not knowing what to say, she sank against him instead and he pulled her into his arms and held her. She knew that loving Spencer when he didn't love her back wouldn't always be easy. He was a hard man, a man who'd been hurt by love. It would be up to her to go about repairing his heart mainly because she believed in the very essence of her soul that it was a heart worthy of fixing.

"It's beautiful, Spencer," she finally said. "Simply beautiful. Thank you."

"You're welcome." Then he said, "The rain has stopped. Are you ready to get dressed and go to my place?"

She looked at him. Her heart was assured that although he didn't love her, he definitely wanted her. "Yes," she said, wrapping her arms around his neck. "I'm ready."

Chapter 10

Spencer stood at the window in his bedroom and glanced out. It had been four days since he'd told his mother about his wedding plans and his phone was still ringing. His cousin Delaney had even called him all the way from her home in the Middle East to congratulate him.

He leaned against the windowsill, thinking the last few days had been sheer bliss. Chardonnay seemed to have accepted the way things would be between them and no longer fought the idea that in less than two weeks they would be getting married.

And their relationship had definitely improved. They were now an engaged couple and instinctively acted the part. They had begun sharing breakfast and dinner each day, would take walks together in the afternoon while he brought her up-to-date on that day's work activities, and at night they shared a bed. He no longer had to seduce her to do so. Each night she would come to him automatically, as though she knew her place was beside him in bed, and a part of him felt that it was.

Last night they had attended a wine-tasting gala in downtown Napa, Taste Napa Downtown. The outfit Chardonnay had worn had been both professional and seductive. and he had felt proud to be the man at her side. When they'd entered the ballroom where the event had been held, heads had turned and more than one person had commented that they made a striking couple.

On that thought he lowered his head as a deep sensation settled in his gut, one he'd tried ignoring over the past few days. Whenever he was with Chardonnay, whether in bed or out, he felt like a different person, a man on top of the world. A man who was starting to live for the first time. To appreciate the finer things in life. A man who was looking forward to his future.

A man who was in love.

His breath paused in his throat. Falling in love was something he never intended to happen to him, but it had. He rubbed his hand over his face, accepting what his heart had been trying to tell him lately, but what he had ignored until now.

Months ago, if anyone would have suggested that he'd give his heart to any woman, he would have laughed in their face, knowing such a thing wasn't possible. But he was living proof that it was possible.

He glanced out the window again when he heard the equipment plowing the earth to cultivate additional land for grapes to be planted in the spring. He was anticipating a good harvest in the coming year and was anticipating becoming a father in that time, as well. But more than anything he wanted to be a good husband to Chardonnay, and he hoped that in time she would get over the circumstances of their marriage and accept the fact they were together and build on that.

Her grandfather had got out of the hospital a few days ago and Spencer found he was spending time with the older man, as well. Daniel's health was improving and he'd been extremely happy to come home and discover his plans and dreams for the winery were coming true. To avoid tiring the older man out, the architect Spencer had hired was meeting with Daniel a couple of hours a day to make sure the plans being drawn were exactly the way Chardonnay's grandfather had envisioned them.

Spencer turned when he heard his phone ring, interrupting his thoughts. He moved away from the window and walked over to the desk to pick it up. "Yes?"

"Something interesting has developed that I think you should know about."

Spencer arched a brow at the serious sound of his attorney's voice. "And what is that, Stuart?"

"Over a million dollars was deposited into the Russell Vineyards bank account this morning."

Spencer's body stiffened as his mind began whirling with questions. He took a breath. "There has to be a mistake."

"No mistake, Spence."

"Then how did it get there? Who made the deposit?"

"It was a transfer that I was able to trace from a Korean bank. An international account in the name of BOSS."

Spencer lifted a brow. "Boss?"

"Yes."

He stared at the floor as various things ran through his mind. He didn't want to consider any of them but knew that he had to. "Find out who owns the account and even more importantly, why they would have deposited that money into the Russells' account."

"All right. You don't think that Chardonnay Russell borrowed the money elsewhere, even though she knew you'd agreed to front the financing for the expansion, do you?"

He inhaled sharply. That was a possibility he didn't want to consider. Over the past weeks he had let his guard down and had done something he swore he wouldn't after what Lynette Marie had done to him, and that was to begin trusting another woman. Not to mention fall in love.

He had to admit that his mind hadn't been on a lot lately, other than making love to her. A dark suspicion leaped to life inside of him. Had she used his moment of weakness to keep him occupied so he wouldn't find out what she was doing behind his back until it was too late?

"Spence?"

His attorney's voice made him aware he hadn't answered his question. "I'm not sure what's going on, Stuart, but I want you to find out."

"I will and in the meantime, be careful how you handle your business."

Spencer knew Stuart's meaning and as he clicked off the phone a part of him thought that his attorney's advice may have come a little too late.

A few hours later, Spencer snapped closed his luggage and moved away from the bed. Stuart hadn't returned his call. That meant the information they wanted was hard to get, which was usually the case involving international accounts. Why would anyone place that much money into the Russells' account unless someone had negotiated a deal elsewhere? And since Chardonnay was the one handling the family's business, he could only assume it had been her.

Doubt and suspicions he didn't want to feel were eating at him, and he couldn't forget the moment he'd received the coroner's report on Lynette Marie. Betrayal of the worst kind had wretched his insides and as much as he was trying not to let it happen, he was beginning to feel the same way now.

He walked over to the window and looked out at the hills and valleys. Disgust and anger ate at him. Although the circumstances were different, the results were the same. He had allowed another woman to betray him. And this time the pain cut deeper because he loved her.

From the beginning she had alluded that in the end, he would regret ever coming up with the idea for the two of them to marry. He had merely brushed her comment aside as insignificant. But Chardonnay Russell had played him for a fool. She had weaved her deceitful web around him, first in the physical sense and then in an emotional sense. Each and every time they'd made love it had weakened him, had turned him into putty in her hands to the extent that all he'd thought about over the past week—besides marrying her—was pleasing her, making her happy, trying to show her that a lifetime with him wouldn't be so damn awful.

And all the time he'd been working hard doing that,

she had been undermining him, setting him up for failure and intentionally messing with his heart.

He turned away from the window when he heard the sound of the key turning in the lock downstairs. It would be Chardonnay. Before she'd left his bed early that morning she'd agreed to return a little before noon to give him a tour of the section of the winery he hadn't yet seen, and to introduce him to all the employees.

He turned back to the window when he heard her footsteps coming up the stairs. Anger consumed him to a degree he hadn't thought possible and it would have definitely been to her benefit if he could have left and returned to Sausalito without seeing her. In his present state of mind, he would have preferred it.

He turned when she opened the door and when his gaze touched hers he felt a hardening deep in his chest. At the same time a sensation of pain surrounded his heart.

"I told you I would be back," she said, smiling and stepping into the room, closing the door behind her.

When he didn't say anything but just stared at her, her gaze shifted to the bed where she saw his packed luggage. He watched as her smile faded. "You have to go away on business?"

He inhaled deeply, not in the mood to play her games, although she evidently assumed he was gullible enough to do so. He moved away from the window and went to stand before her. "Yes, I'm leaving but it's not on business. I'm leaving for good and won't be coming back."

She shook her head as if she hadn't heard him correctly. "But what about the wedding?"

His heart hardened even more when he said, "There

won't be a wedding. You would be the last woman I'd marry."

If her reaction was anything to go by, it seemed that his words had immediately knocked the breath out of her body, sent an invisible slap across her face. She placed a hand over her heart and her eyes widened in shocked disbelief. "Why? I don't understand. What happened?"

Her pretense angered him even more. "Let's cut the bull, Chardonnay, shall we? How long did you think it would be before I found out?"

A confused look appeared on her face. "Found out what?"

Spencer shook his head and laughed, not believing she had the nerve to ask him that. Even now she was standing in front of him with a puzzled expression, as if she had no clue what he was talking about, but he knew otherwise.

"I have to hand it to you. You are one hell of an actress. What did you do to get the money, Chardonnay? Are you sleeping with him like you're sleeping with me?" He watched color drain from her face. Guilt, he thought.

"I don't know what you're talking about," she said in a low, strained voice, shaking her head as if to deny his words.

"Don't you?" he said angrily, his tone bitter. "You want me to believe you have no idea who deposited a million dollars into the winery account this morning?"

"What! A million dollars? You're wrong. There must be a mistake."

He chuckled. "Oh, yes, there's a mistake all right, and it was made the day I set eyes on you."

"No, Spencer, listen to me. There has to be a mistake." She reached out as if to make a plea and he grabbed her wrist firmly in his hand and hauled her tightly against his chest.

His stony gaze met hers. "You played me for a fool, Chardonnay. You never intended to marry me and have my children. You had a plan B all along, didn't you?"

"No, that's not true. How could you think I could be so dishonest and calculating? How could—"

"Enough! I don't want to hear anything you have to say." He released her hand and moved around her and grabbed his luggage off the bed. He headed for the door, paused and then swung around to look at her again. "Tell your grandfather that I will continue to pay those men to clear the additional twenty acres like I promised him I would. I will also take care of any and all expenses associated with any surgery he might have, because deep down I don't believe he knew just what kind of games you were playing, just what a deceitful person you are. And," he said, pausing briefly, "if you're already pregnant with my child then rest assured you haven't seen the last of me. And if you aren't, then I hope to God I never see you again."

He turned around and without looking back again, he left.

"Donnay! What's wrong?" Ruth shot to her feet the moment Donnay entered the house.

Donnay had been hoping her mother had left to go to the winery's gift shop that she supervised and wouldn't see her this way. She hurriedly wiped the tears from her eyes as she moved toward the stairs. None of what Spencer had accused her of made sense. How could he have thought she had deceived him? Although she had called the bank and they had confirmed the million-dollar deposit, she had no idea who had done it, or why.

"Donnay?"

She met her mother's worried gaze and said in a low, shaky voice, "I'm fine, Mom."

"Then why are you crying?"

It took Donnay a while to compose herself before saying, "Spencer has called off the wedding. He thinks I've deceived him."

Ruth looked stunned. "Deceived him? Why would he think that?"

Donnay tried to still her shaking hands as she wiped another tear from her eye. She was angry and upset. "He thinks I never intended to marry him because I was getting the money I needed to save the winery from someone else. He even suggested I was sleeping with someone else to get it."

"How could he suggest something so despicable?"

"Because someone deposited a million dollars into the winery bank account and I—"

Donnay stopped talking upon her mother's sharp intake of breath. She studied her mother's features. Ruth Russell was flushing guiltily. Something wasn't right and Donnay played her hunch by asking, "Mom, do you know where that money came from? I checked with the bank and it's actually there."

Ruth stared back at her daughter and slowly nodded. "Yes, I know where it came from. He said he was going to do it but I asked him not to, because I believed that everything with you and Spence would work out just fine."

Donnay was having a hard time keeping up with what her mother was saying. She placed a hand on her arm. "He? Who is *he,* Mom?"

Ruth drew in a ragged breath and then she said, "Your father."

Stunned, Donnay could only stare at her mother. Her mind tried denying what her ears had just heard. There had to be a mistake. But something pushed her to ask for clarification purposes. "My father?"

"Yes. I told him about the outlandish proposal Spencer had made to you and Chad said that he—"

"Whoa. Back up a minute, Mom. I'm trying to follow you here but I'm having a hard time. Are you saying you've seen my father? Actually talked to him?"

Ruth nodded again. "Yes, he called a few weeks ago and said he was in the area and wanted to see me."

"In the area?"

"Yes. He was in San Francisco on business and decided to rent a car and come to the valley. He wasn't sure if I was still living here, or if over the years I had married and moved away."

Donnay inhaled. "I guess you got around to telling him about me," she said quietly.

Ruth nodded. "Yes. At first he wasn't happy about having a daughter he'd never known about, was cheated out of knowing. But then I explained to him how those letters came back. I'd even kept them and showed them to him so he'd know that I had tried contacting him."

"So," Donnay said slowly, "what has he been doing all these years? Is he married? Does he have any other children?"

Ruth shook her head. "He's a widower. His wife of fifteen years died five years ago and they never had any children. He retired from the army and went into business for himself, some sort of international electronic corporation that has done well over the years. And now that he knows about you, he wants to meet you, Chardonnay."

Ruth smiled slightly. "You should have seen him that first night after I told him about you. He was ready to come here and claim you immediately, but I convinced him to wait until I felt the time was right. Besides, he and I needed to talk, to find out what has been happening in our lives over the years. When I told him about the winery's problems, and how you were willing to sacrifice your happiness to marry a man you didn't love just to save the winery, he offered to pay off the debt. He said he would put the money into our account as soon as it could be transferred. I asked him not to, but like you he's stubborn and has this protective instinct and he did it anyway. I'm sorry if doing so has caused friction between you and Spencer."

Donnay shook her head after hearing her mother's explanation. "It doesn't matter. Our marriage would have been doomed from the start, Mom. This shows just how little he trusted me, and a marriage not based on faith and trust is no marriage at all. I could have survived without love but I have to know that Spencer has faith in me and trusts me. Without it, a relationship couldn't last."

A small smile touched her lips as the picture became clear in her mind. "So, is my father the *old friend* you've been spending a lot of time with lately?"

Ruth actually blushed. "Yes, and he is very anxious to meet you."

"And I'm anxious to meet him, as well." Donnay turned to go up the stairs then, but Ruth's voice held her back.

"He loves you, you know."

"Who, Mom?"

"Spencer."

Donnay chuckled to hold back fresh tears. "No, he never loved me, Mom. Our marriage was going to be a business deal. I told you that."

"Yes, but I have my own eyes, Donnay. That might have been his intent but it didn't last. That night he came for dinner, he couldn't keep his eyes off you. You might not have noticed but your grandmother and I certainly did. Spencer Westmoreland loves you."

Donnay glanced down at her left hand. She had removed her engagement ring and she held it, clenched tightly in her fist. She then looked back up at her mother. "No, Mom, he doesn't love me, but you know what's really sad and probably pathetic? I fell in love with him and was actually looking forward to being his wife and the mother of his children."

Knowing she couldn't hold back her tears much longer, she said, "I think I'll go into town. I need to get away for a while." Then without saying anything else, she raced up the stairs.

Spencer tensed visibly when the phone rang. A part of him knew it had to be Stuart. He placed his wineglass on the table and picked up the house phone.

Arriving home to Sausalito had been a welcome relief. He had spent the past couple of hours opening up windows and blinds to enjoy the view of the Bay from his living-room window. To keep busy he had immediately begun work on another business deal, one that would involve his cousins and brothers. His cousin Clint had retired as a Texas Ranger and was using the ranch he had inherited from his uncle to set up a business much like the one Durango and McKinnon had established.

He picked up the phone. "Yes?"

"I got the information you wanted, Spence."

Spencer remained silent for a moment then said, "All right. Who put that money into the Russell's account?"

"A man by the name of Chad Timberlain."

Spencer racked his mind trying to recall where he'd heard that name before. It suddenly hit him at the same time he heard a knock at his door. He felt a hard tug on his insides at the thought that he might have jumped to the wrong conclusions about Chardonnay.

"Look, Stuart, I'll need to get back to you. I think I know what might be going on, but I'll have to verify it and call you back."

He hung up the phone and headed for the door, wondering who would be visiting him since no one knew he had returned to Sausalito. He snatched opened the door to find a tall, muscular, fifty-something-year-old man standing there.

Spencer inhaled slowly. Although the two of them had never met, he recognized the man's profile as the one he'd seen that night on the path, just seconds before he had taken Ruth Russell into his arms.

"Chad Timberlain?" Spencer caught the man by surprise in asking.

The older man frowned coolly. "Yes."

Spencer stepped aside. "Come in. I really wasn't expecting you, since I just figured things out. But I'm sure you're here because you feel that the two of us need to talk."

The older man gave him a look that indicated the two of them needed to do more than merely exchange words and Spencer understood. If he was in Timberlain's place, he'd do the same thing. "And we need to come to an understanding," Spencer decided to add.

The man's features relaxed somewhat as he stepped over the threshold, and Spencer exhaled as he closed the door behind him.

"So, as you can see," Spencer said sometime later to Chad Timberlain, as they sat in his living room finishing off glasses of Russell wine, "I assumed Chardonnay knew about the money that had been placed in the winery's account."

"Even when she told you she didn't know anything about it?" Chad asked, his gaze boring into Spencer. After the two of them began talking, the older man's manner appeared calm and relaxed. But the more Spencer outlined just what his and Chardonnay's relationship was, the more the conversation between them became somewhat strained. Although Timberlain hadn't been involved in his daughter's life before now, he felt that was neither here nor there since he intended to become involved. Starting here.

There was only one answer Spencer could give and it was one he wasn't really proud of. "Yes, even when she denied my allegations."

The man's gaze hardened under Spencer's direct stare. "I felt compelled to place that money into the account because I couldn't stand there and let you railroad my daughter into marrying you."

After hearing his account of his relationship with Chardonnay—minus, of course, the intimate part—he didn't find her father's attitude the least bit unreasonable. "Yes, sir. I understand and I can also appreciate that."

The man nodded. "So what are you going to do to rectify the situation? Ruth feels that you love Chardonnay and what happened was a grave mistake on your part."

Spencer swallowed. Grave was too mild a word. He couldn't see her ever forgiving him. He had asked her to believe in him and trust him, yet he hadn't done the same for her. He met her father's intense gaze. "I do love your daughter and will be the first to admit I was wrong. If she never speaks to me again I will understand."

He then leaned forward. "But because I love her, I'm going to fight for her and hope that she finds it in her heart to give me another chance. It's no longer about what I can do for the winery, it's about us—Chardonnay and me."

A smile touched the corners of Chad Timberlain's lips. "I've yet to officially meet my daughter, in fact I plan to do so tonight. From what Ruth tells me she can be pretty stubborn at times, so you won't have an easy job."

No one had to tell Spencer about Chardonnay's stubbornness. He was very much aware of it. "I know, but I'm going to die trying," he said, and he meant every word.

Donnay glanced at her reflection in the mirror as she tried to ignore the butterflies in her stomach. She would be meeting her father for the first time tonight. Her heart was already filled with love for him. Without having met her, he had come to her aid by putting that money into the winery account and proving that he would be a father who would always be there for his daughter.

She had hoped that getting caught up in meeting her father would eliminate thoughts of Spencer from her mind. Tomorrow was soon enough to be faced with the task of canceling everything. She would have to call the florist, the caterer and the printer. She wondered if he had told his family yet and, if he had, what reason he had given them for calling off the wedding. No doubt he had convinced them—like he was convinced—that she was someone who couldn't be trusted.

She glanced at the clock on the wall. It was nearing six o'clock. Tonight her family would be hosting a small dinner party to celebrate her grandfather's homecoming, as well as her father's entrance back into their lives. Her mother had confided in her earlier that she and Chad Timberlain were doing some serious dating. Donnay was happy knowing there was a chance her mother might be able to recapture the love she had lost over twenty-seven years ago.

She heard a knock on her bedroom door. Thinking it was her mother or grandmother, she said, "Come in."

Donnay turned to see the door open and instead of her mother or grandmother, her breath caught when Spencer walked in. Fierce emotions welled up in her throat when she remembered his harsh words, his accusations. He had asked her to believe in him when he had no intention of ever believing in her. "What are you doing here, Spencer? What do you want?" she asked in an angry tone.

He moved into the room so quickly that she hadn't been given time to blink. When she did, he was standing there, right in front of her. His voice was gentle yet husky when he spoke. "I'm here to apologize for all the things I said. And as far as what I want...what I want Chardonnay, is you."

All it took was one look at Chardonnay's features to know his apology hadn't softened her any. Anger lined her gray eyes and she was standing stiff, with her hands balled into fists. He noticed that she had removed his ring.

"You accused me of those god-awful things. You played judge and jury. You didn't trust me. You—"

He reached out and tried touching her hand, the one that no longer wore his ring, and she angrily snatched it back. "No! You even accused me of betraying you with another man. How could you think so low of me?"

Spencer saw the tears in her eyes and a deep lump formed in his throat. He had hurt her. He had caused her pain and more than anything he wanted to make it right. "I love you, Chardonnay," he said in a low voice, straight from the heart. "I never meant to fall in love with you but I did. I'm the one who got caught up in all my scheming and manipulative tactics. I have been betrayed before. A few years ago, when my fiancée was killed, I discovered she was pregnant by another man. I made a promise to myself then that although I still wanted a wife and children, there would be no love. But you proved me wrong because you demanded my love without even realizing you were doing it. And when I found out about the money in your account, I felt used and betrayed because I realized you no longer had anything to gain from our marriage and that in essence, you no longer needed me…but I had begun needing you."

Donnay inhaled deeply. Spencer's words from earlier that day had been cruel, unjustified and angry. But now she understood why he had been so quick to judge her falsely. His former fiancée had gotten pregnant by someone else? She couldn't imagine a woman wanting to have any man's baby but his. Even now she was hoping that she was already pregnant.

She saw the strain and pain on Spencer's face. He had admitted that he loved her, which definitely came as a surprise. And she believed him because confessing his love to a woman couldn't be easy for him. And she loved him, too. She loved him with all her heart.

"If I accept your apology, and believe what you say about loving me, what do you expect of me?" she asked in a soft voice.

He placed both hands in the pockets of his pants as he stood gazing at her. "I expect—I would hope that you will take me back, give me another chance to prove just how wrong I've been and to make things right. I would want us to go ahead with our wedding and become husband and wife, but I'll let you set the date. If you prefer waiting until after the holidays then that's fine. I will no longer rush you into anything."

He sighed deeply then continued. "And I would want you to give me a chance to love you in such a way that you would want to love me back." A smile curved his lips when he added honestly. "I will make it almost impossible for you not to do so. And if you're not pregnant already, then I'll let you decide when we'll have children. I won't make it a priority. I want to spend time with you and love you the way you rightly deserve without any limitations or stipulations imposed."

Donnay didn't say anything for a while and then she tilted her head and studied him. She saw the strain lines across his forehead, the tension that had tightened around his lips. But it was his eyes that brought it all home. They were dark, intense and filled with love…for her. "And what if I were to say that I already love you, that I had fallen in love with you weeks ago?" she asked in a tight voice, fighting back a sob that threatened to close her throat. "What if I were to say that, Spencer?"

He took a step closer to her. "Then I would ask you to give me an opportunity to make you never regret loving me, never regret giving me another chance. Never regret becoming my wife and the mother of my children. Will you?"

She slowly nodded. "Yes."

Happiness spread across his features and he removed his hands from his pockets and reached out for her. This time she didn't deny him and willingly went into his open arms. He held her tightly to him, as if he never intended to let her go, and then he tilted up her chin and captured her mouth with his, glorying in the taste of his own personal brand of Chardonnay.

The moment his tongue took hold of hers, sensations rippled through him, pleasure seeped into his bones and desire filled his entire being. If her family didn't have a number of dinner guests downstairs he would be tempted to lock the door and stay in this bedroom with her forever. Besides, her father would not let him do such a thing. The man had given him twenty minutes before he'd threatened to come up and rescue his daughter, if need be. The only need was the one Spencer felt in his crotch.

"I want to make love to you," he whispered against her moist lips.

"And I want you to make love to me."

He smiled. "Later tonight? At the villa?"

She grinned. "Yes, later tonight. At the villa."

Although he wanted to keep her in her bedroom a little longer, moments later Spencer found himself escorting Chardonnay down the stairs. In just the nick of time, he figured, because standing on the bottom step was her father, waiting on them. Spencer held her hand, the one that once again was wearing his ring.

Spencer stopped in the middle of the staircase and turned to Chardonnay. "This first meeting should be your time with him. Go down to your father."

She smiled when Spencer released her hand, and continued walking alone down the stairs. A grin of pure happiness covered Chad Timberlain's face and he opened his arms up to the daughter he only recently discovered he had. Automatically, she returned the affection by walking straight into his waiting arms.

"Dad," she whispered while he held her tight. Chardonnay glanced across the room and saw her mother standing with her grandparents, tears in their eyes. Tonight was very special. The father she'd never met had come to claim his daughter, and the man she had fallen in love with loved her back.

She felt utterly and truly happy.

Later that night, Donnay lay wrapped up in Spencer's arms. After an intense lovemaking session, they had talked. Since he hadn't called his family to cancel the wedding plans, and she hadn't canceled the florist, caterer or printer, they decided to still get married the week before Christmas. Besides, each and every time they made love they ran the risk of starting a family, which was something the both of them decided they still wanted to do.

Donnay smiled, thinking about what he'd told her earlier. "I can't believe my father actually came to see you."

"Well, he did and he wanted to let me know in no uncertain terms that he would not tolerate me taking advantage of his daughter."

"He's really special. To think he put all that money into my bank account to help out."

Her father had explained after retiring from the military, he and three guys who'd served under him in the army had formed an international electronic company called BOSS and it was doing extremely well. He had assured her that giving her that much money had not affected the company's bottom line.

Chad was semiretired and the first of the year he planned to step down as CEO and turn over the day-to-day operation of the company to the three competent men whom he considered surrogate sons. Donnay would get to meet them at her wedding.

"So when do you think your mom and Chad will marry?" Spencer asked her.

Donnay's smile deepened. "Before Valentine's Day. I can't imagine them waiting longer than that. And trust me when I say that this time, she has no qualms leaving here and traveling with Dad, although she'll wait until after Gramps's surgery, of course. She's satisfied that you and I have decided to make our home here and we'll keep an eye on my grandparents. Mom deserves to finally spend time with the man she loves and to be happy."

"You deserve to be happy, as well. I love you," he whispered close to her ear.

She smiled at him. "And I love you, too."

She snuggled deeper into the arms she had once believed were incapable of loving anyone, especially her. He had proven her wrong, and every time she looked into his eyes, she saw the truth reflected in their dark depths. He was a man who, she had discovered, not only had a lot of forbidden passion, but also had a lot of hidden talents. She couldn't help wondering where he got some of his smooth moves and creative positions when they made love.

"Ready again?"

She chuckled as she turned in his arms. She couldn't

say he hadn't warned her about his inexhaustible energy. Reaching up, she placed her arms around his neck. "For you, Spencer Westmoreland, I'll always be ready."

Epilogue

Spencer stood beside Reggie, the youngest of his brothers, who was still a bachelor and who was standing as his best man. Spencer watched his beautiful bride walk down the aisle to him on her father's arm. He thought Chardonnay was a stunning vision in white. The top of her gown fitted tightly to the waist and then flared out in a thousand ruffles.

All the love he never thought possible was flowing through him at that moment and he definitely couldn't wait for their wedding night. After spending the night in their villa, they would be flying out in the morning for Paris where they would spend two weeks.

"You sure you want to do this?" Reggie asked, leaning over to whisper in his ear.

Spencer grinned, not taking his gaze off Chardonnay. "Hell, yes."

His brother Jared, standing close by as a groomsman,

poked him in the ribs, reminding him of the preacher who was within earshot. That didn't bother Spencer. On this day, his wedding day, nothing would bother him.

When Chardonnay reached his side and gave him her hand, he took it and lifted it up to his lips and kissed it. What the hell, he thought. He could definitely do better than that. Then he pulled her into his arms and kissed her lips. She returned his kiss in kind, until a few guests cleared their throats, reminding the couple of their presence.

Spencer pulled back and met the minister's frown. "You're supposed to wait until after I pronounce you husband and wife," the pastor scolded them in a low voice, trying to keep the smile off his face.

Spencer gave the minister a mischievous grin. "I know, sir. I'm sorry. I got carried away."

And then the wedding ceremony began.

When it ended, the minister presented the couple as husband and wife, and Spencer kissed his bride all over again.

* * * * *

Harlequin® *Desire*

ALWAYS POWERFUL, PASSIONATE AND PROVOCATIVE.

A BRAND-NEW WESTMORELAND FAMILY NOVEL FROM *NEW YORK TIMES* BESTSELLING AUTHOR

BRENDA JACKSON

Megan Westmoreland needs answers about her family's past. And Rico Claiborne is the man to find them. But when the truth comes out, Rico offers her a shoulder to lean on…and much, much more. Megan has heard that passions burn hotter in Texas. Now she's ready to find out….

TEXAS WILD

"Jackson's characters are…hot enough to burn the pages."
—*RT Book Reviews* on *Westmoreland's Way*

Available October 2 from Harlequin Desire®.